the LONELY GIRL'S VEGETABLE PATCH

the LONELY GIRL'S VEGETABLE PATCH

Genevieve Plunkett

THE FEMINIST PRESS
AT THE CITY UNIVERSITY OF NEW YORK
NEW YORK CITY

Published in 2026 by the Feminist Press
at the City University of New York
The Graduate Center
365 Fifth Avenue, Suite 6200
New York, NY 10016

feministpress.org

First Feminist Press edition 2026

This book is made possible by the New York State Council on the Arts with the support of the Office of the Governor and the New York State Legislature.

First printing September 2026

Cover design by Sarah Flood-Baumann
Text design by Drew Stevens

Library of Congress Cataloging-in-Publication Data
Names: Plunkett, Genevieve, 1986- author
Title: The lonely girl's vegetable patch / Genevieve Plunkett.
Description: First Feminist Press edition. | New York City : Feminist Press at the City University of New York, 2026.
Identifiers: LCCN 2026015032 (print) | LCCN 2026015033 (ebook) | ISBN 9781558613713 paperback | ISBN 9781558613805 ebook
Subjects: LCGFT: Bisexual fiction | Novels
Classification: LCC PS3616.L886 L66 2026 (print) | LCC PS3616.L886 (ebook)
LC record available at https://lccn.loc.gov/2026015032
LC ebook record available at https://lccn.loc.gov/2026015033

PRINTED IN THE UNITED STATES OF AMERICA

For Robin. I miss you.

1

I MET TRISTAN at Grandview Stable, where he was training me to take over for him as barn manager. Tristan had recently had his heart broken. The woman responsible, who was seventeen years his senior, was married to a man older than her by another seventeen years. It seemed to me a wonderful stack of numbers, seventeen on seventeen, with Tristan at the bottom, trying to extract himself in a game of emotional Jenga. He wanted to quit the horse farm and leave Vermont for good.

Cleo could pull hot bread from the oven with her bare hands, he told me.

Cleo had a gold fleck in her left iris like a grain of mica—that was *her* left, from her point of view.

She had come to Grandview last year to buy some hay bales, and Tristan had been the one to help load them into her truck.

"How many horses you got?" Tristan had asked her, throwing in the last bale. Some dust went up between them and Cleo sneezed, the force of it sending goose bumps down her arms and across her sunburnt chest. She was wearing denim overalls with the suggestion of a sweaty white tank top underneath. Tristan had felt himself get stiff—

"Like, how stiff?" I wanted to know at this point in the story. He looked surprised and then, slightly irritated, asked me if I wanted him to consult the Mohs hardness scale. I told him that would be nice, and he said, with some reluctance, "It was more like half-mast."

Bless you, Tristan had said to Cleo, his crotch mercifully concealed by the open tailgate.

Yes, she answered. Not *thank you.* Just *yes,* which had seemed to Tristan a tad wistful, and so sexy. She climbed into the truck and drove away, tailgate still down, hay bales bouncing lightly. Oh boy.

It seems unwise to get involved with a man who is obsessed with another woman, but I was twenty-one, and Tristan was like whipped cream on an already free sundae. He was like a kid's treasure map. I could not conceive of falling for him hard enough to get hurt. Plus, all the other men I'd been with smelled like strangers sprayed with mall cologne. When Tristan hovered his lips close to mine, he smelled so familiar it was like kissing my own armpit. I was big into smells, which was one of the reasons I drove a scooter instead of a car; how else could I know where I was, without the musk of the world pushed into my face, swilled inside the visor of my helmet?

Cleo worked hard hours in the sun but still wore glitter around her eyes. Painted her toenails pink. Was in love with Tom Hanks and Gordon Lightfoot.

Cleo had a stretch mark on the side of her belly button that made it seem like it was squinting suspiciously at you. She had been married at twenty. Divorced when she was twenty-one. Married again at twenty-two.

I HAD NOT been entirely truthful on my résumé when applying for the barn manager position, meaning that I had exaggerated everything. I knew nothing of equine first aid, only that if a horse was limping, one should not ride it. That probably summed up my riding skills as well: Don't get on a limping horse. My experience came from the two summers I spent as a spotter at an equine therapy center for children with special needs. Most of the young riders were nonverbal, some wheelchair aided—two were legally blind—and it had astounded me how confident they became once they were in the saddle. Their spines stretched tall, their faces opened in the kind of unrestricted joy that somehow put me to shame, as if I had, all my life, been carrying around false and stupid reasons to not feel that way also. I walked hundreds of laps around a dirt-padded indoor arena, keeping my hand on a little leg prone to wiggling or a shoulder that wanted to list. I would have walked an eternity for those children, their happiness the only way forward. The exhaustion I felt after those long days was clean and final—no small latches of anxiety left undone. No question lingering about whether it had been time well spent. What else was time made for?

Sometimes in the spring, when the horses tended to be rowdier, the program's director, Paula, would have me ride them, just to burn off some steam. She would watch me go around at a posting trot and grimace.

"You ride like you're waiting for a bomb to go off," she said, but allowed me to continue—after all, I was only there to exercise the horses, not win ribbons. Once, however, she marched over and took my horse by the reins, stopping it short, then placed a gentle palm on my knee.

"Drew?" she asked. "Have you ever taken a proper fucking breath in your life?"

The therapeutic riding center eventually closed for the same reason that all good programs are forced to end—lack of funding—and I found a job at a women's clothing store where I was forced to model the signature chunky jewelry that they sold. For six months, I was Jacob Marley, rattling my chains at upper-middle-class women who were just there to buy a scarf. I graduated from high school and worked at a doughnut stand stationed at the exit of a corn maze, handing oil-crisped cider doughnuts to disappointed tourists who had been hoping that my stand was the outhouse. When the season ended, I worked at a used bookstore, where I was paid under the table by a fifty-five-year-old man named Byron who once asked me, out of nowhere, how rough I liked it.

"Praying mantis rough," I said, because never in my life had I admitted to taking offense. I was the kind of girl that could dish it back, cool and unbothered. And, as I was quickly discovering, you did not actually have to be clever to be that kind of girl. You only had to position yourself like you were clever, and smile like you knew more than you were saying; the men were never actually listening. Eventually, because I was living in my friend Nico's basement and not paying rent, I saved enough money to buy a scooter. It was a used Vespa, sold to me by a college grad who did not want to deal with transporting it back to California where he was from. He looked at me skeptically and told me that, around here, you only get three good months of riding before it's too cold, too windy. There's too much *winter* here. He shuddered.

"I'm very hairy," I told him, handing him the cash. I swear to God, you don't even have to try. You just have to say the first thing that pops into your head. You can cringe at yourself later, and I did, although it was at fifty miles an hour with the wind fluttering the inside of my tank top. I spent the rest of that summer huffing the grass-sweet air, gulping the fishy odor of wetlands as I zipped by them. I sniffed and sniffed, feeling always that I was searching the outdoors for that perfect nest of soft, green conditions where I could inhale deeply. Paula had been right: I needed to learn how to fucking breathe.

I FOUND MYSELF out on the scooter on one of those sniffing excursions after receiving an email from Byron that read BECAUSE YOU WORE THOSE PANTS. With it, there was an unnamed attachment, which I knew not to open, because I didn't want to see his middle-aged erection. But then I'd begun to doubt myself, because there was a chance that I was misreading things. It seemed too sloppy of him, leaving a digital dick print on my computer, like mailing someone a severed thumb. I knew that I had to look at the attachment, had to confirm with myself that it was a penis, that I was not crazy, self-absorbed, overly sexualized—maybe the pants that I had worn, which were tight, button-fly corduroys, reminded him of something from his own wardrobe that he wanted to show me? Maybe he was too old to be familiar with the traditions of the unsolicited online dick pic. Could he even take a selfie? I clicked. The photo loaded bar by bar onto my screen, and my first reaction—I am sorry to say—was triumph: I had been right. That feeling was followed by a twisted sense of satisfaction: It was an ugly, strained thing, gripped too tightly, as if to keep it from deflating. If it had had a face (thank God it didn't), it would have been a whiny, insulted one, like when Marv from *Home Alone* takes an iron to the forehead. Then, before the disgust and shame rolled in, I felt a sense of resolve: I changed into *the* pants (they would always be *The* Pants from now on), and instead of going to work at the bookstore, I got on my scooter to chase down that green, green patch of unblemished nature that I knew existed somewhere.

That scooter ride did not lead me immediately to the farm where I met Tristan—that would have been too seamless, and I don't usually take to opportunities delivered to me by fate. Although, now that I think of it, everything that would transpire over the next year could be interpreted as suspiciously well-timed—ill-timed? I wish there was a word to describe whatever sort of timing exists in between these two possibilities. Maybe that's what irony is: coincidences that are too creepy to be good and too exciting to be bad. The scooter ride was important because, although receiving a haggard dick pic from one's boss seems like an obvious reason to quit and never go back, for me, it was the ride that solidified my decision. Zipping between those striped hills toward the buttery horizon was like ripping a length of duct tape off my bare skin. Oh! I thought with a shiver. I have free will!

I SAW THE ad for the barn manager job in the paper the next day, and I, still free-falling and looking for a place to land, thought of the circles I used to walk at the therapeutic riding center. MUST HAVE 5 YEARS' EXPERIENCE RIDING AND CARING FOR HORSES. Okay, so maybe I didn't have five years—two summers at best—but I had put in the miles, round and round on the soft dirt, and that seemed to count for something.

Grandview Stable was a tourist destination that offered guided rides on horseback through the woods. It was a place that was especially popular during leaf-peeping season for those peepers who wanted to ditch the tour bus experience. Anyone who worked there needed to be firm with horses, and even firmer with the clientele.

"People aren't going to know how dangerous this is, even if you tell them," said the woman who had greeted me when I arrived. She had a gray ponytail and a resilient notch between her eyes. She spoke to me as if I had already been hired, and I wondered briefly if she was mistaking me for someone else. "You must have danger on the mind at all times, so your clients can enjoy themselves. You understand?" I thought about Paula's words to me: *You ride like you're waiting for a bomb to go off.*

"I'm good at anticipating disaster," I said solemnly. The woman's head ticked slightly backward in approval. I thought: I am going to work here and my arms are going to get so toned.

I started my training the next day and was at first disappointed to find Tristan there, and not the flinty woman who had hired me. Tristan walked across the dirt driveway as I was unclasping my helmet, carrying a pitchfork in each hand like he was going to toss one at me. He was wearing your standard Carhartts, a faded gray T-shirt, and work boots, and his hair was cut uncharacteristically short, even though there was no way I could have known that. He seemed to hold the pitchforks with some humor, which I misinterpreted as judgment, as if he could see already that I was not up to the task. I stood straighter, trying to match this humor, a defense mechanism that I had developed for all kinds of situations. It was especially useful when men flirted with me and seemed like they'd turn mean if I refused them. Around this kind of man, I would change my demeanor, my whole posture, to imply that there was a larger joke going on, one that was greater than his pickup line—something totally omniscient, and I was in on it. It was like hitting an emergency meta switch that confused the man long enough for me to slip away without having to reject him outright. I matched myself to Tristan this way, squaring my shoulders, ready to scoff at his pitchforks, as if I had been shoveling shit my whole life and none of this would come as a shock to me. But as he came closer, I saw that he had a lovely, kind face. A humble, downward smile. How awful, I thought. Now there would be no hope of relaxing. I would have to resign myself to being perceived all morning by a man that I did not find repulsive.

We did shovel shit. We shoveled so much horse manure that I started to suspect that this was no training at all, but a way of tricking gullible people like me into free labor. If so, it was the most scenic trap that I had ever been lured into. All around the property, there were mountains so thick with trees they reminded me of my grandmother's bunched-up knitting. The clouds were firm and unhurried, and all around us there were horses grazing and swishing their tails. They looked drowsy in their mesh fly masks, which fit floppily over their ears like jester hats. After two hours of mucking the paddocks, we moved on to the stalls. Tristan had been showing me his favorite poop-picking method when he stopped. He looked around as if he had just remembered that I was there.

"Do you know all this already?" he asked.

"No," I said. "I don't even know why I was hired." Being around Tristan made my body eager for work. I liked the growing ache in my shoulders, the twisted-rope feeling in my spine. Even then, before my attraction to him became undeniable, I could feel the possibility of that attraction, as well as the allure of allowing it to unfold at its own pace. When the work is tedious, I thought, one would be wise to prolong the seduction. If one *were* wise.

We were a few days into my training, and so far I had learned, besides the correct poop-flinging technique, how to administer a pasty dewormer to the horses via syringe and how to tie and quickly release a safety knot. It seemed that I was learning everything haphazardly. I could tell that Tristan was preoccupied, his mind elsewhere, while he demonstrated how to clean a leather strap with a toothbrush. As if I would ever need to know such a thing. I wanted to ask him, What? What is troubling you?

He told me about Cleo one morning while we were in the upper paddock, attempting to catch a horse named Murray so we could give him a bath. Murray was a short, dun-colored horse with a donkey-ish face. He reminded me of a sardonic butler, someone who could convey a creative range of complaints with a single sniff. It was easy enough to slip the halter on, but after Tristan had led him three steps, Murray's legs buckled, and he flopped down on his side with a groan. This was not a medical incident, I learned, but a strategy to keep himself from having to go to work. Tristan gave the rope a serious tug, and I thought that he was going to laugh and fix the situation, just as he seemed to be able to fix everything else. But what I thought was a laugh was in fact a strange, phlegmy sob. Murray's act of defiance seemed to represent a breaking point for Tristan. He tossed the rope down and let his body land, half humorously, on the sun-hardened dirt. If it had not been for that sliver of humor—a subtle flapping of arms—I might have been truly concerned. Murray mirrored Tristan's theatrics, thudding his donkey head on the ground and blowing through his nostrils. Sometimes, even now, when I see or hear the word "futile," I remember this scene. What was there to do? Man and horse were out of commission. I felt taller than a streetlamp, and just as awkward, standing above them on the peak of that hill. Below us, the stable was a long wooden box. Beside it, there was a fenced-in area set up with various obstacles made from poles and plastic blocks. It reminded me of a room that I was sometimes brought to in elementary school, where a teacher offered me many games to play that all turned out to be tests. I did not blame Murray for not wanting to go. Tristan's sobs turned bitter, then mockingly bitter, and then he was laughing and sighing.

"Are you losing it?" I asked, finally.

He sat for a moment with his hands on his knees, then a surge seemed to move through him. He stood, picked up the lead rope, and began helicoptering the end of it. He brought this spinning end closer to Murray's hindquarters, until I was sure that it would strike him. Murray lifted his head and looked at the threat to his rear without alarm, the same look of resignation that a husband guilted out of a recliner might have. He stood, then allowed himself to be led down the hill as if nothing had happened, his long face as blunt and droopy eyed as ever. Tristan was silent as we passed through the gate and as we hitched Murray to a post near the stable door, where our buckets of soapy water and car-wash sponges were waiting. I had been ready to forget the sobbing incident, to never speak of it, having been conditioned all my life to absorb and break down the particles of male humiliation. I was an emotional bivalve, a mollusk. But Tristan cleared his throat.

"Yeah," he said, as if continuing a conversation that we were already having. "I recently had my heart broken." I dunked a yellow sponge into the water bucket and watched it darken. Tristan's sudden and formal sincerity disconcerted me more than his collapse.

"Her name was—*is*—Cleo. Is. She's not dead," he said. Tristan may have corrected himself that one time, moving Cleo into the present tense along with the living. But from that moment on, we spoke of her in the past, as the perfect ghost that she had become. We pressed the sponges against Murray's hide, creating long stripes of dark, dripping hair, and then swept them with a rubber squeegee, flicking the runoff onto the ground. Meanwhile, Tristan told me about Cleo with the same cadence that he was using to teach me the ways of the farm: temperamentally, fueled, it seemed, by his mood. Now it made sense. Now I could learn from him how to tighten a western cinch, how to find the toothless groove inside a horse's mouth with my finger, all in tandem with these stories about Cleo. As if the memory of her was the driving force behind all our tasks, Tristan's heartbreak the binding logic of our days.

THERE WERE OTHER stable employees besides us: girls who strode in wearing tall English riding boots, with impeccable asses, as smooth as chestnuts. They were athletic but also aesthetically unaware, the implication being, it seemed, that horse girls were too obsessive for vanity. They had a doe-like blend of hyperfocus and obliviousness. If their asses were perfect, let the saddle be the sole beneficiary. I watched for signs in Tristan's face to determine how moved he was by this fleet of summer blonds, but if he reacted to them at all, it was with businesslike cool, with an undertone of slight irritation. Could they *not* walk their horses over the hose? Could they turn their music down when customers were at the barn? These girls were my peers, I understood, but I could not fully accept it. They seemed hardy and capable—and astonishingly friendly—but also like their parents would have named them Harvard had they been born boys.

It soon became clear to me that the girls who were responsible for leading most of the trail rides were headed back to college at the end of the month, and with Tristan leaving, the bulk of these duties would land on me. I needed to learn the route. I needed to get back on a horse before anyone found out how inexperienced I was.

We rode up the mountain path, Tristan leading on a hot-tempered mare while I followed closely on butler-faced Murray. The flies were out, and Murray had taken refuge in the sculpted crease of the mare's buttocks, his fleshy nose resting against the coil of her anus. What tenderness there was in this act. What trust! I did not even need to keep my reins taut, so strong was this link between the bodies of our two-piece caravan.

"Cleo could smell my moods," Tristan shouted from his saddle. "She would sniff the inside of my ear canal or ask me to breathe in her face." As he explained these things to me, I watched Murray huff his lady friend's asshole. Around us, the sweaty summer foliage gleamed, the far-off cornfields shimmered in the heat. I knew that Tristan was showing me the path so that I could navigate it myself someday, but in that moment, swaying and half drunk on the summer air, the notion that I would ever be without him, that I could even survive out here on my own, seemed preposterous.

"She said that I smelled like wet straw when I was lying to her. Like beer and wool when I was coming down with a cold. Maple syrup when she was ovulating."

Oh right, I thought. This was why Tristan knew better than to go after the tall boot girlies in the barn. He was a categorical weirdo.

"What about when you smelled like horse dung?" I asked. Tristan twisted in his saddle to face me.

"That's how she knew I was tired." He smiled, timidly, as if to convey that he was humbled to find me still there, with my horse all the way up his horse's back end, still willing to listen.

When he asked me at the end of the day if he could buy me a drink, I said yes, thinking that this was part of the balancing act of our working relationship; it was a date, yes, but more of a conciliatory one. A clinking of pints to the two weeks I had already spent with him and his heartbreak. We both showed up at the bar wearing a fresh set of clothing, but with dust still in our hairlines and in the moons of our fingernails. What a comfort that was, as if there were no surprises left, no hidden expectations. As we drank our beers, straddling the corner of the bar, I noticed that I had not heard Cleo's name since our ride up the mountain. Cleo was not there with us. She hadn't even made it through the door.

"You must think I'm a trainwreck," Tristan said to me. His voice seemed somewhat untethered. It might have been the change in environment, the need to speak over the jukebox and the idling trucks outside the open door. Also, I reasoned: I had never seen him when he was drinking.

"Trainwrecks are very long," I said. "Long, as in sprawling." Tristan looked offended.

"I don't sprawl?"

The bartender asked us if we wanted another. He was hoodied and grim. It seemed that saying yes or no would annoy him equally, so I told him yes. It gave me a moment to think about what I wanted to say to Tristan.

"No, I think you're better than that," I said. "You're like a department store explosion. Sad and messy, but with no human casualties." I wasn't saying it right, but it did not matter. Tristan cocked his head appreciatively, and I took him then for a man who did not require a constant stream of praise, but merely a show of effort. He was not a narcissist. My stout arrived and his Long Trail. He liked that I only drank stouts, he said, because he found it unusual and a little silly. I agreed, feeling excited that we had both contributed observations about the other and that it had gone smoothly.

I recognized, even then, that this was the moment where Tristan and I could have broken away from the conventions that we had created for ourselves. Here was my opening to ask Tristan about his plans for the future—he had not spoken of where he was headed after my training was done. I might have asked him about his favorite movie, if he had any siblings, pets, grandparents still living. I could have offered a detail about myself that was more intimate than my preference for beers that tasted like burnt gingerbread. Could I possibly convey that my happiest moments had all taken place in a large pinewood arena, walking circles in soft dirt and holding firmly to a small orthopedic sneaker? Or that my idea of a hobby was riding my scooter near wetlands where I could sniff the primeval dishwater of the earth? Maybe I did not have the emotional maturity for such confessions. Maybe I did not believe that Tristan and I could survive on our own, small and unwatched by the past. Or—and this is why I take full responsibility for how events unfolded—it was possible that I was turned on by Tristan's obsession with Cleo, that I had already envisioned us together in her figurative shadow, Tristan showing me what he liked based on what Cleo had taught him. It might grant us a kind of immunity: freedom to experiment within the bounds of Tristan's memory, inside the hot climate of his grief. It would be like roleplaying, except we'd be ourselves, puppets to the whims of a woman who we had granted goddess-like power.

AT A YOUNG age, I had already established myself among a close circle of girls as the one "most likely to." Sure, I had boasted, I'd suck a dick, I'd swallow stuff—lord help me, I did not even know the proper terminology. At the time it had little to do with having any sort of robust sexual appetite. The way I saw it, I was also the girl who collected toads on hikes, who allowed daddy longlegs to crawl up my shins at the school picnic. I sniffed spittlebug foam, rubbed it between my fingers to feel it melt away. Sex seemed like any other sensory experience that most girls were squeamish about and I was not. There was an especially memorable conversation that took place at a friend's sleepover party. Six of us were sharing a tent that the host's mother had erected on the patch of wild, compressed grass behind the house. It was thrilling for us, all eleven or twelve years old, to have this space to ourselves when so many of us were starved for privacy, whether it was from sharing a bedroom with multiple siblings, or, as was the case for a girl named Tiff, who was the wealthiest of the bunch, being forced to use the hallway telephone within earshot of her parents' room. I am sure the inside of that tent was as foul and greasy as the lining of a potato-chip bag by the time we spilled out of it the next morning, exhausted from binging on junk food, holding in our farts, and dreaming up filthy scenarios involving Leonardo DiCaprio (who some of the girls called "Leo," as if they knew him personally) or an eighth grader named Evan (all hot boys were named Evan). Tiff had lectured us on the inappropriateness of fantasizing about grown men, even celebrities. Her father was a detective, she explained, although none of us understood what that had to do with anything.

"Okay, whatever," said a girl named Ashley. "What would you do to Evan if you were locked in a closet with him?" We had all agreed earlier on the locked-closet scenario because, though none of it was real to begin with, the presence of the locked door implicated us even less. To us it seemed that, should you find yourself shut in a closet with a boy, to *not* make out with him would be a waste of time of criminal proportions.

"What do you mean, 'what would I do?'" Tiff was confused, which confused the rest of us because we had been talking about sex for nearly two hours by then. There was a brief and awkward silence during which none of us picked up on the fact that we had, all this time, been narrating what we would allow to be done *to* us, not once considering the acts that we would choose to initiate, whether the door was locked, unlocked, or swinging wide open.

"Well," Tiff said finally. The bulky red flashlight cast her face in unbecoming seriousness. She was about to confess something icky. "If it was dark in the closet—like totally dark—we could do it."

How unimaginative. Another girl tried to help things along.

"Dark because you don't want to look at his thing?" she asked.

"I don't want him to see my orgasm face!" Tiff said, almost shouting. There was silence again, as we digested this statement that was uncomfortable on so many levels. So: There was a face to be made. For those of us who had had orgasms, this realization felt like a sickening line of fine print. For those that were not as far along in their self-exploration, it was met with still more blank confusion. I admit that I was tremendously impressed by Tiff's candor, her apparent lack of dignity-preserving techniques. What she was admitting to was something that I would have never dreamed of admitting to: that it wasn't the swallowing, or the touching, or the looking plainly at wrinkled genitalia that threatened our sensibilities; it was the notion that we might stoop so low as to enjoy ourselves enough to be perceived as enjoying ourselves. It was a terrible, terrible thought.

THE BAR WAS growing crowded. There was a group of guys waiting to order who were standing closer to us than we were seated to each other, and that felt wrong. I knew that the date had not yet built to the intensity that would warrant one of us to propose going home with the other, but I wanted to leave, so I suggested that we walk by the river. Tristan eyed the door, as if the river were out there and he could gauge whether it looked inviting. For some reason, this made me wonder if a river walk had been a bad idea. Why had I even thought of it? But then he nodded resolutely and put down some bills for the tab, and I knew that it was not the river that had needed consideration, but me—did he want to commit more of the evening to me? The answer seemed to be yes.

"What made you think of this place?" Tristan asked when we had walked the few blocks to the floodwall. Here, on the edge of town, the lights from the streets and businesses stopped abruptly and the dark roar of the river took over. It was such a river that if a full-grown tree happened to uproot and fall in, that tree would be swept away like a twig. Again, I had the opportunity to tell Tristan that I sometimes came out here because I liked the smell. The gray rushing water smelled like wet rocks, like a slippery cliff face, with an interesting hint of foulness—moss and sewage. I came here when I still lived with my mother and needed to smell something that wasn't her.

"I dunno," I told Tristan. We walked along the grassy crest of the wall. I could tell that Tristan was trying not to say whatever it was that he wanted to say. I was not giving him anything else to work with, however, so he gave in.

"Cleo and I used to come here," he said. Relief washed

over me. Cleo was back. I wanted to talk about her—I *knew* how to talk about her.

"We came here because it was discreet," he said. "We'd go to Wily's because the people there were not likely to know her husband." Wily's was the bar where we had just been. I felt a thrill pass through me that I can only describe as the thrill of wondering if Tristan had been imagining Cleo, not me, on the barstool across from him. In retrospect, I do not believe that this was Tristan's intent, but the thought excited me. I wanted to take it further.

"Did you, like, ever make out on this path?" I asked. We had stopped walking.

"Oh, sure," he said. "One time it started to rain and all you could hear was the crashing of water. I'd never kissed anyone in the rain." He paused, and I could feel his hesitation, maybe wondering if he had gone too far. "It was kind of . . . slimy," he said. He was suddenly irresistibly vulnerable, his arms slack at his sides, his waist small, and his shirt tucked into his work pants.

"Show me," I said, and I could feel his relief as his arms came up and folded me in. He smelled faintly of pine dust and the deep, earthy scent of the horses. Beneath that layer was the smell of someone who came from a clean house, who slept on clean sheets. And then deeper still was something tangy and unidentifiable, like the core of a distant planet. I pressed my mouth hard against his and he broke away, looking me up and down.

"You're taller than she was."

"What else?"

"What do you mean?"

"What's the same and what's different?"

"Your hair is straighter. Your teeth are rounder."

And so we kissed and pressed our bodies together while he gave me the list.

Back at the lot where his car was parked, I started to ask him, "Did you two ever—"

"Yes," he said, and pulled me into the back seat. It was clean back there, with only some light dust in the crevices of the upholstery, wood shavings from the barn. He sat and I straddled him and we waited like that, with our clothes on, until the interior light turned off. It was unnecessary to pretend that back-seat sex was anything other than an ingenious idea, one that Cleo herself had invented and that Tristan and I were helplessly fated to reenact. We quickly separated for long enough to pull our pants off—Tristan had the male privilege of only needing to lower them to his ankles—and then I got back on, although not *on* on. Not yet. In the darkness and with the enclosed feeling of my head pressed into the ceiling, I couldn't help but think about the locked-closet scenario, about Tiff's fear of being seen, and how it connected to my own sense of liberation: that Tristan's eyes were aligned with my breasts, not my face, but also that if, by some miracle, I managed to come and Tristan managed to perceive it, we would both be concealed by the darkness, as well as the warm bluff of alcohol in our bloodstreams and the illusion that we were merely humble reenactors in the first place. There were too many safety mechanisms engaged to worry about one of us accidentally stumbling into unflattering reality. I was hovering, ready to lower myself onto him, while he tore open a condom. For some reason, I got it into my head to make a joke to distract him, and to maybe take away the seriousness of the condom. Condoms are crucial, yes, but yet another ego violation, like plugging your nose before diving into a pool. Nobody wants to be seen plugging their nose. I gathered up one of my breasts and wagged it at him, as if to say, *I am up here and impatient.* Tristan acted pleasantly offended. He finished with the condom, then pressed his mouth over my nipple and sucked.

"Did Cleo like that?" I gasped. He nodded his head without pulling his mouth away, and I resisted dropping down, because I guessed that Cleo would want to tease a little. She was the one that got away, after all. Outside, the darkness of the parking lot was broken only by the sheen of the windshields of other parked cars. These cars had the look of vehicles in it for the long haul, some with cardboard-patched windows, or tires so flat that they pooled cartoonishly. Still, I did not want to become too complacent and forget that we were now naked in a public setting. With Tristan buried in my tits, I had to be the eyes for both of us. I felt his hands on my sides, pulling me gently downward, angling his hips upward, caught helplessly, I imagined, between the ache of memory and the ache of now. Also, was there any man worth having other than a man tormented, a man who sees you as the remedy? Was there any other sex worth giving into? And here I was about to give in, when I saw a flicker at the edge of the parking lot. No, it was more of a blinking. I thought for a moment that it was a bicycle headlight.

"What?" Tristan was out from under me in an instant, working his pants back up. I felt compelled to give him an answer, even though I was still trying to figure out what I was seeing for myself, so when I said *cop,* it wasn't necessarily that I believed this, only that I had come to realize that the flickering was the beam of a swinging flashlight.

My friend Nico, whose basement I was living in, had left for her first semester at college. I was three years older than her, although only a grade above in high school—she was a smart, young August baby, while I was a kindergarten delinquent who had been held back at the urging of a concerned school counselor.

"It's more of a *social* delay than an academic one," the counselor had explained to my mother, which was her way of saying that I was a freak who liked to hold my breath when I went to the bathroom until I passed out. I am not certain why I did this. I only know that navigating the beige-tiled school restroom always felt superstitious. You were lucky if you found yourself alone in there, with no one going number two in the next stall. You were lucky if the powerful flush did not spit water back at you. If the faucets did not have a slimy skin of wet paper towels. At some point, I must have started holding my breath—either to stop these things from happening or as a kind of self-defense—and it is very difficult to stop a strange little habit once you start one.

Nico was pursuing one of those majors that I did not fully understand, the kind that had a dad seal of approval. Solid, and vaguely scientific. Nico had always been practical in high school. A mid-height-ponytail girl with cuffed jeans and tractionless tennis shoes. But she had a soft heart. Not like an ASPCA softy. More like an alleyway mattress. Nico was so undiscerning with her affections, it made me wonder if her sheltered upbringing had backfired. If you're not allowed to watch the bad guys on TV, I reasoned, then how are you supposed to identify them in real life? In ninth grade, she dated a druggie named Pat, and wore his Slipknot sweatshirt to school for a whole week when he got suspended. Sophomore year, it was a wrestler who got so irritable from cutting weight that he pushed her into the trash cans in the cafeteria. Junior year, she swore off boys, but then allowed the math teacher, Mr. Pursley, to convince her that becoming truth pen pals with him was a totally normal arrangement.

"What the fuck is a truth pen pal?" I had asked her.

"Like, when you play 'truth or dare,' and you pick truth. They can ask you anything and you have to answer," she said. We were in the cafeteria and she was eating yogurt, which somehow made her seem even more infuriatingly nonchalant. She scraped the rim of the container with her spoon and then held it near her lips, displaying the little pearl of excess yogurt that she had produced, and said: "Mr. Pursley says it's good to have someone to confess to on a regular basis. But it's hard to find the right person." She licked the yogurt pearl and looked thoughtfully at the streaked spoon. "You need to make sure that the person is mature enough not to judge."

"Mature, like a sixteen-year-old girl?" I asked her.

"They're just letters," she said. Then added, "He writes in *pencil.*" As if that were the mark of true integrity.

I couldn't challenge Nico too heatedly on these matters, because I felt indebted to her for allowing me to live in her basement, which I had been doing since the beginning of my senior year. It was one of those finished basements that all the ranch-style houses had. The kids with these basements always had robust gaming systems and stay-at-home moms who decorated for every holiday—not just Halloween and Christmas. Nico's mom decorated for Earth Day, which, looking back, was probably a red flag, but it seemed that all mothers were so unlike my own that their quirks never struck me as anything other than signs of fierce normality. To wake up in a sheet-covered bed to not only find your mother in the kitchen where you left her the night before, but also holding a pan of blue-and-green-dyed corn muffins for Earth Day? That was peak emotional security.

And so I adopted the role of cautious obedience, while Nico received letters through the vent of her locker that read, *Last night I dreamed that I found semen in the wool of a lamb. I woke up full of jealousy and wanted to break the rules. I drank black coffee instead. I watched the moon.* Unable to decide which line was most horrifying, I pointed to Mr. Pursley's handwriting and said, "Uh-oh. He used a pen." Nico, expressionless, folded the letter, as if to hide this fact, and tucked it into the overstuffed pocket of her three-ring binder. There were so many letters in there. This was getting out of hand.

"What's next? His own blood?"

"People are allowed to feel things, you know." She slammed the locker shut.

"What rules was he talking about?" I asked. But she was already walking away. Was she wearing her ponytail higher? I felt the world tip sideways, like a waiter holding a tray while turning a corner too fast. I put my hand against my locker, not sure if I was worried about Nico or worried about myself. The night before, I had heard Nico's parents arguing above me through the drop ceiling, and my first thought was that they were fighting about me; I had been there too long, was eating too many snacks in the middle of the night. Maybe they had found one of my used tampons improperly buried in the bathroom wastebasket. Any small mistake could very well be the last straw.

They were going to throw me out. When the suspense became unbearable, I climbed the stairs and stepped into the kitchen. I found Nico's mother and father in front of the stove, the mother kneeling, with her hand over an overturned plastic container. The father was holding a broom. They had been arguing because Nico's mother was too afraid to lift the container, beneath which they had captured a mouse, and Nico's father was becoming impatient with her. Once, my own mother had found a mouse in our cupboard and made a cracker-crumb trail from the kitchen to the living room, where she planted herself supine on the couch, a lone saltine resting on her stomach. She waited there all day for the mouse to follow the trail and find its cracker. What was her plan for when it reached her? I never found out, but I guessed it had something to do with companionship, the feeling of committing to an act of kindness, even if it was a strange and unsanitary replacement for the real thing. And, despite everything, I found that I understood my mother's logic more than I understood Nico's mother's unwillingness to lift the Tupperware. Still, I was relieved to discover that no one was angry at me, that my place in their household was not yet under threat. I offered to take charge of the Tupperware, and when I lifted it and the small brown mouse skittered free, Nico's father trapped it once more beneath the soft bristles of the broom and struck the pitiful lump that it made with a hammer.

I OFTEN THINK about what Nico said to me in front of the lockers that day. "People are allowed to feel things." It was a statement that was inarguably true, and perhaps very simply amended by the one implied exception: *as long as it does not hurt anyone.* Yet there was something about it that left me unsettled, because the statement itself demanded to be examined without the presence of feelings. Was this the second exception?

I had always allowed my mother to feel her feelings, and I suppose that, to some extent, I had established a system of emotional hierarchy that gave me permission to feel things about my mother's feelings, without overshadowing them. Her feelings were free-range; my feelings were caged. Her feelings were a heap; my feelings were a pile of salt.

IT DID NOT occur to me to question why Tristan felt the things that he felt—why he could not get over Cleo or what made the barn so painful that he had to change occupations. I suspect that the reasons did not matter so much to me because Tristan had been forthright from the beginning. It seemed a gift that someone would want to share what made them messy. In my experience, people concealed their mess until it was an emergency, and then once they hit that point, they threw open the door—ruined!—and cried for help. Could it have been that I conflated Tristan's honesty with neediness, and it was the perceived cry for help that I was attracted to? I cannot know. At the time, I only ever turned to self-analysis when I thought there was a problem, or when I feared that someone might be angry with me.

THE MORNING AFTER our failed attempt at car sex, Tristan and I were scheduled to lead our first trail ride together. The idea was that I would watch and see how it was done so that I could lead the next one with Tristan shadowing me. That I would soon be on my own was a reality that I still had not fully allowed myself to comprehend. I felt as though every moment was insulated, barely touching the next moment, like a string of pearls. Like how my head felt in my motorcycle helmet: a little clumsy, but sealed from danger. I could not possibly be put in charge of five inexperienced strangers on five giant beasts out in the woods where there were bears and no cell service. Surely some kind authority would intervene at the last minute, or I would find myself moving as if through the plasma of a dream: our horses carousel horses with marble eyes, the landscape soft and made of sugar.

I was excited to see Tristan when I pulled up to the barn, and curious about how he would behave toward me now that we'd become something—even if that something was still undefined. After we had discovered that the police officer coming toward us with the flashlight was not a police officer but a lone dog walker, light in hand so he could bag up poop from the sidewalk, we found that our adrenaline was spent. Our buzz flattened. And ahead of us, the next day, we both knew there were hours of barn chores, flies, and direct sunlight. Tristan offered to drive me home, but I lied and said that my Vespa was parked around the corner. I wanted to walk across town, to smoke a cigarette and listen to my boots on the street. I wanted to feel the trophy slickness in my underwear and daydream about what the future held for me and Tristan. But I found that the more future I allowed in, the more alone I felt. Curiously, the moment that I wanted to replay in my mind was not what little had occurred in the car, but what Tristan had said to me on the floodwall: *You're taller than she was. Your teeth are rounder.*

"Your teeth are rounder," I whispered to no one. "Your hair is straighter." I kept myself occupied this way, repeating these words quietly as I walked, trying to preserve the cadence with which Tristan had said them. There had been a sweet splintering of relief in his voice, like the smell of green twine.

CLEO'S MIDDLE NAME was Buster because her parents had been huge Buster Keaton fans.

"Why not use Keaton then?" I had asked.

"Because that would make too much sense," Tristan said.

"Cleo *Buster* Bonneville?"

"That's her," he said. There was pride in his voice.

"I'M SORRY, but you are going to have to ask that woman how much she weighs." It was the first thing Tristan said to me when I found him in the stable. He was brushing a pony with one hand and balancing a western saddle on his other arm. His face was wiped clean of the night before, replaced by a concern that I did not recognize. I did not know what woman he was talking about.

"Which one?"

Tristan stopped his brushing and gave me a look. "You know which one." He flicked his chin toward the stable door and, in the same motion, hefted the saddle onto the pony's back.

It turned out that, in my eagerness to see Tristan again, I had completely missed the family of five that was waiting at the picnic tables around the side of the stable. Immediately I could see what Tristan was talking about. The other day I had learned that each horse had a specific weight limit that could not be exceeded, ranging from 110 pounds for the smallest ponies to 250 for the draft horses. The problem always was, however, that no one in the history of humankind has ever given their actual weight when asked. It was a stupid system, because if we suspected that we had been given a false weight, we then had to make our own assessment anyway. Why not just save ourselves the awkwardness in the first place? Tristan had had this same conversation with Cleo, not surprisingly, and she had sided with the stable's policy.

"It's a question of morals: vanity versus animal rights," she had told Tristan last year. "Even if the customers lie outright, they're going to have to sit on that poor horse for the next hour and feel each forbidden pound bearing down into its spine."

"So, is the idea that they feel bad enough to lose weight, or to tell the truth?" Tristan had asked, and Cleo had looked at him, furious.

"Weight has nothing to do with it."

I reminded myself to ask Tristan later how much Cleo weighed. If she had always been truthful about it. If her number was higher or lower than mine.

The family of five looked tired already, the youngest two girls shoving fingers under the rims of their riding helmets to scratch their scalps. The oldest boy slouched against the picnic table, barely conscious. The dad was a goatee dude who looked like he had been forced to tuck in his shirt for the first time in his life. And the mother, I saw with a mixture of awe and despair, was a giant Joan of Arc dressed unconvincingly as mortal. A warrior princess who had probably won her goateed husband as a prize in a watermelon-crushing contest. I saw right away that the problem was not so much asking this woman about her weight, but that we would have to put her on our largest horse, while the rest of her family—husband included—rode alongside her, Sancho Panza–style, on their ponies. It would be a glaring visual joke, and this woman, who could smother an Arabian between her thighs, would either have to take it in stride or forever remember this day as the day she tried to create a nice family memory, and instead became the front-runner of the Big Woman parade that she may or may not have been avoiding all her life.

"Can I have the children's heights and weights?" I asked her, adding in the height factor as a distraction. She gave me the numbers, and I acted like I was doing calculations in my head. "And yours?" I asked, staring up at her.

"One-fifty," she said. I took this straight to Tristan, back in the barn, even though I knew that 150 was impossible. The last time I had stepped on a scale—a quilted one, mind you, in Nico's mother's bathroom—it had read 145. At the time I had not known what to do with that number, having no one to compare it to, except my own mother, who had always been scrawny, unable to focus long enough to eat a full meal. I suppose I was lucky to have escaped the body image circus that most of my friends had been a part of since before puberty. It was only because I still considered myself a growing child with a lingering belief that, whether my weight was high or low, it was still evening out in some way, waiting for me to fully mature. In other words, I would worry about it when someone told me to worry about it.

"SHE TOLD ME one-fifty also," Tristan said to me after the ride. It had not been a total disaster. The mother had ridden her Clydesdale without contempt and with what I imagined to be a certain level of gratitude, maybe due to the exaggerated space between her and the rest of her family. The morose teenage son had straightened out after his pony sneezed and almost sent him flying over its neck. The girls were terrified, but determined to appear braver than their brother. And the goateed father, seated stiffly on Murray, had allowed himself to follow in the shadow of his wife, while Murray took great, perverted gulps of air from the depth of her horse's enormous ass. I couldn't help but hope, for the father's sake, that this aligned with his own long-standing and deeply felt perversions. That maybe he understood Murray's compulsions more than anyone could ever know.

"If she already told you one-fifty, then why'd you make me ask her?" Tristan was going from stall to stall, taking off each horse's bridle and hanging it on his elbow. He looked a little like a dream catcher with all that leather hanging off his arm. I was following him, empty-handed.

"You're a girl," he said. "I figured she'd tell you the truth." In the tack room, he untangled the bridles one at a time and hung them on their designated hook: Murray, Whiskey, Blondie, Ranger, and the big one, who was insensitively named Bertha. I did not know where to take this conversation. I did not want to talk about the large woman anymore, because she was not Cleo. How, I wondered, could we bring the conversation back to Cleo? How could Tristan and I revisit the context of last night that had allowed for that ease of comparison—the things that made me like or unlike her? Tristan went back into the aisle, walking hurriedly between the stalls, and began the task of unburdening the horses from their sweaty saddles.

I followed, knowing that I should be helping more, worried that he was rushing because he wanted to go home. Had I paid attention at all to how the ride had been conducted? Somewhere along the trail, toward the top of the mountain, one of the girls' ponies had veered to the side and dipped its head into a patch of grass, grazing with such passion that a green froth had developed around the bit in its mouth. The girl had pulled and pulled at the reins, but was not strong enough to direct the pony back onto the path. I could see in her small, embarrassed outrage that she had believed all her life that the reins on a pony were like the handlebars on a bike. Now that life had shown her that this was not true, I wondered: Would she love ponies less? And then: Could it be that I was proud of myself for having been the kind of girl who would have loved ponies more? Tristan had turned his mare around and, ducking his head to avoid the tree branches, rode over to the girl. Without dismounting, he reached for the bad pony's reins and tied them around the horn of his saddle, thus tethering girl and pony to his side. How did he know to do that? How was he so certain that the pony would accept its leash and not flop down insolently on its side like Murray had done in the field? There were so many possible disasters that could occur once you left the safety of the stable—bad ponies, overconfident tourists, rain, wind, slow horses, fast horses, bees, turkey vultures, lost garments, loose saddles, dropped cameras. Once I had gotten a taste of what could go wrong out there, the list would continue to write itself in my mind. *I'm good at anticipating disaster,* I heard myself telling the flinty woman who had hired me. Why would anyone want such a skill?

"What's up?" Tristan was thrusting a saddle into my

arms, the underside hot and furry like a dog bed. The now-saddleless horse behind him wore a dark indent of sweat on its back. It reminded me of the creases on the side of my face after a deep sleep. How could I tell Tristan that I was freaking out? That all I wanted was to be thrown back into last night, where the rules were strange but somehow very clear to me? He had tasted my nipple. I had felt his erection poking my leg. Where did that leave us, and, more importantly, how could we get back to that, without things seeming forced and awkward? The thing about car sex was that it required spontaneity and fear—couples in movies were always kissing and walking backward and unbuttoning each other and panting. Their passion was cinched tightly by a musical score and quick close-ups. In real life you had to create your own drama, and last night the script had been tragically cut short. I would have to create it again myself, without the alcohol this time.

"How much did Cleo weigh?" I asked Tristan. I wanted his reaction to be what it always was: sly, eager, and slightly guilty. It was the mixture of eagerness and guilt that I liked the most—the purity of it, exaggerated further by the artlessness of his shaved head. But he was quiet—politely quiet, I thought. The way people are when they have lost feelings—and it made me uneasy. I adjusted the saddle in my arms and thought of how I might salvage the moment. Make a joke. Create an absurdity larger than the one I had just spoken into existence. Tristan turned to another stall and began working the cinch loose from the horse there. I knew that I was supposed to shelve the saddle that I was holding and make myself available for the next one, but I just stood, watching. It was possible that Tristan had, sometime between last night and this morning, decided that it was best to move on from Cleo. Had the words that we had spoken, which I had all too comfortably treated as foreplay, been, from Tristan's viewpoint, the opening and reopening of wounds? Maybe what I thought was sexy was, in fact, keeping Tristan suspended in a raw and painful limbo. I hurried with my saddle into the tack room and looked for its place on the wall, but could not remember which horse we had just taken it from. The brass-plated names looked ridiculous; here we were, assigning male and female personalities to these creatures, naming them like children, giving them their own shelves, as if they cared how aesthetically we stored their torture devices. When I was stressed, my mind liked to fixate on details like these, picking apart all the ways in which the things we were accustomed to were, in reality, nonsensical, brutal, or terrifying. I chose a wooden beam at random and heaved the saddle onto it, and when I walked back into the aisle, Tristan was not in any of the stalls, or in the feed room, or outside by the water pump. The horses turned their heads toward me. Their ears swiveled in unhelpful choreography. I felt that I had done something unforgivable, and that I had not worked hard enough. Tristan had given me half the tip after the ride, and I had barely been able to keep my horse from falling behind. I deserved to be abandoned like this.

No sooner had my heart settled on this matter than I heard a rattling sound from the front of the stable. Tristan was coming through the door pushing a wheelbarrow with a hay bale in it. I felt a strange emptiness as we began with the rest of the day's chores. It seemed that Tristan was not angry with me for mentioning Cleo, but I did not feel the invitation from him to bring her up again. I did not know if this meant that he and I had slipped back into the category of coworkers who flirted, or if we were still coworkers who planned to undress each other at the end of the day. If the latter was the case, then would we undress strictly as ourselves, or would we continue to adhere to the guidelines of the night before? It was all very confusing; meanwhile Tristan told me that my next task was to learn how to reverse the small tractor through the doorway of the hay barn.

"Without hitting anything," he added.

Two girls around my age showed up who had been recently hired to take over the work for the summer girls. These were the autumn girls. According to Tristan, autumn girls arrived every year from the nearby college with high hopes, probably envisioning that their days would unfold like an L.L.Bean campaign: mornings spent at the library in vintage sweaters, afternoons in the crisp air, petting horses. Wearing vintage sweaters. And every year, half the autumn girls were gone by the first frost, or after the first time they were forced to complete the morning feed with a hangover. There was a saying: "The first to stub her toe on frozen shit." The autumn girls were never trained to lead trail rides, because it wasn't worth it; even if they stayed on through winter, tourist season was over by November. I wondered why I had not been hired as part of one of these seasonal batches. Was it so obvious that I was not a college student? Did I look like someone who would stick through a harsh winter, and was that a good thing?

Tristan left me momentarily in the cab of the tractor while he met the two new autumn girls. I watched them watch him as he walked across the driveway. They were both pretty, but the tall one had a look of competence that made me immediately jealous. She nudged her friend subtly with an elbow, as if to send a message about Tristan that was either approving or cruel. Both scenarios made me hate her. She had bangs that caught endearingly on her eyelashes, and she was wearing duck boots with quilted cuffs, even though it was hot out. I shifted the tractor into reverse and began inching carefully into the barn. The movement made the girls look up, which was what I had hoped for. Consciously, or subconsciously, they would acknowledge that I was here before them, and I had already reached tractor status. Duck Boots waved at me, which I resented. Tristan turned and gave me the "one minute" finger with eye contact, and I felt a new stirring of loyalty. The tractor rattled beneath me. The world chattered like teeth, and I thought about Cleo and her truckful of bouncing hay. Tristan's respectful erection.

ON THE AFTERNOON before my first date with Tristan, I had returned from the barn to find a new email from Byron. I had not heard from him since the dick pic, not even after I failed to appear at the bookstore that day and the next. It was the kind of job where I was often alone, in charge of opening and closing when the boss wasn't there. It was completely possible that my not showing up had resulted in the store not operating for a span of days. The subject line of the email was NO TITLE, which meant that he had typed out the words *no title* instead of leaving it blank and relying on the parenthetical, autofilled *no subject*. This bothered me. I left it alone and got dressed for the bar, but then feared that maybe he was demanding his keys back, or that he was angry, or worse, remorseful.

Dear Drew,
I am not sure what you want me to say. I am a man of complex needs. Just a man. Perhaps you have it in your head that I am something else.

The note reminded me of the "truth letters" that Mr. Pursley left in the vents of Nico's locker. What was it with these men? There was a similarity in tone, the tone suggesting that they thought highly of themselves, but were also aware that they were full of shame and ugliness. The implied hope seemed to be that we, as girls, should find that shame and ugliness to be attractive because we were, in part, responsible for it. I had closed my email and left for the bar, trying not to think too hard about any of it. Was not my ex-boss allowed to feel what he felt, and wasn't the only problem that his dick looked like half-burnt Marv from *Home Alone* and I did not want it? It was possible that all dicks looked like Marv, but that the ones attached to the men that I desired were forgiven by way of selective blindness. They did not jump out unsolicited. They were not photographed head-on with flash, the way you'd snap a picture of a boil to send to your mother: *Does this look normal?* I quickly forgot all of this once I arrived at Wily's, satisfied with the quick, makeshift conclusion that penises were inherently wrong and ill-intentioned and that anyone dealing with them had to be like a prison volunteer: cautious but compassionate, with a "meet people where they are" kind of attitude.

I thought about all this again while I waited for Tristan to save me because I had backed the tractor too far into the hay barn and toppled a wall of hay bales on and around myself. There had been a crunch like breaking wood that I did not have the stomach to investigate. How could I sit here judging men when I was so obviously incompetent? Across the gravel drive, Tristan led the autumn girls away from the stable toward the dung heap. They fell out of view where the ground dipped, and I looked for a moment at the gridwork of trembling white-fence ribbons across the property, the rough bouquets of weeds where the ground was not grazed. Above the paddocks, the mountain seemed dangerously close, accessible in a way that I had always assumed mountains should not be. And yet, we had scaled it in less than an hour, our horses dropping their turds without ceremony, the tourists assailed by so much raw countryside that I doubted they truly saw any of it. It occurred to me then, still sitting behind the wheel of the tractor, that I could just leave. While Tristan and the girls were out of sight, I could get on my scooter and drive silently away. I could find a job that did not require me to be responsible for strangers' lives, and yet was still less soul draining than the bookstore. No imminent danger and no surprise penises. Such a life had to exist out there. Instead, I climbed down from the cab and tried to assess what damage had been done, but all I could see was hay—some still holding its form, some loosened from the fall. I had heard about fires starting in hay barns such as this, something about damp hay creating heat so intense that it spontaneously ignited. It was all very vaginal, if you asked me. I could not see what thing I had backed over, so, fighting my instinct to run, I began to restack the bales that were still intact. I soon uncovered a crushed wooden pallet. There were about a hundred such pallets employed for various purposes throughout the farm. Relieved, I dragged it to the back of the barn and tucked it upright against a far wall, where it fit in with some loose boards and draped cobwebs. There were swallows back there, diving in and out of a square of light high above me.

Tristan was waiting when I returned to the tractor. He was alone. Even though I had hidden the broken pallet, it must have been obvious from the tractor's strange angle that something had gone awry. The look on Tristan's face told me that he understood everything that had happened, but that he was not going to be angry. I felt as if I were wrapped inside layers of indebtedness: because I had taken the Cleo thing too far, because I was useless on the trail ride, incompetent at driving the tractor. Because I was not as fresh and teachable as Duck Boots. Oh, to be fresh and teachable again! Tristan walked around the tractor, hands in his pockets, looking at me.

"She never told me," he said. He came closer, and when I took a step back, I felt the haystack against my shoulder, warmer and more solid than I expected. What was he talking about?

"And she carried it differently." He put his hand on my side and held it steady, as if appraising that part of me or taking a mental measurement. I could see the humor rising in his face, and I understood that he was not only answering my question from before—*how much did Cleo weigh?*—but also anticipating my next one. *Am I bigger or smaller?*

"Where?" I asked. "Where did she carry it differently?"

"Here." He kissed me. "And here."

We climbed the tiered haystack easily. Even in the rush of it, I was still aware of a voice in my head, a sarcastic commentator who wanted to know if this was any less cliché than the car sex. What had happened to the dog-hair couches and flabby air mattresses of my past boyfriends? And what was next? Elevator sex? An infinity pool? When we reached the ceiling, Tristan made a fist and pushed upward. A shower of hay particles fell over us, and I saw that he had swung open a trapdoor. A loft. I followed him through. In the center of the loft there was a large square of floor missing, and I could make out the top of the tractor below, which looked like a kid's crookedly parked toy. Above the hole there dangled a hook and pulley system, bright in the concentrated beam from a square window. This struck me as something from an old photograph: this raw moment of industry seized by the relentless, artistic light that would not leave it alone. The floor was slippery with loose hay. Tristan closed the trapdoor, wiping it clear of dust so that we would be able to find it again later. He looked at me intently.

"Don't fall through the hole," he said. I laughed and leaned in to kiss him, but he stopped me with his hand. "I mean it," he said, still serious. So I said, "I won't." I could see that he was being my manager, trying to avoid a workplace injury. How was it that this was the right thing to do, of all things? I wanted to be consumed by the narrative of the moment, for Tristan to lay down the rules (number one: don't fall through the floor), and for me to abide by them. Craving a narrative was like desiring a specific flavor of air: mountain air, salty sea air, sweet, musty hayloft air.

"You and her are very different, you know," Tristan said. He worked my tank over my head, brushed my hair back when it fell over my eyes. "I don't know if this is going to work."

"How can I make it work?" I asked. *How can I make*

sure you don't stop? He unclasped my bra and the tight shell of it fell away. The air was so warm that it almost felt too natural, being naked with all that space around us. Like I could have walked out of there and not noticed.

"Here," he said, pushing me gently until I was lying on my back. "I am going to show you what to do." The way his voice was in that moment, I would have jumped through the hole for him.

I soon learned that what Tristan really meant was that he was going to show me what to *like.* I did not have to do anything. He was going to be thorough, and he was going to be generous, even though I had been stumbling around guiltily all day, assuming that I was undeserving of any kind of attention, much less this slow but consistent pressure. Normally, I would stop a guy using this technique, or at least subtly redirect—it is my opinion that the tongue is not a shovel, but more of a rebellious, lock-picking feather—but I was not me, and *not me* was strangely okay with it. I wondered if all of this had been orchestrated. If Tristan had meant to be aloof earlier so he could undo me like this. Why was that so hot? I squirmed to try to get him to change pace, but Tristan held strong, taking my legs and pushing them against the sides of his head. Did he want me to squeeze? I squeezed, and he made a sound into me that made me squeeze harder. Did I taste like her? Did I sound like her, through the earmuffs of my thighs?

Cleo was afraid of olives. Not when they were isolated in a drink, Tristan explained, but when they were crammed into a jar. She said it gave her a "formaldehyde" feeling of dread. Cleo maintained many different categories for dread. There was Hiker's Dread: the fear of not having the energy to complete something once you reached the halfway point. Mortal Dread: this was self-explanatory, but also made Cleo feel strangely compelled to clip her fingernails short. Dental Dread was the worst kind of dread on the planet, followed closely by Bus Stop Dread: the terrible feeling that you had forgotten to pick up a family member, or a child from school, even if no such person or child existed.

I could tell that something was off when I returned to my basement room at Nico's house. I always used the ugly back entrance because it was more private, although it was not my privacy that I was trying to preserve, but that of Nico's parents. How jarring would it be for them to have an inherited houseguest unlocking their front door in the evenings, walking timidly behind the television while they were in the middle of *60 Minutes*? There are some things that people deserve to do without random non–family members watching: wearing a towel turban or eating a wet salad. I went inside and immediately smelled Pine-Sol. My belongings had been piled neatly on the futon where I slept, and the ash-white wall-to-wall carpeting was newly raked by a vacuum cleaner. I could smell the airing out of sheets, the spritz of disinfectant at the bottom of the trash bin. Someone had done a deep clean of the entire house while I was at work. Cleaning always put me on high alert. When you arrived home and your house was mysteriously clean and smelling of chemicals, it meant that your mother was gone and some busybody relative like your paternal grandmother had swooped in and thrown away everything in the kitchen. I set my backpack down and tried to pry off my boots without showering the carpet with flecks of dried mud. I am too filthy for this place, I thought, bitterly. Except for where I've been licked clean.

"Drew!" It was Nico's mother, at the top of the basement stairs. She was cheery, which concerned me even more. Nico's mother was one of those women who seemed to have traded aging for a slow dehydration. She had a long, anxious neck and wore startling blue eyeshadow, both of which I did not find off-putting. At the time, she had not let go of her eighties perm, and it gave her a leonine silhouette of authority as she walked carefully down the stairs.

"Drew, I want to talk to you." I stood frozen. I knew what was coming; I just did not know how it would be delivered. I hoped not too warmly. That would give me nothing to hold against her, would only increase my sense of ineptitude, guilt, and that awful accumulation of dread that follows a person whenever they are fully reliant on another. (What would Cleo label it? Deadbeat Dread?) The story was that Nico's parents were going on vacation for three weeks to the Virgin Islands. They wondered if I might house-sit for them. They would pay. (Here I must add that I had never been charged rent for the three years that I had been with them.) Nico's mother was quiet and pleasantly smiling for a moment too long, which told me all that I needed to know: This was it. I had three weeks to find a new place to live, and they were sending me off in the most painfully generous way. Jesus himself could not have conceived of a gentler extraction.

"That's perfect timing!" I said, my face matching her brightness. "My boyfriend and I were just talking today about finding a place together." The relief that washed into the room was palpable. The tendons in her neck disappeared, as if someone had dropped them like reins.

I showered and then dressed myself in clean jeans and a tee, even though I did not plan on going out again. I could not bring myself to wear pajamas—even sweatpants felt too homey, settled in. I had three weeks, I knew, but my body was now incapable of spreading out. What I had said about the boyfriend was not even the thinnest stretch of the truth. For one, I did not consider Tristan my boyfriend, or even boyfriend material. My heart was too literal for that. He had told me from the beginning that he was not sticking around, and I did not find that it was my business to hope otherwise. Furthermore, the idea that we might ever live together, in any capacity, was so unnatural it was embarrassing. Domesticity was the death of anonymity. It meant that every insignificant decision you made would now be perceived: the brand of hand lotion you bought, the peanut-butter jars that you were too lazy to recycle, the fried hair in your hairbrush. When you lived with another person, you were always accounted for in some way, your spinning globe stopped abruptly by the finger of shared bills and timed showers. I removed my belongings from the futon. When they were lined up like that, they looked even more pitiful and slumped. A toiletries bag, a laundry bag, a cloth grocery bag still holding a can of soup from the last time I went shopping. Just an out-of-shape bag family. It was only five, but I turned off the light and lay down under the quilt, still in my clothes. I imagined myself caught beneath Nico's mother's overturned Tupperware, wanting neither to stay where I was nor to be released into the cold, fluorescent world.

THERE HAD BEEN a therapist who appeared after the first time my mother went away. I was ten, and I could tell that the therapist, who was the first person I had ever met with frameless spectacles, wished my mother was more competent, and it annoyed him that she was not. I tried to explain things about her, like how she was incapable of taking a shower when I was home. It worried her too much to know that I was moving around, possibly knocking over her piles of stuff, when she was concentrating on washing her hair. Similarly, she could not cook with the television on, or when she had a headache, or when I was asleep. There were certain noises that could not coincide, but then there were noises that were also not allowed—like the gong of pots and pans—against a backdrop of silence. We ate a lot of takeout, and at odd times of the day.

"I bet that was stressful for you," the therapist said. I did not want to reward him by agreeing, so I rolled my eyes.

"Life is stressful."

I could see that this phrase had only confirmed whatever he already believed about me: that life with a negligent mother had hardened me. I would soon develop an attitude and, possibly, if no one got through to me, a drug habit or a teen pregnancy. I did not like the way his blue eyes shifted behind the floating glass of his spectacles. Blue eyes already lack boundaries, and his had been set loose like some kind of deconstructed fishbowl. What the therapist did not understand—what no one understood—was that my mother was anything but negligent. She explained everything to me. She knew herself as much as it was possible to know oneself, and she was full of sorrow and regret for her flaws. She may not have been able to make a grocery list, but she could hold me on her lap and tell me the ways that she wished she could be better. When she laid it out like that, in the shadow of the world's turmoil and her own suffering, none of it seemed that bad. So what if she couldn't make small talk with the other moms at school pickup? So what if she sometimes let important letters fall into the crack between the stove and the counter? The crack was a poor design anyway.

The therapist liked to encourage me to imagine myself elsewhere when my environment became overwhelming. That was his word. "Overwhelming" to me was a dodgeball game, or a surprise flock of seagulls, not a messy house and a mother with a wet towel over her eyes. Still, I humored him and narrated a nice scene with grassy hills and blue skies, and a tiny stone cottage near a lake. I could tell that the mention of the cottage touched him.

"Tell me about this *cottage*," he said. "What is it like inside?" His eagerness gave him away, and I knew right then that he expected my imaginary house to be the opposite of my real house. What he wanted was for me to want what everyone else thought was normal. And of course I wanted that. Of course I wanted the tiny stone cottage with rugged shutters and plump hedges all around it. But it was imperative that I live my life without being perceived as wanting any such thing. I could not be so obvious, especially not in front of a man who pronounced the word "cottage" as if it were stuck to the roof of his mouth.

"The floor is covered in trash," I told him. He tried to look patiently incredulous.

"Drew," he said. "*Your* cozy little cottage?"

"I never said it was cozy."

I PUSHED MYSELF deeper into the crook of the futon mattress and felt something tickle my face. It was a blade of hay. Earlier, I had ground my head so profoundly into the floor of the loft that my hair had become woven with hay like a scarecrow. Tristan knelt in front of me, trying to brush it out with his fingers. While he was doing this, I noted the front of his pants, the button that looked like it was ready to pop. I touched him. He was so hard he didn't even feel human.

He pulled away.

"Maybe next time," he said, shielding himself with his hand. I was stunned. What rules were we playing by now? Was I supposed to insist? Convince him? All my life I had been led to believe that a man would never do this. If he did, it was to cover up an insecurity, or to create some kind of twisted upper hand. They never just *didn't want to.* I placed my hand over his and pushed gently. His breath caught a little. Yes, I thought, I think you should reconsider. I was still mostly undressed, which felt exciting and unfair. I wanted Tristan to look at me, and for it to weaken his resolve. He placed his other hand over my hand and removed the hand that was holding his crotch, so that I was holding him now, through his pants. He pressed me there.

"I said, 'Maybe next time.'"

I thought about it, lying in the crook of the futon, wondering if Tristan was changing the rules sporadically, or if there was a higher logic to it all. But what were the rules? Was I a stand-in for Cleo or a gateway to her memory? Either way, why would he punish himself by walking away, when he had me right in front of him, naked and crowned with wild, hay-pricked hair? Pondering all this threw me into yet another state of horniness and confusion. I pushed my face into the futon and slid my hand down the front of my jeans, which were zipped so tightly that all I could do was hold one finger to myself, like holding the *off* button on a laptop with a frozen screen. Maybe horniness and confusion lived symbiotically. Maybe that's what people meant when they talked about keeping the mystery alive—if the brain was allowed too much clarity, would it shut down the body's impulses? Would lust become gruesomely dissected by reason? I rocked my hips into my stationary finger. I could have unzipped, but Tristan had taught me this: to wait for it, to trust that it would be there. I imagined him as he had been in the loft, the sound that he had made when I squeezed his head between my legs.

No, that wasn't it.

I imagined the slow bullying of his tongue, too insistent, then not enough, then mean again.

That still wasn't it.

How distorted his pants were afterward. His hand against it.

That was closer.

I looked at the scene through Tristan's eyes. I liked that better, and my mind, showing mercy, removed me from the picture and replaced the woman in the hay with someone else. Someone *not me.* As Tristan, I could see it clearly: how he had Cleo where he wanted her and where she could not leave him, his head vised between her legs, her body a single, electric plea. I could see how he would respond to this plea on his terms, generous, then stingy. *Maybe next time.* Tristan had not been punishing himself at all.

I drove to the stable the next morning with a sense of renewed determination. Somehow, I had stopped caring about my new eviction notice, and all I wanted to do was convey to Tristan that I was willing to let our game evolve. Yesterday, it had been unclear exactly what my role was, but now it made perfect sense: I was here to help Tristan punish the woman who had broken his heart. I did not have many useful skills, but I was open-minded and I had not felt this excited about anything for a long time. Since Nico left, I'd been trying to find something to do with myself, like a hobby—not because I was bored, but because I felt suddenly that I needed to be something more than just the friend left behind to rot in her parents' basement. I had asked myself, What activity would be the least creepy? If you had a directionless girl living beneath you, what would you want her to be doing? Quilting? Writing poetry? Listening to French lessons on tape? I tried taking novels home from the bookstore, but there was no ambience, and I felt cheap and unsophisticated, which was the opposite of how I wanted to feel when I was reading a book. The ceiling was too white, the walls whined with plumbing. One of the ground-level windows was blocked by a garden-hose rack. The other showed the strange underbelly of a shrub.

The sky was cloudier than yesterday. Showy and melancholic. It didn't feel like morning, or any other hour for that matter. Time seemed as immovable as the silver pitchers in somebody's dining room. I took a hard turn, gulping in the scent of lilacs and the pungent odor of curing roadkill, and I wondered if you could decide to make sex your hobby. I believed that you could make a case for it if you were having specialized sex, like people who ate bizarre food—in other words, people who did what everyone else did, but threw in a twist. Yes: I was honing my sex strategy, giving serious thought to the psychology behind my next move. Still, I worried that it wasn't quirky enough to earn it kink status. One might make the argument that Byron's dick pic was kinkier, just in terms of sheer brazenness, plus the added camera, which could be considered a prop. Tristan and I had no such props, but we were surrounded by leather daily, and I knew how to wield an English riding crop, so maybe that counted for something. He and I had another trail ride that morning at nine, and this time I was supposed to lead. Such a task required confidence, strength, awareness, and people skills. I wasn't sure what frightened me more: that I had to go through with it, or that I would have to go through with it under Tristan's supervision. It was like trying to make friends on the playground with the teacher watching.

When I pulled up, Tristan was already there, bringing in the two Haflingers, Trick and Treat, from off the hill. We tried to use Trick and Treat for rides whenever we could because they were stocky and strong, and they walked so close together on the trail that you could almost count them as one horse. I was annoyed with Tristan for getting there before me, and then more annoyed when Duck Boots appeared from inside the toolshed just in time to open the gate for him. I had forgotten about her and her slightly less pretty friend. Today she was wearing an oversize flannel shirt, tucked in the front, which was something that I had only seen affected people do, but somehow looked natural on her. Along with her almost-too-long bangs, everything about her seemed to fall together in the right places, like a quilt that someone decides to purposefully push off-center, to make the room look lived-in. I was further irritated and amazed to learn that her name was Diane. There was something so heartbreakingly vintage about that name, like a name given to someone in witness protection. Her friend introduced herself to me in the tack room as Aurora, which was a name that I did not find charming and that did not suit her at all. Now that I was seeing her closely, however, I decided that I liked her quiet ruggedness. She had thick eyebrows and a good center of gravity. I walked around the stable, getting ready for the ride and acting like I was showing Aurora the ropes, when I was really using her as a human shield, so that if we bumped into Tristan, I would not recite to him the monologue that I had rehearsed on the drive over: that I wanted to help him punish Cleo. That he could do anything he wanted to me within reason, and he would not have to pretend that it was just for fun, or only half sincere. If he needed it, I was ready.

MY CLIENTS FOR the morning were a newlywed couple from New Jersey. They were both the same height and had matching blond-eyebrow looks of amazement. The Haflingers, Trick and Treat, were similarly blond, which made the couple want to take pictures, and led them spiraling into a discussion about which one of them was more suited to ride a horse named Trick and which one deserved to ride Treat. It was gross. So as not to contaminate their bliss, Tristan helped the man into the saddle, and I boosted the woman. I gave them a lesson on how to hold the reins—like ice cream cones—and how to steer gently if their horses went off course, then slipped my hand beneath the saddle cinches to make sure that the horses had not bloated and sucked.

"What on earth does that mean?" the woman asked me. I explained to her that horses had their games, just like children. Sometimes they puffed out their tummies when you were tightening the saddle, only to suck in later, which could send the saddle slipping sideways or worse.

"Imagine a loose fanny pack," I said, and the man and woman shrieked like it was the funniest thing they had ever heard. Fanny pack! Bloat and suck! Tristan, from atop his horse, gave me a look of approval. Maybe I was better at this than I thought. I sat tall, resting one casual hand on the back of my saddle, and urged my horse up the trail. When the Haflingers followed eagerly, I felt powerful. *Drew has always been a leader,* said an imagined narrator. *She just had to stop holding her breath in the bathroom.*

There were more pictures to be taken at the top of the mountain, which was not the true top of the mountain, but a clearing where the trail ended. An opening in the trees looked out over a cliff—again, not a true cliff, but a dramatic slope—from which one could look down at the buildings of the closest town, which looked like muffin crumbs scrunched together on a plate. The newlyweds wanted to be photographed on their horses in front of the view. It was a reasonable request. It was only when the wife suggested that their horses be posed touching noses, to capture a sense of symmetry, that I began to get nervous.

"I want it to be like Jackie and Carson's wedding picture," she said to the husband. The husband looked questioningly at the view, which had been darkening steadily since we set out. I could tell that he was not convinced of his wife's vision.

"Jackie and Carson had a sunset," he said. "And a professional photographer." At this, the wife turned her attention to me, extending the camera by its strap in my direction. I could see in her expression that, to her, the problem was that she had been carrying an expectation in her heart and that expectation had already been dashed some time ago. Now, she was here, and perhaps no one could know what sacrifices she had made to arrive at this particular summit in her life, riding a horse named "Treat," when maybe that was not the persona that resonated with her soul. I looked warily at Tristan, but his face said, *Give the woman what she wants.*

I AM CONVINCED that we would have made it to the stable without incident had we not spent so much time forcing two side-eyed prey animals to face each other head-on. Even if the pictures came out decently, which I doubted that they would, I still wondered what the point of it was. It's one thing to capture a moment in passing, but to manufacture a scene to look poignant seemed depressing. Did the wife intend to lie to their friends when they got back, as if to convince them that these matching blond ponies had spontaneously posed in a show of anthropomorphic affection, and that was supposed to reflect positively on their status as a married couple? I could not imagine being in a relationship where you were meant to conveniently forget the labor behind quaint details. *Remember how I mowed down that kid in the mall so we could buy the last singing Santa Claus? Remember how I bullied the waiter into giving us the more scenic table?* Not that I could imagine myself in a relationship at all. And, because I am the worst devil's advocate I know, I started to wonder, as we were filing down the mountain trail, if perhaps what Tristan and I were attempting was a similar kind of hypocrisy. All morning, I had been anticipating my next move in becoming Cleo, forming a plan so I could embody her without overdoing it. In other words: how to be sexy without revealing my hand.

Since leaving the summit, we had been following a section of the trail that was shielded by a canopy of trees. So, when the path opened near the foot of the mountain, we could see that the storm had already formed. The dirt was pocked by rainfall. The tall bushes bent at pale angles. I felt my horse pick up her feet, the whole world going up on its toes, and I worried that I was about to be thrown. But it was Trick, the husband's horse, who spooked and took off galloping, away from the trail and into the neighboring hayfield. Tristan shouted at me to grab the wife's horse, and then, seeing that they were not a flight risk, urged his own horse after the husband's. Life became cinema then: the sky a panoramic band of darkness, the two figures tearing across the horizon. Tristan leaned forward and, stretching beyond the saddle like a stuntman leaping from a speeding car to a locomotive, reached out to take control of the runaway. The two horses stopped so abruptly that they each twirled on their haunches. From where the wife and I stood, it seemed almost pleasantly choreographed, like an old Western. It helped that neither husband nor wife fully understood the danger that they were in. I believe they viewed the situation as if one of them had been humorously carried off by a rogue golf cart. That was fine, I supposed. The couple would return home feeling as though they had lived something authentic. They tipped us each thirty dollars, and I suspected that it was not just for Tristan's heroics, but for the whole scenario, as if we had had control from the start. That was also fine. It made me think about the importance of scenarios. Was there any real thrill without a story to support it?

I COULD TELL that Tristan was shaken by the events. After the blonds left, he sat down on an overturned bucket and put his face in his hands.

"That could have been so bad," he said. He looked up. "But you did good."

"*I* did good?" I was bewildered. This got the attention of Aurora and Diane, who wanted to know what had happened. I told them, because I could see that Tristan was too humble, and Diane stepped forward.

"You two should take a break. Go get lunch." Anyone could have said it, but coming from Diane, the suggestion sounded like a stroke of fresh paint. How satisfying to take a lunch break after a harrowing experience. Other people did such things; why couldn't we? Diane and Aurora promised us that they knew how to untack the horses and let them outside. They were horse girls, through and through. I had my doubts, but I wanted to believe them, and I appreciated how they were treating Tristan and me like an established couple who needed a date night.

We took Tristan's car into town. I was happy to be the passenger. Being the leader was exhausting. Being a failed leader was even worse. The storm had already moved on and the sky was steely and timeless again. Tristan drove quietly, seeming to have recovered his nerves. Finally, as if reading my mind, he said, "That shit happens too often."

"You going all cowboy?" I could tell that he liked the sound of that, even if he was trying not to. I could also tell that, underneath it all, he was weary, and it had nothing to do with the runaway Haflinger.

"Why did she leave you?" I asked. I had meant to put this in a certain flattering context. As in, *You were incredible out there, plus you're not a jerk. What's Cleo's problem?* We rumbled over the train tracks, past the abandoned signal tower, where I cranked open my window to try to catch a whiff of the comforting creosote. I didn't even do it consciously; it was like a reflex. Tristan stopped at an intersection and turned left, which brought us downtown.

"I told you she was married?" It was not really a question.

"Was that her reason?"

Suddenly, we were on Main Street and Tristan was parallel parking, looking over his shoulder and spinning the wheel with his palm.

"Well, did I tell you I got her pregnant?" This was not really a question either. We got out of the car and started up the sidewalk. Main Street was the only part of town with walkable businesses. The rest were about a mile away, nestled awkwardly into shopping centers. Just one block ahead and across the street was the used bookstore. I hoped that Byron would see me from inside and wonder why I was strolling around in muck boots with a farm boy. I know it's cruel, but part of me wanted him to see Tristan and to feel inadequate.

Tristan told me the story while we sat on a sidewalk bench, eating hot dogs and potato chips that we had bought from a cart. He said that he had been stupid, assuming that Cleo would not get pregnant because she was forty—and not because he thought that forty was too old biologically, but because he had this idea that women would have figured out how to not get pregnant by then. I liked that he was opening up to me, but at the same time, I felt a weight lowering in my gut, the sensation like staring at a piece of fruit that starts to look less and less appetizing. Selfishly, I wanted the Cleo story to remain the dark-humored jewel that it was in the beginning: full of obsession and heartbreak, but nothing so unappealingly somber as a baby. Tristan said that when she told him, he felt a new door open in his heart, and now that she was gone, it was still swinging open, tormenting him. I knew, from the way that he was talking, that the baby was also gone, and I waited fearfully for him to reach that point because I did not know how to talk about the loss of something that never was. It's funny how, when you are young, you can be so irresponsibly compassionate, but also self-serving, to the point where only stupid but well-meant decisions are ever made. No real sacrifices; no real cruelties. Tristan said that Cleo lost the baby. She was alone when it happened, and obviously could not go to her husband for comfort.

"Sometimes I think that I'm more upset about failing her in that way than I am about never knowing my child," Tristan said calmly. It was the saddest thing I had ever heard a man admit to. Why was I always surprised when any man showed depth, and what was this new shame? The bad fruit feeling from moments before became a thing that I wanted to push my thumb into, to wet my mouth with. I placed my hand on his back and thought about saying, *It's not your fault.* But the phrase had been ruined years ago by the therapist with the incomplete eyeglasses. Instead, I asked, tactlessly: "Did she blame you?" He inhaled, looked up at the shoppers moving across the street.

"No," he said, like the answer interested him. "But she didn't like how broken up I was about it."

"She didn't want you to be upset?"

"I'm sure there was more to it than that." He crumpled the foil from his hot dog. I could sense that the action was mirroring something internal. He did not want to go back there in his head. Or he didn't want to reveal to me that he was back there. Maybe he was afraid now of being emotional because it had backfired before, catastrophically.

"She had a filthy mind, you know," he said then, standing. "But when she got hurt, or hit a curb when she was parking, she'd say, 'Oh, biscuits!' instead of *fuck* or *shit*."

"She sounds like a real treat," I said. I hoped that he would take my sarcasm as the peace offering that it was meant to be; we could move on from the sad stuff, but he could still say whatever he needed to say.

We continued walking up the sidewalk, slowly, like sightseers. We passed the bookshop, and I allowed my eyes to touch upon it lightly. The store had an attractive front with a crosshatch window, where old leather-bound books were displayed—even if they had boring titles—because it sparked the imagination, made people remember why books were seductive in the first place. I don't know if any of this was true, but that was what I had been told when

I was hired. As we walked, Tristan seemed to be easing back to his old self, or at least the self that I knew. I felt certain that, if not later tonight, then at least soon, we would have sex, and it would be full of wonderfully cultivated tension. We could even use props, eventually, if the props conversation came up.

"You know what the Jersey man said to me after I saved his life?" he said suddenly and stopped walking. His finger was out, comically, about to convey the line. I could only imagine what the blond husband might have said out of earshot from the women. Would he have been grateful and vulnerable, or would he have tried to recover his pride? I watched Tristan's finger drop to his side. He laughed. It was a strange laugh—defeated, a tad unhinged.

"Don't tell my wife I shit myself?" I said, offering my guess. But Tristan was looking at something behind me, over my head. I turned around and saw that we had stopped in front of a vacant storefront. I recognized the place as having once been a greasy but comforting breakfast spot, and before that, a family-owned pharmacy. When I was a child, the stores and restaurants on Main Street were of great significance to me. I assumed that they were immovable like monuments, and filled with items that existed only within the context of those stores, on that street, in that town. On the rare occasion that I was shopping downtown with my mother and saw another child from school, the intensity of worlds colliding, proving that everything was in fact real, was dizzying. When shops started closing and lying vacant, I thought it was tremendously sad. Until one day, it was just how things were. The storefront, on closer inspection, seemed shinier than I remembered it. I could make out through the glare of the window a gleaming wood floor, as if newly renovated. And above me hung an oval wooden sign with the words BUSTER'S CAFÉ burned rustically into the surface. I waited for Tristan to finish the story, oblivious to the significance of the sign, although I suppose if I had truly been paying attention, I would have caught on earlier. On the glass doorway there was a handwritten notice in deft lettering that announced an opening-day celebration later that week. Tristan cupped his hands around his eyes and peered through the window, then backed away. He looked faintly impressed, and also like he wanted to cry.

THERE WERE NO trail rides booked the next day, so Tristan and the autumn girls and I decided to wash the tack, which meant hauling out every saddle, bridle, and piece of leather from the stable, spreading it out in the sun, and scrubbing it with special soap and conditioner. The chore was not totally unfamiliar to me from my time at the therapeutic riding program, and I was further relieved to find that it was the kind of busywork that was more for the purpose of saying that you did it, rather than making anything look truly clean. I also suspected that Tristan was spiraling and needed a task that was meticulous and hyper-focused, which was why he had been the one to suggest it. We sat outside the stable, Aurora and Diane at the picnic table with toothbrushes and sudsy water, and Tristan and I on the ground, working some kind of lotion into the stiff flaps on an English saddle. Tristan had been quiet on the subject of Buster's Café, so I asked him again, "Are you sure it's her?" I didn't care that the autumn girls could hear us. I always liked if someone was eavesdropping, but only if they were far enough away that all parties could believably pretend that it wasn't happening. Tristan looked forlorn.

"It has to be her."

"She's not the only Buster in the world."

Here, he looked up from the moistened saddle in his lap and stared like I was being purposefully obtuse, until I said, "I suppose people are allowed to spontaneously open cafés if they want to." At this, Tristan lowered his eyes again, started polishing vigorously.

"There's nothing spontaneous about it."

Diane, it seemed, did not understand the rules of eavesdropping and let out a clear and musical, "What the fuck are you talking about?"

"There's been a resurrection," I said. Tristan scoffed. I didn't know why he was being so moody. It wasn't as if Cleo having a business downtown changed anything. Geographically, she had always existed within a certain sphere. Now, if anything, that sphere would be more predictable.

"I don't know what that means," Diane said cheerfully.

"I think we should go," I said to Tristan. "To the opening."

THAT AFTERNOON, I received another email from Byron. RE: NO TITLE. This time I opened it eagerly, hoping that he had seen me and Tristan walking past the bookstore the day before.

> *Drew —*
> *Last night, I went to see a community theater production of* A Moon for the Misbegotten, *and the young lead actor looked so much like myself that*

I wondered if it was possible that I had fathered a child at some point in my life and not known. Isn't it strange that you, like me, will grow older, yet never be in the position to experience this type of fracture?

I had two theories. One: He thought that he could cover his misdeed by filling my inbox with an abundance of nonsense, like someone trying to conceal a sex toy in their underwear drawer. Two: He was twisted enough to believe that, because I had seen his penis, we were somehow bound to each other. I was now his personal diary.

I toyed with the idea of responding with something even more cryptic but decided that I didn't really want to spar electronically with Byron (even though I knew I would win). The curt but also decadent tone of Byron's last two emails reminded me so much of Mr. Pursley's truth letters to Nico that the two men became indistinguishable in my mind. It could have been that my mind was trying to be economical, or maybe it was a warning. Sometime in the middle of senior year, Nico had told me that Mr. Pursley had taken her out of town to see *Amélie,* that movie about the French girl who is too pretty to function properly. She said that Mr. Pursley had made a strange remark as they were leaving the theater.

"Your friend, Drew," he said. "She's got a bit of an Amélie thing going on, doesn't she?"

"He didn't mean looks-wise," Nico had added, a little too readily. "Just, like, your *demeanor.*" I'd shrugged at this, but inside I was reeling. I had not been prepared to be noticed by Mr. Pursley, especially as anything other than Nico's disapproving older friend. I'd wanted to go see the movie right away, as if this one comment could provide the lens through which to see myself—my *demeanor*—as others saw me. It was unthinkable, however, to sit through an entire movie for vanity's sake. It felt too exposing, as if anyone who saw me there would know that I was just as self-absorbed as the next teenage girl. As an alternative, I'd walked to the record store and bought the soundtrack on CD, and then listened to it on my Discman when Nico wasn't around. The music was almost too whimsical to bear, like a meringue. The accordion a sound that I had never considered. It was not a tidy instrument, but it was full of purpose and imagination. It seemed to represent everything that my life was not. A life that was well-dressed, healthy, and inspiring. I'd pulled off the headphones and threw them into a corner.

The next day at school, I'd purposefully taken the hallway that would bring me past Mr. Pursley's classroom. I don't know what I'd been hoping for, except maybe that I would walk by the open door and glimpse him at his desk. Maybe he would see me and I would know, through that micro-meeting of eyes, whether his remark had been in earnest. It troubled me that, overnight, my distaste for Mr. Pursley had morphed into this shaky fascination. All it had taken was one offhand comment, the laziest allegation of interest. I'd stopped just short of his classroom and willed myself to turn around. He was wrong about me anyway. There was no angle to my life that shimmered.

I still needed to consider where I would live after Nico's parents returned from vacation. The money that I was making at the stable might cover the cost of a rented room, but it would leave me with nothing left over. The summer was winding down, which would limit my ability to drive long distances—or at all—on my scooter. The image of my mother's house appeared in my mind: at first just the front porch with its empty bags of potting soil and the nubs of chalk that had been there, slimming in the rain, since I was a child. Then the dark front room, folded away from the sun by long curtains, layered and pinned. A patch on the curtain that shone more brightly, like a yellow lampshade. The too-thick rug. Like being trapped in someone's sweaty slipper. Going back there was incomprehensible. It seemed that the only solution was to take the Vespa out again as a distraction. I would gulp the air before winter turned it thin and smoky. If I was incapable of enjoying the moment, then at least I could hoard it, and along the way, I could pretend to look for FOR RENT signs.

As soon as I started riding, I stopped thinking about my living situation altogether. The problem slipped away somewhere into the reeds and the mixed grasses. It is difficult to wring urgency from warm weather. My brain said: *You are running out of time.* My body said: *Big deal. Just sleep under the stars.* I drove for a long time along cow pastures and cornfields, watching my shadow every now and then make its flip-book-like appearance across the side of a hill. I thought: *I will go to Buster's alone. I will order a drink, sit at a table, maybe look for apartment listings.* That's as far as I got. The rest of the plan leapt back into the depth of my mind, like my shadow when there was no green hillside to carry it.

That morning, after the tack had been scrubbed, metal bits soaked, and all leather massaged, I'd found Tristan alone in the tack room.

"I liked you better when you talked to me," I said, aware of how ridiculous I was being. As if he was not allowed one day of sulking. He gave me a look that was kinder than I deserved, and I could tell, from that one look, that Tristan was a reasonable person. He was emotional, yes, but he would never do something shocking or irresponsibly hurtful. He would never be too much. I felt this so strongly that I opened my mouth to apologize.

"She has her hooks in me," he said before I could speak. His voice sounded like a haggard confession, like maybe he needed my help with the problem. I stepped closer, pulled his hands to my waist.

"I can help you with that," I said. We could block the door with a saddle stand. He could lift me up onto it. We could be quiet. I could be quick.

"I bet you could." He was purposefully not kissing me, holding his lips a centimeter away. He smelled like work and leather and sweat. I let him breathe on me.

"Please, Tristan," I whispered. "Take me back."

"No." He kissed me so hard I had to steady myself on the row of bridle racks behind us. A bridle fell to the floor, making a sound like a dropped dog leash. Tristan kicked it out of the way. I imagined one of the autumn girls walking in and finding Tristan grinding onto me against the wall. Aurora would be shocked, I decided, but the sight would send Diane into a full recalibration. She wouldn't be able to march around anymore looking at the world as if it were a runaway scarf on a windy day. She'd be forced to accept that everything was half steeped in wrongness, that Tristan was wounded and I was a bad influence. I reached for Tristan's belt, and felt him there again, solid as a copper pipe. When I undid his pants, he reached a hand down to straighten himself. I wanted to live in that moment, crawl inside it. The ache of his dick hardened against his zipper, the easy motion of his hand, so familiar with this specific maneuver: straighten and set loose. His dick did not look like Marv from *Home Alone,* but even if it had, I would not have cared. I knelt and touched him with my tongue. He stepped away.

"You want me to take you back?" he asked me, gripping himself.

"Yes."

"How bad?"

I found that I was shivering, as if truly desperate. When had the lines between acting the part and living the part dissolved?

"Please, let me," I said. It was clear that Tristan wanted me to beg for forgiveness, as if I were Cleo. At the same time, we both knew that I was begging him to let me suck his dick. We could be in both worlds at once. Both worlds needed each other. Tristan's hand started moving then, slowly.

"Don't do that," I said. "I'll do it for you." He looked down at me, eyes narrowed and distant. His hand pumped faster, as if in defiance.

"Just let me try," I said. Then: "Give me a chance." His eyes closed and he fell back a step, but he didn't stop. He kept going and I kept begging, caught in the agony of wanting to watch him forever, but also wanting the thing that I was asking for. Knowing that as soon as he came, I would be slapped back into myself. But also dying for him to come. Saying: "Let me, let me." Thinking: Don't ever let me. Don't you dare.

He didn't. He braced himself with his forearm on the wall above my head and hunched over me, his come rippling past my hair, drops landing on the leather bridles, the wall. Everywhere but where I had asked for it.

I PULLED THE Vespa into a Stewart's to refuel. I felt foolish at gas stations, especially when there were real bikers there with real motorcycles. The Vespa's fuel tank was located beneath the long camel-colored seat, so I had to flip it up and shove the pump awkwardly into the hole, which never looked natural and always looked like I didn't know what I was doing. Plus, my full-face motorcycle helmet felt like a pumpkin head. I was a space girl who was also trying too hard, and it was obvious. The late sun was so bright, I felt that I was seeing everything out of the sides of my eyeballs. The people walking from their cars to the store were lit matches. Every window and windshield was a knife blade. I replaced the gas nozzle, slammed down the seat, and got back on the Vespa, facing away from the sun. It was the season right before the leaves changed colors, but you could sense the turning before it happened. The tone shifted, goldenrod exploded onto the scene like a fortunate man's plea: *Let this never come to an end.* After the tack room, Tristan and I had finished the last of our chores as if nothing had happened. It wasn't a shameful silence, but it wasn't exactly gleeful either. I could tell that he was still thinking about the café, and I was irrationally hurt that I hadn't cured him of that by letting him jerk off into my aura. I drove back into town with the sun still behind me. The drivers headed in the other direction squinted, ducked their heads, and threw up their hands against the harsh light. That evening would burn itself into my mind—all those orange, twisted faces flying at me like some kind of credits rolling. I thought about Pompeii, the masks of people frozen in their last moments. I thought about how, if I could be frozen forever in a moment, I would choose the tack room, Tristan hunched over me, his arm working faster and faster.

2

I NEVER EXPECTED horses to become a theme in my life. When I was a young girl, I didn't see them as animals so much as a child's bedroom aesthetic, something that other girls—not me—chose to decorate their school binders with. The first time I met a horse up close, at a state fair, I was overcome by the unexpected smell of it. It was salty, dripping with thick saliva that did not strike me as icky, but somehow hard-earned, like motor oil. A man—probably the owner of the horse—asked me if I wanted to sit on the horse's back. I pondered this. Now that I understood the proportions of such an animal, sitting on it seemed like serious business. I worried that I would not fit the part. I might make a strange face while I was up there. I might not understand the deeper significance of what it meant to sit atop a creature with as much presence as a horse seemed to have. The man interpreted my hesitation as fear and told me that it was okay. Maybe next year I would be bigger and braver. As soon as he said "bigger and braver," the horse let down his penis until it nearly touched the ground. It was pink and flakey like a sunburn. All around us, people laughed out of discomfort—I imagine because I was standing eye level to it and I seemed like a sweet child who maybe didn't deserve the shock, and what else could you do but laugh? Until then, I had not been aware of the crowd, or that the whole interaction had been observed by so many strangers who now thought that I was a coward.

I TOOK THE next morning off to drive Nico's parents to the airport. They acted like they were doing me a favor by letting me drive a car for once and said that as long as I replaced the gas in the tank, I could use it to move my belongings to the apartment that they still believed was lined up for me. On the drive back into town, I rolled down every window, letting the wind thud against my open hand, whip my hair, dry out my teeth. Even with all that air on me, I still felt trapped. The steering wheel looked preposterously bulky. The icons on the dashboard seemed unnecessary, the way outdated technology can appear naïve: *Don't the buttons know they can be smaller?* Instead of bypassing Main Street to avoid traffic, I rolled through at a comfortable speed. Here was the benefit of the metal box: I could spy on Buster's Café and the used bookstore without giving myself away. The bookstore was dead as always, but the café had added a new element. A sandwich board with a balloon attached. TOMORROW, it read. My thoughts turned cottony, my hands stuck hot to the wheel.

The next day was windy. The horses were on edge, snorting as if to filter the chaos. Voices were tossed around like buoys. Diane was a blender of hair and plaid, while Aurora moved solidly, pushing a wheelbarrow.

"I'm a Taurus," she told me by way of an explanation.

"Oh wow! I'm a Libra!" Diane said, because she thought we were just throwing out signs for fun. Tristan, in the middle of putting down new wood shavings, looked at me shyly through the dust clouds. Had he missed me on my day off?

"You look—" he said, coughing. "Interesting." It was because I was wearing a very thin layer of concealer and two flicks of mascara, and I had chosen a shirt that fit me. I told myself that I had taken these steps because I would not have time to change before going to the café later. As if I had an appointment with the place. I was tense. I gave Tristan a jumpy reply.

"Don't call me interesting."

We had two trail rides lined up that morning, but one turned out to be a mom wanting a pony ride for her four-year-old son. Tristan assigned it to the autumn girls because it only involved leading the pony around the property, then giving the kid a sugar cube, telling him to hold his hand flat so he wouldn't be bitten. I was envious. Didn't they know that walking circles was my specialty? I threw myself into the work of getting the horses ready for the other trail ride, going over the basics with the riders—a mother and teenage daughter this time—and leading the way up the trail. The wind did not relent. Manes and tails were a mess. There was a pillow fight in my eardrums. All the while, I was thinking about the café, imagining that it would be Cleo herself behind the counter, steaming milk, tamping espresso grounds, chatting casually with customers. There was not much about my little excursion that I could plan—how many options does one have in a coffee shop? So, it came down to my entrance: my pace and style of walking through the door, and whether I would find a table first, or go straight to the counter. Would I talk to her right away, or let my presence slowly build, my eyes dancing in her direction until she asked me a question? Was I from around here? A college student? Were those muck boots on my feet? I imagined her looking me up and down and understanding from my plainness and my shrewd expression that I did not fit with the summer girls or the autumn girls. I was of a separate category, one that I barely understood myself. We were almost to the clearing where the trail ended when the tree limbs ahead seemed suddenly fuller and darker. Black shadows expanded and floated down, and I thought, with alarming serenity: The branches are falling on us. I saw right away that it was only a group of turkey vultures, hopping down from a tree like black umbrellas onto a dead squirrel. They positioned themselves in a dark council. (Later I would learn that it is called a *committee* when vultures gather and a *wake* when they close in to eat something, and I would tell far too many people this fact.) The mother gasped, which I thought was a strangely delayed response. I halted my horse and turned to look at her. She had her hands in fists, holding the reins up by her face, as if to shield herself.

"They're horrible!" she said.

You're horrible, I thought.

"Fun fact," I said to the grimacing mother, "if you get too close to a turkey vulture, it'll projectile vomit on you. Roadkill." I turned back toward the path and urged my horse forward before I could see Tristan's disapproving face. I had, earlier and with amusement, considered what it would be like for me to become obsessed with Cleo, but it had already happened. I was so eager to get to Buster's Café and lay eyes on the woman that I was becoming irritable, resentful of anyone who was in my way.

We were mostly quiet for the rest of the ride, hearing

only the strange yawning of tree trunks in distress. When we were done, the mother handed me a tip and smiled apologetically before getting into her car. This caused me to feel such remorse that I went into the stable and pressed the bills into Tristan's hand.

"What is up with you?" he asked, not angry. (Heaven forbid he react poorly to anything.)

"I have my period," I lied.

"Do you need some dark chocolate with paprika?" Diane asked. She was in a stall, leaning on a pitchfork. "I have some in my bag."

"Of course you do," I snapped. She wilted only slightly.

"Why don't you head home early," Tristan suggested. I felt like an unruly child banished to the outdoors: liberated and skittish with guilt.

WHEN CLEO WAS a girl, she went to one of those schools taught by nuns, where you could get in trouble for breathing. Cleo got in trouble for trying to poison the water fountain. She was always an overachiever.

When she was twelve, she raised a pair of prizewinning steers, which her father made into hamburgers on her thirteenth birthday. She has been a vegetarian ever since.

Cleo had an emergency appendectomy at fifteen. When they put her under, she claimed to have seen the future: a world where technological implants were the norm, but only men were allowed to have them.

KNOWING EVERYTHING THAT I knew about Cleo, I could not imagine her as anything less than ferocious: well structured, proud eyes. Anjelica Huston, Angela Bassett, Sigourney Weaver. Images of these women spun in my head like the portraits of queens. I could see all my weaknesses through their eyes. It made me want to clean under my fingernails, sit up straight, brush the back of my tongue.

I parked the Vespa in a public lot two blocks from the café and walked up the sidewalk with my helmet tucked under my arm. I liked to think that it gave me a certain unconscious swagger, but I am not sure that the rest of me—muddy boots, skinny arms, flat hair—supported this. Still, I walked like someone on a mission, passing the bookstore and checking my reflection brazenly in the many-paned window. That girl is on a mission, I thought. Let Byron see me and wonder what I am up to. Ahead, the sandwich-board balloon, swaying in the wind, said, *This way, this way.*

She was already looking at me when I walked in, which startled me so much that I forgot my plan entirely and approached the counter before finding a table first. I fell in line behind a large man with a blond, braided beard who I would one day know as Amos, but who, in that moment, I was only using as a buffer so I could collect myself. Soon, I would know practically everyone in that place—by drink order, first name, and private nickname. It's funny to compare your first impression of a space to the intimate knowledge of it as time passes. Standing in line, hiding behind the big man, I saw the shop as spare but inviting, like a rectangle of sunlight on a hardwood floor. I had no idea how dramatically that impression would change through experience, as if experience were a can of spray paint, complicating every surface with all the moments I'd spend there. The big man paid for his drink and stepped away, and for a moment Cleo had her back to me while she prepared his order. I knew it was her, even though it could have easily been an employee—who was to say that the real Cleo wasn't in the kitchen, in the back office? There was still the possibility that all of this had been a colossal instance of jumping to conclusions on Tristan's part, and that the name Buster had been chosen at random for its mass appeal. Who wouldn't like a place called Buster's?

"What kind of bike do you ride?" She had turned around, and was leaning her elbows on the counter, pleasantly and unhurried, even though it was obvious that the place was packed, the line behind me still growing. "I've had my eye on a little mustard-yellow Honda. Listed online," she continued. I knew that she had seen my motorcycle helmet. I knew that she was expressing interest in this thing that she assumed we both knew something about—that is, riding motorcycles—but I could not figure out what to say. My mind was filled with what Tristan had put there, and yet empty at the same time. I forgot how much I was or wasn't supposed to know, how to act like I was totally ignorant of her.

"It's just a Vespa," I told her. Then: "But I had to get my motorcycle license to ride it." She liked this, and I sensed that she approved of my need to tell her, as if we both desired to be tougher than your average scooter girl. She was cuter than I expected. Short, with wild, curly hair held back with a twisted scarf. Her features were small and direct, and I suspected that if she had been wearing makeup, the result would have been too on point. There were the hoop earrings that I had heard about, the flash of mica in her left eye. I was unexpectedly moved to see these things. I felt a rush of fondness toward Tristan for being truthful and reliable, then a similar fondness for Cleo for unknowingly keeping her end of the bargain.

"What kind of coffee do you like to drink?" She wanted me to order, of course, to keep the line moving, but the question felt personal, playful, and somehow flirtatious. I was moved a second time.

"Hot?" I said.

I sat in an armchair by the front window. It was all that was available. I regretted that I had not thought to bring something to read, or at the very least a newspaper that I could pretend to look at. But I had a decent view of the counter and the café's steady stream of customers. I watched them wait in line and grow impatient, especially as it became clear that there was only one person taking orders, making drinks, and working the register. I was worried that someone would complain about the wait or storm out, but with every person it was the same thing: When it came their turn, Cleo smiled and somehow bewitched them into passivity. From where I sat, I could see her face and the way her eyes were filled with genuine mirth—which is not a word that I have ever wanted to use, but was the only one I could find to describe her. Her front teeth were turned slightly inward in way that made her smile utterly captivating. I wanted to see it again and again, as if it were a mechanism that I was trying to better understand. When she had handed me my mug, winking at my request for "hot" coffee, I had felt as though she was totally invested in me, and that she had appreciated my deadpan humor, as if no one else that day had thought to ask for coffee so cleverly. *You're not fussy*, her eyes said to me. *And I like that about you.* I soon realized that I had not been the only person to have this experience. From my armchair I could see each new customer turn away from the counter, cup or pastry in hand, visibly lighter than when they had walked in.

At last, there was a lull in the crowd, and I watched Cleo cleaning up from the rush. She brewed more coffee, loaded the dishwasher, and stacked the trays from the display case that were now empty. The lingerers brought their dirty dishes to the bus tub, wiped their mouths one last time with a napkin, and waved to Cleo, their faces saying, *Nice job! Thanks! Good luck!* Was it possible that Cleo was known already throughout town and that all these people had come to support her on her first day? It seemed improbable to me, but perhaps no more improbable than the notion that she had won over an entire town of strangers. I would conclude later that it was a little bit of both, which I guess was the only realistic option. Eventually, it was just me and a man with large headphones. I supposed I was waiting for him to leave, although I couldn't say what I planned to do once I found myself alone with Cleo. I was so disoriented that I did not even know what time it was. Maybe the shop was already closed and Cleo was politely waiting for us to clear out. I stood and brought my cold mug to the counter.

"Hey, Vespa Girl," Cleo said. "How was it?" She took the mug from me in both hands. That was one of her moves; when she handed you something—a cup of coffee, a book, a muffin—she held it close to her chest first, both hands around it, as if warming it for you. It was the same for objects that she received—a borrowed pen, a hair scrunchie. This was not something that Tristan had told me, but something that I would learn for myself. I hadn't thought about Tristan all afternoon.

"Everything was good," I said. "Sufficiently hot." Cleo seemed to look me over. I wanted to say more, to somehow justify my presence or to make myself interesting in her eyes. But, again, I couldn't think of anything. My mind was as whitewashed as Nico's basement. A feeling came over me then, like the feeling you get when you're about to hear yourself confess a secret. *I'm afraid of my job. I am running out of time. No angle of my life shimmers.*

I was saved by the door opening and slapping shut behind me. A man with a closely trimmed white beard approached the counter, waving a five-dollar bill animatedly like a child excited to buy an ice cream cone.

"Got any coffee left?" he asked. He looked so sincere that I wanted to hide. I quickly moved out of the way and got my helmet from under the armchair. Somehow, I knew that this wasn't for me. Whatever this was.

"Bye, Vespa Girl," Cleo called. I left her behind the counter with the rosy old man. Even though Tristan had told me the logistics of her marriage, it did not occur to me that the man might be her husband, that she would have anyone so wholesome and ordinary in her life.

AT TWENTY-ONE, I was not very sexually experienced. I had only had penetrative sex with two guys, the first a boyfriend who did not last long as my boyfriend, but lasted a very long time in bed. He lasted so long that I started to dread having sex with him because I had to mentally block off at least an hour to complete the task. Afterward, I felt wrung out and scuffed like an over-licked dog toy. In just the three short months that we were together, we developed a carefully choreographed routine, one that seemed to be the only surefire way to get him to come within a forty-five-minute window. I was the triple axel champion of tummy-to-back flipping, never missing a beat for fear that we would have to start all over again. The guy after him was terrified of getting me pregnant, so we mostly had oral sex. He was the opposite of Captain Endurance, and somehow got it into his head that this should be a point of shame. I did not understand why we couldn't just reframe it as me being exceptional at blow jobs.

"I'm so sorry," he said every time we were finished. "I don't know what's wrong with me."

"It seems like everything is working fine," I told him, but he couldn't get over himself and insisted that I was lying to make him feel better. It's too bad. It was an empowering and time-efficient two and a half weeks.

All of this is to say that I had a vague understanding of how couples walked the fine line between the art of getting each other off, and the chore of it. Each time, you drew from the same tool kit, but tried to change up the sequence in an attempt at making those tools seem ingenious. What Tristan and I were doing seemed to want to contradict these terms, in that every encounter so far had the benefit of seeming spontaneous, reliant on the novelty of the situation. Could he just approach me whenever he wanted, say the same lines, and expect the same scenario to unfold? I was not convinced. This led to a sense of finality that made it difficult for me to gauge my next move. I was not even sure that it was my move to make. When the hinge of lust is heartbreak, shouldn't the heartbroken have the power?

I think it was this anxiety that led me to slip up and tell Tristan that I had been to see Cleo. We were in the stable, and it was raining so hard, all we could hear was the tin roof crashing like a cymbal. The good news was that our rides for the day were canceled, which meant that I had been gifted one more day of pretending that I would never have to go out alone. Lately, my dreams had been swarming with runaway ponies and malfunctioning gear. The night before, I dreamed that I was trying to lead a trail ride, only I had mounted my scooter by mistake and I kept leaving my clients behind in the dust.

Diane was out sick. When I asked Aurora what was wrong with her, she looked puzzled.

"Why would she tell me?" she asked. She was wearing a waffle weave shirt under loose-fitting denim overalls, like a schoolkid from 1995.

"Because you two are friends?" I said. But she raised an eyebrow.

"I barely know her," she said, then climbed into her rain parka. I don't know why every small surprise threatened to undo me, but this information wounded me in a place I didn't know was woundable. I had been unknowingly invested in the assumption that Aurora and Diane were an unlikely, albeit inseparable, pair, and now they were just *nothing*. I watched Aurora swish away toward the paddocks to clean the horse shelters.

"They don't even know each other." I crossed my arms over the railing of the stall that Tristan was mucking. "Can you believe it?" He leaned on his rake, as if bracing himself to hear me out.

"The autumn girls!" I said, when I saw that he was not going to get worked up about it. He gave me a look of strained sympathy and beckoned me to come into the stall. His tolerance of me was so tender. It made me want to be less annoying, for his sake. More annoying, for mine.

He wrapped his arms around me, still holding the rake. It was the first time he had held me, and I was not relaxed enough to enjoy it. Instead, I told him that I had a confession. He pulled away.

"Okay?" he said. Above us, the rain crashed. If Aurora had been outside getting eaten by bears, we would not have heard. I told him that I had gone to Buster's Café on opening day, and that I had sat in an armchair and watched Cleo until late in the afternoon. I asked him if he thought it was weird of me. I could sense that the way I had brought it up, and my strange timidness, was what made it weird, and not the act alone. He sifted the rake through the wood chips, looking away.

"How did she seem?"

I remembered the long line of customers, Cleo greeting each person as if they were her first one of the day. How, when she called me Vespa Girl, it made me feel cute and fresh, like Diane. It was as if I had not considered the possibility, until that moment, that my life could be defined in any simple, likable way.

"She makes everyone fall in love with her," I said.

If visiting the coffee shop without Tristan had been the first betrayal, then the second betrayal was going back there the next day, résumé in hand. This time, I walked from Nico's house, instead of taking the scooter. Part of me wanted to see if Cleo would remember me without the helmet acting as a visual cue. When I arrived, she was leaning over the counter where I had left her the afternoon before, talking to a thin man in a suit with a perfectly round bald patch on his head. The man's posture was so rigid it seemed as though he were trying not to let the bald spot fall off.

"Here comes Vespa Girl," Cleo said, not to me, but to the man, as if she hadn't needed to look up. My face got hot with pleasure and embarrassment because I had been recognized and now I had no choice but to approach and make my business known. The man in the suit stepped back, as if giving me the floor, and I had the impression that he assumed that Cleo and I were friends, that she had been expecting me.

"What can I do for you?" she asked me. I gave the suit man a wary look, and he took another step backward, holding up his to-go cup in a salute. I said nothing, just slid the résumé across the counter, mortified.

"I've gotten quite a few of these this week," she said, picking it up. My heart dropped at the thought of the long line of people—dashing young men, girls cuter and wittier than me—all eager to work there. "Drew Harding," she read aloud, as if picking up a nominally interesting book at the library. While she was focused on the paper, I looked at her closely, as if to make sure that she was exactly as Tristan had described: the fine glitter around her eyes, her large breasts and the curve of her tummy, the strong lines framing her mouth. Her arms were a Noah's Ark of tattooed animals—birds mostly, a rabbit, the silhouette of a galloping horse. She had lived my life nearly twice over already. I felt a sense of loss at this notion, for myself, not for her. As if I could have spent the last twenty-one years being a better, less risk-averse person.

"Reason for leaving your last job: dick pic?" She frowned thoughtfully. "Reason for leaving current job: mortal terror." She narrowed her eyes at me.

"I have nothing to say for myself," I told her. She fell back on her heels in consideration, a hard but not disapproving expression on her face.

"Well, good," she said finally. "Take a coffee and go sit over there." She handed me an empty mug. Since yesterday, the coffee carafes had migrated to a self-serve counter. I filled my cup with the one that said *noir* on the tag, forgetting that cream and sugar were even options, then sat in my armchair like I was told. I hadn't listed Tristan as a reference on the résumé. I had provided Diane's number instead, not daring to mention the flinty woman or the name of the establishment for fear that Cleo would recognize it and draw some kind of conclusion. It helped that the flinty woman was never around, and when she was, she was too busy hunting down a veterinarian to be bothered. I did not know why I was even troubling myself with any of this, considering how many people I must have been competing with for the position. I watched customers come and go. Cleo remained behind the counter, brewing new pots of coffee, wiping smudges off the glass of the display case, flattening bills from her tip jar. I did not know if I had been made to wait because she needed time to deliberate, or if she was playing some kind of game with me. Her demeanor reflected neither of these conditions. I waited. I had nowhere else to go, no other hope in my mind.

I had tried to call Nico the night before, but because I did not own a cell phone and had to use the phone in her parents' kitchen, she, probably seeing the number and thinking it was them, didn't pick up. I wasn't even sure what I would have told her. If she got wind that I was being kicked out, she might launch into a rescue effort, and that would be unbearable. Mostly, I just wanted her to tell me about college, about the boys she had met there. I wanted to know that she was making the same mistakes, but that everyone still loved her and she was still getting A's. Nico seemed to attract chaos in an aloof, distracted way. The people around her were always falling apart, getting arrested, sleeping in their cars, and yet she never seemed in danger of succumbing to the same fate. She was like the blow-up boxer that my therapist had used once in a session with me. The thing had been shaped like an egg, with a twisted cartoon face, a squinting black eye. Whenever you punched it—and no matter how angrily—it would pop upright again. The therapist had wanted to watch me punch it. He said, "Why don't you give this guy a shove?" But then he'd settled into his chair with too much mustered casualness, and I knew that it was another test. I'd made my face porcelain and punched the grimacing face, watched it tip back and then slowly rise. This did not surprise me. At first, I assumed that the trick was to not get frustrated, that the therapist wanted to see how many futile swings it would take to break me. I would never break, not in front of him. I'd punched again, erect and emotionless. I think I slipped away for a moment, in that perfect meditation of punching and waiting, willing myself to shrink deeper and deeper away from his eyes. Eventually the exercise was framed as a lesson in perseverance, and I saw then how easy it was to take an object that was literally hollow and fill it with whatever meaning would benefit you. I'd wanted to say to the therapist that, in my storyline, the boxer represented the cruel and relentless world springing back to bite you in the ass. You could punch it and punch it, and it would always, someday, best you. I doubted that anything would best Nico—she was an opossum: too cold-blooded for rabies, immune to venom. I couldn't look away, couldn't fault her, and yet, I was somehow not envious.

A group of out-of-towners came in, gaping around for a menu, as if one should exist on the ceiling. I watched Cleo's patience with them as they asked for sandwiches.

"No sandwiches here," she said cheerfully. "But you could buy two cookies and a brownie and make that a sandwich." The out-of-towners did not know how to process this suggestion. The woman in the front looked helplessly over her shoulder at her family, then turned back to Cleo, speaking with insulting politeness.

"Could you recommend a place where we could find a sandwich? You know, like a deli?" Cleo's look of absolute serenity reminded me of how I must have appeared facing the inflatable boxer, except hers was more of a jeweled disdain. It went deeper than what was happening in front of her. I could see, suddenly, how terrible it must be to be hated by her, or even cast outside her circle. How unbearable it must be for Tristan, to have had her and lost her.

"That depends," Cleo said to the woman, full of conspiratorial friendliness, "on how far you are willing to walk, versus how comfortable you are with the idea of salmonella." I watched the group leave, stunned, and wondered who had been in the wrong in this interaction, if anyone. For some reason, it was almost impossible to tell. Cleo beckoned me to the counter then, and I hurried to her.

"Here's the deal," she said. She was pouring a glossy stream of black coffee beans into a jar. The bag of beans was so enormous that she had to balance it on her shoulder. "I have this friend, a painter, and I've been sitting for him every weekend since June." She looked at me around the bag, as if to make sure that I was listening. I nodded.

"The painting is finished now. It's huge. It's beautiful." She moved on to another enormous bag, snipping the corner open with scissors, and hefting it up to pour. The beans in the second bag were a matte brown, their smell earthy, sweet, and as engulfing as the scent of leather in the tack room. She continued: "It's also full-frontal, and it doesn't take much imagination to see that it's me." She curled the top of the now half-empty bag and held it firmly like a handbag. "Now, you might be thinking that I am asking you a yes or no question. I am not. I am asking you a *when* question."

"Okay," I said.

"If I hang it now"—and here she put down the bag and extended her arms out toward the empty wall facing the counter—"is that too . . . on the nose, too territorial? If I wait, and hang it, let's say, in three months, would that be disingenuous?"

"Is this a test?" I asked. The door opened and a young couple walked in. I expected Cleo to put our conversation on hold so she could take their order, but she only peered at me.

"Yes and no," she said. I felt put on the spot, caught between the enigmatic look on Cleo's face and the customers, who I felt somehow responsible for, even though I did not work there—did not even know whether I was being considered for the position.

"Frontal, as in . . . ?" I gestured toward my crotch. I was buying time.

"Full. Bush," she said.

The customers waited, a little skittishly, in puffer vests

and big sunglasses, the uniform of weekenders from the city.

"Ah," I said. "That sounds very territorial." Cleo twisted her mouth.

"So, I should wait to put it up?"

The male puffer vest cleared his throat.

"No, I think it's a good thing." I made a small fist-pumping gesture. "Set a precedent. Claim your space. Et cetera." Cleo smiled, and I understood instinctually that I was allowed to step out of the way. The couple approached and ordered espressos. I returned to my chair, dazed and feeling triumphant in a hundred unexpected ways.

I GOT THE job. Cleo called me at Nico's house that evening, introducing herself as the lady from Buster's, as if I didn't already know so much about her. As if she hadn't been holding the only candle in my mind since the moment I woke up. She wanted to know how much I knew about coffee.

"Only as much as what's decent," I said.

"Ah, yes," she said. "It is completely possible to know too much." I knew that she would like this answer. Since our conversation about the nude painting, I had been overcome with a kind of mania. I knew what to say to make her like me. I knew how to say it. And the more positive feedback I received from her, the quicker my wit became. I was oiled up, spring-loaded. I would have worked for her approval alone.

I was there when the painting went up. It was almost five feet tall, and Cleo and her painter friend spent all morning getting it on the wall. The painter was a thin, hunched man, who wore a style of top hat that I had never seen before. He and Cleo took their task seriously, stopping many times to examine the placement of the painting. It was more impressionistic than I had originally imagined—I'm not sure why I expected all nude portraits to be milky realism—but clearly depicted a naked woman leaning over a claw-foot bathtub to test the water with her hand. I liked the illusion of the fingers sliced diagonally by the surface of water, which wasn't blue, but a blending of reflected colors that made more sense than a photograph. The pubic hair was a tasteful afterthought. A cluster of brushstrokes that seemed to have been applied without analysis. If any part of the painting was intellectual, it was the breasts, for their blue tinge, and the way that they expressed something transcendent about the woman. The breasts told a story that only an older, wiser person would think to tell. I saw the burden of them and understood their absolute necessity. Cleo saw me staring.

"I told you it was good, Drew-Bug," she said. I had graduated from Vespa Girl to Drew-Bug, which was sometimes just Bug, or the even more elusive Drew-Baby (pronounced *bee-bee*). Like the installation of the painting, the nickname struck me as something best delivered early on, before I had a chance to grow accustomed to anything else. It was *now*; it was fresh. It was as unpretentious as the painted pubes.

I was riding high at this point, intoxicated by my sudden and complete initiation into Cleo's world, while also finding myself more caffeinated than I had ever been in my life. My heart was as wired as a hummingbird, and any thoughts of Tristan felt like a soggy weight in comparison. I had left him stranded, for the remainder of tourist season, at a job that he had been intent on leaving. When there was a lull at the coffee shop, and my mind slipped toward Tristan, I hiked it up, as if it were a saggy pair of tights. Poor Tristan, I thought. We might have had fantastic sex. Never: Poor Tristan, disposed of so easily, when he was nothing but good.

I had not been so terrible that I left him without any notice. There was a trail ride that Sunday, which I completed in a state of blissful detachment, sailing on the notion that I would never have to lead another ride again. I would not have to get on another horse if I did not want to. Without Tristan riding behind us, I was even a little cocky, letting my feet hang loose from my stirrups, leaning over in my saddle to pluck an apple from a tree and feed it to my horse like all of this was just a dreamscape and I had complete control. I made jokes with the tourists, flexing my new confidence. I told them that I only rode open-air vehicles—scooters and horses—so I could smell the big country.

"I can smell rain twenty-three hours in advance," I said. "On a good day, I can smell whether a person is lying. A lie smells like wet straw."

"And truth?" the people asked me, their faces blankly skeptical in the shadows of their helmets.

"Truth smells very faintly of charcoal, which makes sense, I suppose. Isn't that the stuff that makes you throw up?" I didn't wait for an answer. Even though I was making it all up, the sound of my voice was familiar. Had I had this conversation before?

I met Howie officially on my second day at Buster's. He walked in, exactly as he had before, waving his five-dollar bill like Santa Claus on his way to a kids' bake sale. The nude painting was going up at the same time, and I had been enjoying watching each customer come in, look around, spot the canvas, and react in their own way. I didn't expect anyone to be scandalized—this was 2005, after all—but it was still vaguely interesting, the way unpacking Christmas ornaments can be vaguely interesting, just to see the varied shapes and styles. Howie seemed to be the only person who didn't see it right away, because he was so focused on getting to the counter. When he saw me there, he paused.

"You must be Rebecca," he said. He was tall and squarely built, but his voice wasn't booming like I expected. It was sincere, almost womanly.

"I'm Drew," I said. He followed my eyes to the wall where Cleo and the artist were now standing, hands on their lower backs, in a pose of serious contemplation. I watched him take in the painting, and saw that he was familiar with it, his eyes warm and steady, with no glint of surprise. He stared at it in a way that no other customer had dared: with esteem, almost fatherly if you didn't know any better, which I still did not. Howie walked toward the artist with his hand extended, and I watched them shake, Howie's strength evident in the way the artist lost momentary control of his arm. Then he reached over to Cleo, wrapped his arm around her, and kissed her lightly above her eyebrow. The three of them walked toward the counter, and I tried to read the look on Cleo's face. She didn't seem unhappy. Now, I would probably describe her expression as one of suffocation, how mothers sometime seem when their children are crawling all over them.

"Drew, this is my husband, Howie," she said to me. I did not want her to see my shock, so I masked it with fake astonishment. *Oh my God, what an honor to meet you!* Inside I was seething. Howie, with his tucked plaid and his apple cheeks, seemed like an interloper, even though, realistically, if anyone was an interloper, it was me. I stepped aside so that Cleo could make him a latte and felt a pang of outrage as he dropped his change into the tip jar. It was like watching your grandfather tip a stripper. Before he left, I overheard Howie tell Cleo that he had mistaken me for someone named Rebecca.

"Rebecca wasn't right," she said, almost as if to shut him up. Had Cleo already hired someone before I came around? Had she chosen me over this Rebecca girl? I felt warm all over and brought a pile of dirty plates into the kitchen so Cleo wouldn't see my face redden. She found me in the walk-in freezer stacking trays of frozen puff pastry. She came in, let the ice-covered door close behind her. Above the handle, someone had posted a large notice the shape and color of a stop sign that read STOP. YOU ARE NOT LOCKED IN. I didn't know why it was necessary to stop, unless the sign wanted to prevent panic-induced hyperventilating, but I appreciated the sentiment. *You are not locked in.* How many times could I have benefitted from someone telling me this?

"He's gone," she said. "You don't have to hide anymore."

"I wasn't—"

"Howie is incorrigible."

"He seemed very nice to me," I said. Cleo sighed.

"That's just it. You see now why I couldn't hang the painting at my house."

I did not see. I didn't understand at all.

I THINK IT is common for people to divide their lives into *befores* and *afters*. Sometimes a historical event, like 9/11, is the divider. Sometimes it is a personal trauma. There's before and after having children, before and after divorce. I would describe my life like this also, except there were two defining moments, so my story was less like a folded piece of paper and more like a Venn diagram. One circle is labeled *Drew Before Cleo*, and the second circle is *After Howie Died*. The eye-shaped segment in the center represents the month that I spent working at Buster's—after meeting Cleo, but when I was still just her employee, someone who clocked out and went back to her own sad home every evening.

The only other person that I knew with this life structure was my mother. Hers would have looked like this: First circle—*Mom Before Drew Was Born*. Second Circle—*Mom After Drew Moved Out*. The oblong slice in the middle is colored with black marker.

3 I WAS STILL living in the basement when Nico's parents returned from their vacation. Actually, on that particular morning, I was asleep on their couch with the TV still on from the night before. It was playing that show about the IVF parents who birthed a set of quintuplets when they already had triplets. I would have turned it off if I had been conscious. Nico's mother had a slick, sleepless look, and the father was unshaven. Since I was technically house-sitting, I knew that they had not expected me to be gone, but they had probably thought that I would be packed and showered, and that I would have had the decency to close the kitchen cupboards and take out the trash, which was dripping an unidentified amber liquid over the side. I sat up, bleary, but not surprised. I had known that this day would come, and that I would need to explain myself. Still, it was humiliating to be found like this—being discovered in a state of unkemptness was a big fear of mine, bigger than being walked in on in a public restroom, or even being caught naked. It was a thing that I had been trained to avoid since childhood. Don't open the door. Don't take Polaroids in your room with a messy bed behind you. Never invite a friend over, period.

"Drew, honey, are you ill?" Nico's mother approached me with a palm out, as if to check my forehead for fever. I balked, tried to remember the night before. I had run out of gas on a back road and rolled the Vespa into the side shed of a strange barn, then walked into town and stole the gas canister from Nico's garage. The sun was setting by then, and I knew that my arms would give out if I tried to walk all that way with the canister, so I called Cleo and asked her meekly if she could give me a ride back to the hidden Vespa. She showed up fifteen minutes later, her truck rattling, blaring Hank Williams. I had forgotten the exact road where I had left the scooter, so we drove for forty minutes, studying the landmarks, Cleo asking me to orient myself based on the bald spot on the mountain, or the *War of the Worlds* Martian legs of the distant grain factory. She laughed the entire time, giddy, it seemed, to be going on this Easter-egg hunt with me, while the canister on my lap funked up the inside of the truck. We rolled down the windows and turned up the heat against the chilly air. I felt weightless, drunk on fumes, cruising around at the hour when the earth had already turned cold and shadowy but the sky was light with coiffed pink clouds. The mixture of sharp wind from the windows and the heat pumping at my feet pricked me with goosebumps. It felt as if we were floating through space in a bathtub filled with hot water. Finally, I spotted the barn and its beaten shed. It was farther from the road than I had remembered, and in the darkness, it appeared to be set deep in a kind of rural insignificance that made me depressed. Cleo found some wooden boards that we used as planks to get the scooter back onto the road. I gassed it up and told Cleo thank you, and that I'd pick up the canister from her tomorrow. She leaned against the truck and cocked her head.

"Do you play pool?" she asked.

"I know how to look like I do?"

I followed Cleo's truck for about two miles through a town called Whitebridge, freezing, until she pulled off onto a dirt patch outside a building that resembled a weathered barn. The windows were papered, but I could see the glow of colored lights behind them, the focused points where some of the lights were pressed against the paper itself. Inside, the bar was pushed against the far wall, and I felt exposed walking across the floor. There were three brightly lit pool tables in the center and two booths, snug against another wall, far away. It seemed that the safest place to be was along the edges. Cleo patted a barstool, signaling for me to sit, and she waited for the bartender. I did not know if this was the right time to tell her that I didn't have my wallet or my ID on me, or if that would break the flow of whatever was supposed to happen. There were men seated at the bar who stared down at us with pained looks of interest, as if wondering outright whether they preferred us to be mother and daughter or just friends.

"That your mom?" the one in the middle called. His face came down out of the line, like a marionette, and stayed there, waiting for our answer. I looked at Cleo, but she only brushed her fingers through my hair and stared at the man. I had a vision of Tristan then, remembering that his sadness over Cleo had led him to shave his head, and I wondered what it would be like to want to be rid of a part of yourself because you could still feel another person in it. Now I had that person in my hair, on my scalp. What kind of catastrophe would it take to drive me to do the same? Already, Tristan had become the distant past. There was something about a change in location that could form a greater wedge in time, make yesterday seem like a different era. The man jerked back into the line of faces, and there was a muffled chatter among them. Cleo ordered me a Pepsi and a beer called Double Bag for herself, and we brought them to the pool table farthest from the bar. I liked how she dipped her hand into the pockets to gather the balls, as if selecting eggs from a chicken coop. Her movements, around the pool table and when she was at the café, were deliberate, never jerky or anxious. She was continuously alert, like a robin scouting for insects across a lawn. I studied her cleavage as she racked the balls. Her breasts were not pushed up or manipulated. They did not signal anything, which did not mean that they were not sexy.

"How are you liking the job, Drew-Bug?" Cleo handed me the cue to break with. I wanted to stay cool, so I said, "So far, so good." I struck the ball, trying for the same deliberate movements that I had seen in Cleo, but the break spread out slowly.

"And the people?" I liked how Cleo's jewelry dipped whenever she bent over to aim, her necklaces and bracelets a compass needle against the rest of her. I thought Cleo was referring to herself in the third person.

"My boss is pretty cool," I said, picking up my glass. "But she won't buy me alcohol."

MY TEETH WOULD not stop chattering after the ride home from Whitebridge in the dark. It seemed that my body had locked up. My muscles felt like a seatbelt when it decides to choke you for no reason. I took a shower, leaned against the wall, still shivering, the water as hot as I could stand it. I removed the detachable showerhead and pointed it at myself, painting my torso with pressure, bringing the hard stream between my legs, although I was not sure I wanted to make that kind of commitment: holding it there, shuffling scenes in my mind. Images of Tristan were stamped with a big *NO*, and trying to settle on some other man—real or made-up—was like searching for a word that has escaped you. It was too cerebral, too much like a pop quiz. I brought the nozzle closer, and thought about Cleo with her pool cue, her sun-freckled cleavage, and the way the men at the bar had watched us to see if we would touch again. Whenever Cleo handed me the stick, she'd graze my lower back with her hand, just to give them the bare minimum. It was understood, wordlessly, between the two of us, that the men were not what we wanted, but that didn't mean that their gaze was totally worthless. I wished that I could look at Cleo the way that they did. They seemed to have an advantage over me when it came to ease of blood flow. Tristan had taken one look at Cleo in overalls and a sweaty tank top and had gotten hard. How was it that I only liked the idea of Tristan's dick when it was hard for Cleo, and I only liked the idea of Cleo's tits when Tristan's dick was hard for them?

What kind of dread was it when you knew that your days with your favorite detachable showerhead were numbered?

Afterward, I was still cold, so I went upstairs and lodged myself on the couch with a bottle of wine. I drank it until I could feel all the walls of my stomach.

"MY BOYFRIEND BROKE up with me," I said to Nico's mom. The inside of my mouth was crusty velvet. "We were supposed to move in together, and now I have nowhere to go." She looked back at her husband, and I could almost see the air tighten between them. Nico's dad righted the suitcases, pushed their retractable handles in, and went into the bathroom without saying anything.

"I don't want you to worry," said Nico's mom. Her eyes touched on the wine bottle on the coffee table, then lowered. A kind person's instinct.

"I'm a failure," I whispered to Nico's mom, already forgetting that there was a fake boyfriend to be sad about. On the television, the IVF mom made her way down a line of baby bouncers, shaking and handing a bottle to each of her children. There was no other furniture in the room, just the bouncers and a white carpet. Could that truly be what her life looked like?

"No, no," said Nico's mom. "You just need some coffee." I saw her face push aside her own weariness, as if weariness were an egg that could be swallowed whole. A magic trick.

"You're a magical woman, Gina," I said, flopping back down on the couch. I knew that by the time she had brewed the coffee, I would already be leaving for work.

CLEO HAD NOT been asking about herself in the third person at the pool table. Her question—"And the people?"—referred to the customers. From that moment on, she never called them customers again. Not clientele, not tourists, not patrons. Just "The People."

"*The People* are ravenous today."

"If *The People* keep demanding flavored coffee, I am going to make them drink decaf."

"Get the plunger. *The People* blew up the restroom again."

Cleo and I spent the rest of the game discussing our growing crowd of regulars. At first, I wasn't sure of the conversation's tone. Were we reviewing the week light-heartedly—gratefully—something to lift our drinks to and say, *We did it*? No. That wasn't quite it.

"What about Scoops?" Cleo walked back from the bar with a new bottle and a second Pepsi for me because mine had turned watery. I thought about it.

"Mm, don't think I know him."

Cleo chugged.

"Scoops is a *she*." She put down the bottle on a wooden stool, and raised her hands, pointers extended. Her lips tightened into a prim smirk. She was doing an impression.

"One toasted bagel, scooped out," she mimicked in a clipped, fussy voice, then dropped back into her own: "I said, 'What's that?' and the woman looked at me like I was being intentionally idiotic. It was pure, freshly squeezed irritation." I watched her line up her shot and point at the ball with the tip of her cue, as if all she needed to do was tell it to wait there. She thrust it quickly into the pocket.

"She explained to me that there are these little things called *calories*," she continued. "Apparently, if you rip the guts out of a bagel and just eat the shell, you ingest fewer of them."

"So, what she really needed was half a bagel," I said.

Cleo gave me an over-the-cue look.

"I told the lady that what she was asking me to do was inhumane." She plugged another clean shot, circled the table.

"Then what happened?"

Cleo shrugged. "I gave her what she wanted and slapped on extra cream cheese, just to be nice."

"So, she's never coming back?"

"No, she comes in almost every morning. I'm surprised you haven't met her yet."

SCOOPS WAS NOT the only member of The People who had received a nickname that night at the bar. When I walked in the next morning, Buttload Guy was at the counter, talking rapidly and leaning in as far as his tummy would allow. Cleo was listening, dead inside. When she saw me, she grew an inch taller, threw her dish rag over her shoulder.

"Bug!"

I knew then that I would never get used to this kind of attention. It was like walking into a dressing room and finding the lighting exquisite. Everything fit you. Your skin glowed. I hurried into the kitchen to grab my apron and came out as Buttload Guy was heading out. Cleo approached me, clapping in excitement.

"Sorry I'm late," I said. I was hoping that no one else would come in until I had brewed myself at least one double espresso.

"Oh, that's nothing. Wait until you hear what I just learned."

I looked at her skeptically.

"Did he tell you that it's not 'nip it in the butt?' It's always been 'bud?'"

She opened her eyes wide. Shoved my arm.

"How did you know that?" She followed me to the espresso machine, talking over my shoulder as I tamped down the potent black powder. I wanted to rub it on my gums like a cocaine addict.

"I figured there was a theme developing here?" I said.

Buttload Guy had earned his title because last week he had held Cleo and me hostage in a long-winded and unprompted explanation of how *butt* was a legitimate unit of measurement, rendering *buttload* an inarguably and totally not-funny thing to say. When, later that day, another man took us through the origins of the saying *shoot your wad* and how it was an artillery reference never meant to be sexually explicit, we thought it was the same guy, only with his beard shaved. He said "shoot your wad" so many times I started to get turned on. It was not until Shoot Your Wad Guy and Buttload Guy happened to be in the café at the same time that Cleo and I realized that there was more than one man with this particular compulsion. They would not be the last.

I drank my espresso and felt the caffeine send its little whips around my body. I hadn't said much to Nico's mother after lying about the breakup—and nothing at all to her father, who'd spoken in low, dangerous tones about a basement renovation project when he thought I had already left. I knew what would happen: The father would remind his wife about whatever plan they had agreed on about me, and she would draw out of him one more month. I wondered if Nico's mother was the kind of woman who submitted to sex to get her way, or to apologize for already getting her way. Did I want to coast on one more month, gifted to me by my best friend's mom's vagina and/or mouth? I did not know what choice I had, except to work as many hours at Buster's as possible, subsist on stale pastries and complimentary espressos. Stop wasting gasoline on joyrides.

"Can you take a joyride in a vehicle that you own, or does it have to be stolen?" I asked Cleo.

She was stacking muffins on a small pedestal.

"You should have asked Buttload Guy when you had the chance."

AND SO, it was like that for the remainder of the day, and for the rest of the days that week. Cleo and I drank endless cups of coffee, treating each one as if it were the first after a long night. I stayed out front for the most part, fulfilling drink orders, while she moved back and forth from the kitchen, carrying new batches of scones, croissants, lemon bars, and sticky buns. She would talk for long stretches with the customers, twirling her hair, her little sneaker pointed behind her like a pony's hoof. People of all sorts wanted to talk to her, even the pair of cops that patrolled the block. They walked in, boxy in their vests, and told Cleo that she would get more business if she put some protein on the menu.

"There's walnuts in the banana bread," she said, then sent them down the counter to me, where they ordered twenty-ounce coffees and almond croissants, chewing them in a daze.

Once, Cleo tried to meet The People halfway by preparing a quiche for the lunch crowd. Its surface was tight and gleaming, with small, charred bumps where the broccoli broke through. She sliced it to order and zapped it in the microwave until it sizzled. Immediately, we attracted a quiche diehard, a short woman with wandering gray eyes, who called it eggy pie: "Can I get a piece of that eggy pie?"

"I just can't," Cleo said after the third time we served the Eggy Pie Lady. "She's going to turn me off quiches altogether." She wiped it off the menu board with her bare hand.

BUSTER'S WAS BUSY most of the time, but there were moments between customers when I would wander back to the kitchen to deliver an empty scone tray, or to search for a new whipped cream charger. I would linger, watching Cleo roll out the pie crusts and cut the lemon bars, her knife sliding along a ruler and emerging clean because she had made them perfectly. On the edge of the pan, she left a half-inch crust, which was chewier and slightly darker than the central pieces. This crust could be peeled off in a long rope and eaten. Cleo and I discussed how much of the lemon rope we thought equaled a whole bar if you were to mash it into a square. I argued that it was the length of the pan itself. She said that looks were deceiving, and it was only the width of the pan. We both agreed that we had never had this debate without getting sick. Still, Cleo never brought out the food scale, because then we would know the truth, and the truth sucked.

"Lemon Bar Dread," I said. "The fear of knowing too much." Cleo looked at me, let the crusty pan slip into the murky dishwater with the mixing bowls and batter-coated spoons. She seemed to flip a suspicion over in her mind.

"Oh?"

I don't know what had made me say it. Maybe it was the sugar rush. Or, sometimes, when life is going all right, you find subtle ways to push your luck. I heard the rubber groan of the front door opening and wiped my hands on my apron, signaling that I was going to go out front. Cleo stopped me.

"Wait—" she said. I wondered if she was suddenly seeing through all my bullshit. What would she think of me if she knew how far back my knowledge of her life stretched? Would she feel violated, betrayed?

Cleo brought her finger to the side of her mouth and made a scratching motion.

"You have a lemon bar mustache."

I wiped my face with the corner of my apron and hurried out front, feeling like I had avoided a disaster: I could not let Cleo know about me and Tristan. Whatever friendship was blossoming between us was something that I had never thought was possible, but now it was all that I wanted. I would do anything to protect it.

The giant with the braided beard, who I had hidden behind on opening day, was standing at the counter. He said, "You're not Cleo," in a cheerful, interested way. Either I was delusional, or there was something going on with the men in town. They all seemed to want as much face time with Cleo as possible—which was not surprising—but when they got me instead, a small light flickered in their faces that said: *How disappointing. But then again, maybe not* too *disappointing.* The attitude was similar to the one I'd detected from the man at the bar who had asked if Cleo was my mom. Although not everyone was so explicitly lecherous.

"I'm Amos." The giant man smothered my hand in his. Amos wasn't being lecherous, I could just tell. He was sexy, in his bearish way. He asked for a pot of green tea.

"You met Amos?" Cleo asked later. She was carrying a blueberry pie with a little heart cut out in the crust. The dark filling had bubbled up just enough to stain the edges of the heart a deep burgundy. I resisted the urge to stick my finger in it.

"He's a big dude," I said.

"I know," she said. "Can you imagine?"

"Imagine what?" I asked. I watched her place the pie under a glass dome. I knew what she was inferring, but I wanted to hear her say it. Instead, she shrugged one shoulder somewhat haughtily.

"And here I thought you had a robust inner life, Drew."

It is possible that I felt more slighted than was necessary. So, in an act of totally immature rebellion, I smudged the clean pie dome with my greasy finger as soon as Cleo turned her back to me.

Drew—

It's been a while since I wrote. I suppose you are wondering how the bookstore is faring without you. I never told you this—it didn't seem appropriate, given your age and your position as my employee—but you had a way with the customers. How can I say this? You were a natural flirt. Natural in the sense that I doubt you even knew of your power, and sometimes I feel guilty for not bringing this to your awareness sooner. I just want you to be careful out there, wherever you have ended up. Some bosses may not be as tolerant as I was.

With your safety and happiness in mind—

B

I had just returned from the café and was only checking my email because I needed to feel like I had lounged sufficiently before getting in the shower. For some reason, walking through the door and straight into the shower was depressing; it was what burned-out doctors did, and cheating husbands. I hadn't expected to receive any emails, but now I was all worked up: How dare Byron flip the narrative on me like that? I typed my response, every drop of good sense in my mind evaporated by rage.

Hi Byron,
You're right. I've already been through two new bosses. The first one I fucked right away. The second one I am giving a little more time.
Yours,
Drew
PS—the second boss is a woman.

Someone flushed a toilet upstairs and the sound of plumbing rained down around me. I was going to go crazy in that bleached-out basement. Under the futon, I had stored two weeks' worth of tips, held together with a rubber band. I didn't know what the bundle would look like at the end of the month, whether it, plus my wages, would amount to anything constructive. In the box with the cash, there was the check that Nico's mother had written me for "house-sitting." Three hundred dollars. It was three hundred dollars more than I deserved, but I knew that I was just exacerbating the problem by not depositing it.

My inbox made a bubbly notification sound. Byron had already responded. I clicked it, ragged with self-loathing.

Drew,
How interesting.
I can sense your excitement in telling me this.
Byron

Fuck you, Byron.

There was a second flush inside the walls, which enraged me. *Get it together!* I wanted to shout through the ceiling, as if a double flush were a sign of total incompetence. It was almost seven o'clock, but I needed to get out. The Vespa was low on gas, however, and the thought of going through the indignity of the Stewart's parking lot was too much for me. It was cold, anyway. I slammed my laptop shut and threw on my jacket and scarf.

Nico's parents lived in a cul-de-sac neighborhood of mostly pristine retirees and some young families who were not as tasteful in their plastic Halloween décor, their cheap Slip 'N Slides, and their semi-neglected dogs pacing the lawns into dirt. I walked through the neighbor's backyard to a border of young trees and yard litter, which I crossed through to another yard, and then another, letting the stillness and anonymity of the houses lull me. Figures moved behind sheer curtains. Upstairs bedrooms were a mood ring of colors. I knew where I was going, of course, and the thought of how many blocks I'd have to walk made me crave a cigarette. I'd like to say that the only reason I never developed an addiction was because smoking blocked out all the good smells—which was also why there were some places, too steeped in memory, that could only be endured behind a veil of smoky foulness. I ducked into a corner store, only to find that my jacket pockets were empty. I had snapped every dollar I owned into that bundle beneath the futon. I went back outside and was halfway up the sidewalk—still a residential street, although more eclectic and scrubbier than Nico's cul-de-sac—when someone whistled at me. It wasn't a catcall whistle. More like I was a collie who required a swift command. I saw Amos standing on a porch, cigarette held at eye level, as if he had moved it for the sake of whistling.

"Oh my God," I said, walking toward him. "Do you have another?" He was one of those guys, I could tell, who would give me the cigarette, and stand silently while I lit it. Monuments like him did not chitchat. I found right away that there was no use standing next to him, craning my neck, so I sat on the porch step to take my first drag. The instant head rush gave everything a uniformly bleak vibe that said: *Life is garbage. There's nothing to worry about.*

"Is this your house?" I asked Amos.

"It's my client's house—well, his mother's, but she's too old to do the heavy lifting." He jingled a lanyard that was around his neck. I bent backward to look up at him and saw that it was a picture ID.

"I've got to go back inside in a minute to force-feed him a pill." He stubbed the cigarette on the railing with patient precision.

"Is your client a cat?" I asked. This earned me a one-syllable laugh.

"What about you?" he asked me. "What are you doing out here?"

I stood and turned to him, holding my cigarette dramatically in front of my face. I'd never mastered the art of smoking like I wasn't smoking.

"I'm going to go spy on my mom," I said. Saying it aloud made it feel less shameful. I was grateful for Amos's presence. I considered how I had chosen to take the high road with Cleo the other day when it was obvious that she wanted to speculate about his penis size. When had I ever turned down such an invitation? And what's more:

When had I ever taken the high road? It was unlike me. But here with Amos, I felt a platonic, unhurried ease. He was a caretaker. A boulder. Talking to him was like talking to someone's grave; you felt the cool acceptance, the certainty that your secrets would be kept safe. He nodded, like what I had said needed no further explanation. I thanked him for the cigarette, gesturing with it too obviously again, and told him I'd see him around.

My mother's house was technically a bungalow, but I disliked the term. It felt too unwieldy, like those seafood restaurants that decorate their interiors with nets and lobster traps. *Bungalow* was only one notch higher on my Ick List than houses that were described as *Arts and Crafts*. Could there be anything more demeaning to a structure?

Since I'd left home, my mother had taken to opening her curtains again. I had already known this, from previous spy missions. As I approached the one-story house, I could see that the front windows were lit, the curtains pulled neatly to the side, with only a length of white gauze between the glass and the rest of the room. This layer of grandmotherly lace, slung atop the warm interior, was not something that I was prepared for, although I thought I had prepared for the worst. I wished that more of my cigarette was left to protect me. I wished I had not come, and not because the sight of the house was painful, but because pain and curiosity had a way of becoming perversely entwined. People who have not experienced subtle, slow-burn trauma usually don't understand how perverse it can get. There's a dangerous allure to the places where the trauma unfolded, like a grimy tent in the middle of a snowy forest. You think to yourself, It's smelly, yes, but it's warm inside. And there is the indent of my body, still visible in the sleeping bag! You think, What if I lay down and closed my eyes, just for a moment? And before you know it, you're back there, entrenched in everything that you worked so hard to escape. My cigarette was spent. I dropped it on the smudge of dirt at the base of the tree that I was hiding behind. There was an unfamiliar car parked in my mother's driveway. Brown, early nineties model, with a faded hood. Again, the perversity rushed in, and I found myself hoping that it was a man's car. I pictured my mother, inside, entertaining a man. The record player fixed, its platter no longer wobbly. A place for their tumblers of whiskey on the coffee table that was not stained, or sticky, or ringed with years' worth of coffee mugs. Why did I want this? Because fantasies have a long leash. They can wander into many unexamined corners. It wasn't a Daddy thing. It was that I had always known how charming my mother could be beneath her despair, and it seemed that the world, in some way, should grant her an audience. A figure moved behind the lace in one window, then crossed by the second window, and my weirdo heart swelled at the continuity of it. I turned around, not wanting to spoil this small discovery, which was no discovery at all.

I avoided Nico's parents as much as I could, which was easy with her father, but not always with Gina, who often paced the hallway folding endless piles of laundry, or carried out zany decluttering missions during which she would try to give me old hats that Nico had worn as a child for nonconsensual JCPenney photo shoots. *Lady,*

I wanted to say to her, *I cannot even pull off a motorcycle helmet convincingly, much less a plaid beret.* I could see the contradiction in her eyes whenever we crossed paths: her need for company versus a kind of armor—against my influence, against her own responsibility. I was the stray dog that her daughter had brought home, toward which she could never fully express her resentment, fearful that it would all come pouring out. She would not ask about the undeposited check. The other unspoken thing was that Nico would be returning for Thanksgiving break and I had to be gone before then. I knew, somehow, that when she came back, she would be different. Her intellect would be provoked. She would be armed with a new vocabulary that could be used to define every uneducated person whom she had left behind, rendering them small, boxed into their own categories of irrelevance. She would always be softhearted—I did not doubt that—but I feared that the down of her heart would be swapped out for pity. I could not bear to be pitied by Nico.

THE NEXT MORNING, I arrived at the café to find Amos eclipsing the kitchen doorway.

"Excuse me," I said, squeezing by so I could get to the rack where my apron was hung. Amos hugged the doorframe. Cleo was kneading a lump of dough on the kitchen table, white to her elbows with flour.

"Amos was just admitting to corrupting you last night," she said when she saw me. Her necklaces clinked with each lunge she made into the dough, cleavage shuddering above the tight squeeze of her bra.

"I was already corrupted," I said. I looked at Amos, who just lifted his shoulders in a *leave me out of it* shrug.

He remained in the doorway. "Is my having one cigarette such a thrilling topic?" I asked, my voice more defensive than I meant it to be.

"No, no," Cleo said. She twitched her nose and looked at the ceiling, willing away an itch. "We'd already moved on to the question of alpacas."

"They spit," said Amos in a way that suggested he had already mentioned this. Cleo pinched some flour from the bin and slapped it onto her dough ball. I was beginning to understand that Cleo's need to scheme was not just a personality trait; it was a compulsion. Yesterday, she'd asked me if I thought that the state of Vermont should secede from the union, which evolved into a lengthy—and mostly one-sided—discussion about how it might be possible to convince enough people that the secession had already happened for it to become a real movement.

"People are always more impassioned if they think they're going to lose something," she had said. "Get them used to the idea, so when they find out it's not true, they'll be more likely to fight for it."

"I can see this means a lot to you," I said, and she looked mildly distraught, like the time I told her that I didn't think marshmallows on sweet potatoes were such a crime.

I could see now that she had lured Amos to the kitchen so she could talk to him about whatever new idea she was brewing.

"Are we starting an alpaca farm?" I asked, looping my apron strings behind my back and crossing them over to tie a knot in the front. According to the state health code, Cleo and I were supposed to wear full bib aprons that covered our torsos, but we thought the topless ones, barely the length of a miniskirt, were cuter. Cleo slapped the dough again.

"I'm trying to convince Amos here to take advantage of the gap in the market."

"For alpaca meat?"

"Ew, no. Traveling alpaca studs." She placed each one of these words into the air with her flour-covered hand, as if envisioning a banner.

Amos shifted in the doorway. I could tell that he wanted to escape the alpaca conversation. He was wearing a weathered messenger bag over his shoulder that he slid down his arm.

"Oh, by the way," he said. He reached into the bag and pulled out a folded green cloth, holding it in his extended palm. "You wanted this?"

Cleo wiped her hands on her apron and took the cloth by two corners, letting it fall open. It resembled the American flag in composition, except where the stripes would have been, the material was solid green. There was a circle of blue stars, uncorralled, in the top left-hand corner.

"It's inspired by the flag of the Green Mountain Boys," she explained to me. "But we're going to tell The People that it's their signal to go rogue. It's already happening, Drew-Baby."

At this, Amos lifted his eyes to me. I could not tell if it was a reaction to Cleo's apparent mania, or to confirm that he had heard her call me *baby.* But he just nodded like his job was done.

"Have a nice day, ladies," he said.

WE HUNG THE flag over the kitchen doorway. The Green Mountain Boys were a band of Yankee revolutionaries from eighteenth-century Southern Vermont. No one who wasn't from the area knew about them, much less what their flag sort of looked like, and those who were local had probably not thought about them since fifth-grade social studies. Most people walked by our flag without comment, but there were a few who asked questions.

"It's your signal to go rogue—" I started to say to one boy, a college student with a guitar on his back. Cleo elbowed me.

"She's a weirdo. Pay no attention," she said to the boy, and snatched the tissue-wrapped scone that I was about to give him so she could hand it over the counter herself. He looked at me sideways before tucking the scone inside his jacket.

"You can't just give it away like that, Bug," Cleo said after he left. Her face was full of conspiracy, and that always-present pinch of mirth. There was a little pocket of intensity between her eyes. It is difficult to explain the wave of comprehension that hit me in that moment. It was as if I was reading Cleo's complete manifesto in one flash. The gist of it was this: We—Cleo and I—owed the world nothing, and we owed ourselves only joy. Chaos was the only plan. Laughter was the only language. And I—Drew-Bug, Drew-Baby, Bug-Bug—would never be the butt of the joke as long as I was on her side.

When there was a lull in business, Cleo and I huddled over the stainless steel table in the kitchen to discuss our first serious scheme: what to do about lunch. Cleo was adamantly against any kind of sandwich—not cold, or grilled, or wrapped. She said that sandwiches were a slippery slope. They gave The People too much power, too many options, and way too many openings to make amendments to the menu.

"Everyone wants a sandwich named after them," she sighed.

Another point was that sandwiches required assembly. Cleo explained that this would mean hiring another employee. I studied her closely. I wanted to make sure that what she really meant was that hiring another employee was unthinkable and would never happen.

"Making pie is cute," Cleo said. "Making a sandwich is degrading."

"And quiche is definitely not—?"

Cleo cut her finger across her throat. The Eggy Pie Lady had apparently traumatized her. She still came in most days, looking for another slice. I was kind to her, offering to cook her an egg in the microwave—maybe she just needed a fix?—but she only sighed and said that she would try again tomorrow.

"No! No tomorrow!" I told her. "Please. The quiche was a mistake. An experiment gone wrong." I wrapped a vanilla chip cookie in wax paper and closed her hand over it, like I was trying to smuggle it out of the building. "Take this," I whispered.

"What else do people eat?" I asked Cleo. "Salads?"

"Same issue as the sandwiches: too much assembly. Too much power to The People."

"Premade?" I asked, wincing, because I did not need Cleo to tell me that premade salads were suffocating. "Soup!" I interrupted myself before she could get a word in, and she rocked back on her heels, peering at me. I kept talking because now that I had said it, it did not seem like such a bad idea. I listed the pros on my fingers. "One: No meat. Two: Ingredients like potatoes and beans keep longer. Three: You can make it in big batches. Four: No assembly." I wanted one more point so that I could use all my fingers. "And The People have no power. They can't even see what's in it." I held out my thumb in triumph and Cleo took it in her fist, brought it to her mouth, and bit it.

"You're brilliant, Bug," she said.

Forget Tristan's beautiful solo exhibition in the tack room. This was my new moment. I wanted to seal it in a globe and place it on a mantel.

THE NEXT MORNING, Cleo placed the produce order, then slipped out after the early morning rush to buy Crock-Pots while I dealt with a woman who Cleo called Quad Bitch, but who I, feeling that Quad Bitch was too harsh, had privately named the Brownie Bragger. She worked at the insurance company on the corner and was the only woman I knew who wore real, knee-length pencil skirts and five-inch heels. For a small town where nearly half the residents did not bother to change out of pajamas to go the bank, I found this kind of dress to be unnecessary. It messed with the population's expectation curve, especially because she was already moderately attractive, which meant that she was basically a bombshell. Her hair was layered in that sawed-off style that was popular, and her eyebrows had been plucked into an expression that reminded me of a mean aerobics instructor. Also, she was thin. If she had been a trail ride tourist, I would have put her on our smallest pony. All of this would have been tolerable but for the fact that she ordered a brownie every day, and every day she took that brownie out of its to-go bag, set it on the counter, and explained to whoever had given it to her that she never ate an entire brownie all at once.

"I keep a little plastic knife in my office desk," she said. "And what I do is I take the knife and I cut the brownie into four equal squares." She said this part in the same tone and with the same inflection each time. It gave me an irritated sensation in my spine, similar to how I feel whenever I hear the uncanny voice-over for an infomercial.

"I allow myself one square after lunch, another after my workout, and one more for an after-dinner sweet treat."

"That's only three," I'd said the first time I heard this story, which was what she had been waiting for.

"Ah, because I save the fourth square for the next morning!" She smiled with closed lips, like she was trying to push her teeth back into her mouth, then put the brownie—still intact—carefully into the wax paper.

"I was going to suggest she try the fourth rectally," Cleo had muttered as we watched her walk away.

"No, you weren't."

"Yes, I was."

WITH THE CROCK-POTS set up, the spices purchased, and the recipes laminated and strung on a line across the kitchen, all we had to do was wait for the vegetables to arrive, and Cleo and I would be soup ready. I started coming to work earlier, when it was just the morning commuters looking for a no-fuss cup of coffee. Some of these customers were quiet and bleary and still smelled of shaving cream, while others carried on a kind of pre-dawn chattiness that was soothing to me, like being a child and listening to grown-ups discuss matters that you don't understand. The fake blue-and-green flag still hung in the kitchen doorway. Cleo had selected a few countercultural types to divulge its meaning to. I could not tell if there was any momentum there, but it seemed that more people were coming directly to Cleo, unrelated to the flag conspiracy—artists, students, and some spiritual types—to share with her their own schemes. *All I need is a projector and an abandoned lot. What we really need is a van. A can of paint and someone on the inside.* These talks took place in the mornings while Cleo paused to drink her first real coffee of the day (not the shots of espresso she tossed down at five a.m.). Sometimes I would marvel at the sheer breadth of it: What had she done with her life before all of this, besides having an affair with a farm boy seventeen years her junior? Tristan had said she owned horses, but where had all that gone, if she was here now from five in the morning until late afternoon? From the little that she had told me about her home life, I gathered that Howie was some kind of half-retired financial consultant, although I did not even know if it was possible to be half retired. He still came in regularly, chest and belly puffed with fatherly pride. I could feel Cleo's jaw tighten whenever she watched her husband push a dollar into the tip jar, the slow rise in her shoulders. She was not afraid of Howie, or particularly unhappy with him. It was just that he carried in a different air, like when someone brings a baby to a party and you feel the need to turn the music down. Howie was closing in on sixty, but Cleo, as far as I could tell, was barely beginning her midlife crisis.

I was helping Cleo with the early morning setup when our produce order came rolling in on stacked crates. The delivery guy was dimpled and sandy haired. He was one of those young men who looked like he had been bullied into becoming an adult, who would have otherwise played happily in a creek bed all his life. He gave me the order slip to sign, then leaned on the dolly with his arms folded, looking at Cleo.

"Can I help you stack these somewhere?" he asked her.

"The girl and I are strong," she said, "but thanks." I tried to give him back the clipboard, but he ignored me.

"What are you gonna do with all these squashes?" he asked. Cleo took the top crate from under his arm.

"It depends on how girthy they are," she said, carrying it into the kitchen. This seemed to jolt the delivery guy back into reality. He looked at me, as if seeking confirmation in my face for what Cleo had just implied. I nudged the clipboard at him again, and he took it, slipping it under his arm.

"Did you bring us a fat batch?" I asked, looking into the next crate. It was filled with thick carrots, all about a foot long and ringed with soil. I was teasing him because Cleo had started it, but also because I was annoyed that he seemed so immediately smitten by her—and not only that, but he was unwilling to conceal it. Where was his tact? Cleo was not a 24/7 Jiffy Mart that you could just drunk-walk to in your flip-flops. She was a private club. She was the French Laundry. I carried the crate of carrots into the kitchen just as Cleo was coming out for the next one. When I walked back out, there was an eggplant sailing toward my head. I caught it with both hands like a football. It was long and streaked purple, not like the black, nearly spherical eggplants you find at the grocery store.

"Heads up, Drew-Bug," Cleo called to me, even though she had already thrown it. She was standing next to the delivery guy, looking devilish. "Another one for the Lonely Girl's Vegetable Patch?" she asked me.

"The what?" The flying eggplant had rattled me.

"The Lonely Girl's Vegetable Patch," she said again, pulling out another bulbous eggplant. She slapped it into her palm like a baton, while the delivery guy gaped.

"Oh, right," I said. "I thought we didn't talk about that."

The days got colder. Most mornings, I could not get past the driveway without my helmet visor fogging, or the joints in my hands seizing up. I wrapped the Vespa in a tarp, belting it with bungee cords, in a ceremony of defeat. All wrapped up, it looked like a deer in a body bag. It was only the first day of November.

Our first batch of soup, a winter vegetable stew, coincided with the arrival of frost, and The People walked in blowing on their hands, stamping their feet. They gazed gratefully at the menu board.

"Soup!" they cried. "Just the thing for a day like today!"

"They are way too happy about this," Cleo muttered under her breath, but handed the warm two-cup containers across the counter as if delivering her own precious heart. The People beamed. Cleo beamed back.

"Let's make chilled gazpacho tomorrow," she whispered to me.

"Don't be a baby," I said.

We had made a batch of chili the day that Cleo got the call. She had made it extra spicy and put no notice on the menu that it was completely vegetarian. She wanted The People to love it, to admit that it didn't need meat to taste good. It was not a jab against carnivores, she insisted. She just thought they needed to be taken down a notch—heart health and all that. She kept serving herself little shots of chili in espresso cups, eating with the tiniest sugar spoon.

Her eyes welled with the heat of it. It gave her a look of poignancy, like someone watching a heartwarming film.

We were both out front, Cleo holding the tiny spoon between her front teeth. We had been making a list, on a strip of receipt paper, of how many male customers felt the need to tell us that spicy foods were an aphrodisiac. We had four so far, and the lunch rush had not even hit us. If we reached ten, Cleo had announced to a full room of customers, then she and I would make out for a full minute. Of course, we would not really—it was only to see the men deflate when we told them that they had just fallen short of winning the girl-on-girl jackpot. I was excited by the ease with which Cleo had proposed it, as if the idea of us kissing existed in an alternate world that could be accessed as effortlessly as dipping your hand in a fish tank. It was perhaps our most childish game yet. Still, hadn't the men started it? Weren't we just punishing them accordingly? And not for their audacity—we could handle audacity—but for the painful lack of creativity? We were starved for originality.

The phone rang. Cleo answered it, with the spoon still in her mouth.

"Buster's?" she said, through her teeth. I watched the spoon start to sink like the needle on a dial going down, down, until it dropped. Her expression did not change, even after she hung up and went into the office for her scarf and mittens. I picked up the spoon. It was warm in my hand.

"Drew-Hunny," she said when she came back out, her tote hanging on her elbow. "If I'm not back before close, just shut everything off and lock the door."

"What's happening?" I asked.

"Maybe blast the milk steamer a few times. And check the soup burners."

"What's happening?"

The pocket between her eyes deepened.

"Don't forget to keep the list going."

THOUGH IT WAS normal for me to be at the counter by myself, The People could sense that something was off when they came in the next day. I had done my best to open alone—had only burned one batch of apple turnovers, and whipped into creation a lumpy abomination that was supposed to be cream cheese frosting—but it was obvious that Cleo wasn't there. The music was somehow too loud, and there was a sour, baby-puke smell permeating the kitchen that I could not locate. Even the heating system seemed to want to prove how eccentric it could be.

"Her husband is in the hospital," I shouted over Patsy Cline. The People did not like the word *husband* any more than I did. "Co-ma," I enunciated for them, leaning over the counter.

"*Husband??*" was their only response. I served the reheated vegetarian chili, and no one made any uncouth remarks about spiciness. Even the Brownie Bragger seemed tired. She shivered in her belted pea coat and stared at her brownie with a strange and hungry hatred, as if she wanted to cram the entire thing in her mouth and scream through it. I don't even think her attitude had much—if anything—to do with Cleo being absent. It was just the energy of the day. Gina had also been moody that morning when she woke to find me leaving the house at five.

"What's the matter?" she asked me, hugging her bathrobe.

"Nothing," I told her. "I just have to go to work early."

"What kind of place opens at this hour?"

I was about to explain to her that I needed enough time to preheat the oven, scoop the muffin batter into the muffin tin, and allow the bread dough to rise, but then I caught something in her expression that chilled me: She did not believe that I was going to work, because she had stopped believing anything I told her a long time ago. I could not guess what kind of delinquency she thought I was up to, but I recognized the inevitability of it. She knew too much about my past to admit to me that I had become a burden. She also knew too much about my past to be able to envision anything brighter for me. I left the house. The anger that I felt kept contorting back toward me, no matter how forcefully I twisted it away. Yes, Nico's mother might have the wrong impression about me on a very basic level, but as long as I was dependent on her charity, I felt that I had no way of proving to her that I was a decent human being.

WHEN I WAS ten, my mother went to live in a halfway house for two weeks. The night before she left, she lay with me in my bed and listed the reasons why she had to go, and how they outnumbered her reasons for staying. She stated it plainly for me, while she traced shapes on my back with her finger.

"Some people are born with a bad story," she said. "They go through life collecting all the good stories they can, and they pile them like sweaters. But eventually something happens where they get too hot under all those layers and have to take them off and start over." Her finger moved in a figure eight between my shoulder blades. If someone were to say these exact words to me today, I would not know what they were trying to tell me, but sometimes, when you are very young, it is easier to understand. My brain was a clean paper towel beneath the leaky pen of my mother's words, soaking them up, cell by cell. As she spoke, I had a vision of a long black eel, or tapeworm, that my mother had swallowed as a baby, and I saw that it threaded through her completely, end to end. I saw a doctor trying to pull it from her mouth with spaghetti tongs, but suddenly it was a long black ribbon, like something a magician might try to extract that just keeps coming out. I must have been half dreaming, because in my vision the doctor got tired of pulling on the eel ribbon and took a pair of scissors from his doctor bag and snipped it. *There,* he said. *Now I have solved the problem.* But everyone knew that the problem was still in there, yards and yards of it, still inside my mother's body.

Contrary to what many people have assumed over the years, I was not upset with my mother for the way that she was, or for the halfway house. The only part of the situation that bothered me was that her ailment had not been more straightforward, dramatic, or sudden. I wished that I could have told my friends and teachers that my mother had been dragged away by force, so that they would feel sorry for me in a clean, righteous way. Instead, I felt their pity like breath fogging a window; their pity was breathing down my neck, wanting to know, *Why, exactly?* I could not tell them about the infinity tapeworm that sometimes confined my mother to her bedroom for days, or on other occasions made her walk through the house with her hands up like blinders.

"If I see those pillows, I will get off track," she explained. "If I am reminded of the shopping bags, I will lose another day."

These days, people are too familiar with terms like depression, anxiety, OCD, ADHD. It is helpful, yes, but I suspect that other, more subtle problems get mopped up by these diagnoses. The depression sponge comes along to absorb my mother's highly specific demons, denying them their features, which were all carefully drawn like folk art. So, I find myself with the same issue as when I was a child: I cannot talk about my mother without her being lost to the common denominator.

Your mother was absent?

No, my mother was in too many places at once.

Your mother was depressed?

No. She suffered from many facets of dread.

Your mother left you?

She would never leave me.

AMOS WALKED IN as the midday rush was dying down. I had run out of the chili by twelve-thirty, so The People were especially irritable, and I was nowhere near as talented at talking up the banana bread as Cleo. Amos read the exhaustion on my face.

"I'm only looking for a pot of tea," he said. He always asked for a pot—never a mug or a to-go cup—and I could appreciate the slowness of it. Like a ritual that modern life had forgotten. I threw the tea bag in and ran the hot water over it, watching it dimple, then puff.

"There was a man parked at her house," I said to Amos. "My mother's. She's put up lace curtains. When I was a kid, lace curtains only existed on *Masterpiece Theatre*." I placed the steaming pot on the counter, along with a small overturned cup on a saucer.

"I didn't tell Cleo about your spy mission."

I stared at Amos's photo ID slung around his neck because that was the Amos that I was eye level with. I wondered why I was not attracted to him and feared that I was guilty of a kind of bias that I called the Gentle Loner Spiral, whereby a perfectly decent man gets overlooked, because he has been overlooked. I supposed he was too old for me, but I failed to see how that mattered. Would Nico's parents disapprove? Would Amos himself? Sometimes I felt that I was beholden to no one at all.

"I know you didn't," I said. "But Cleo and I have no secrets." This was not true, of course, but I believed that it was possible and only a matter of time before I was drinking wine on her couch, answering her phone when she was in the bathroom, saying, "Cleo's phone!" Holding her while she cried over Howie.

It was still unclear what had happened to Howie. I had received two updates via phone that were not really updates.

"Nothing yet. Another round of tests."

"What can I do?"

"Ask Buttload Guy about the origins of *kick the bucket*."

"Is he going to die?"

"Put in an order for cucumbers."

"Cleo?"

"I am going to make that gazpacho as soon as I get back."

SHE WAS BACK two days later, storming through the door in a dramatic burst of cold air, her scarf unwound and skimming the floor. I had not opened yet. The kitchen was stacked with dirty baking sheets, the steamer wands were crusted with milk, and I had forgotten to warm up the espresso machine. She walked through the kitchen and into the back room without speaking. I heard the clap of the freezer door opening, and she appeared again with a bucket of frozen raspberries, which she began to eat nervously, as if they were popcorn. It was like watching someone bite into an ice cream cone.

"I'm a little behind with the baking," I said. I could not decipher the look on her face, so I, self-centered and sleep-deprived, assumed that she was annoyed by my failure to keep things running smoothly. I again experienced the shame of being caught red-handed in my own mess.

"My husband was killed by a horse," Cleo said. "And I don't know which one of the bastards did it."

I watched her continue to eat raspberries and tried to make sense of this new information. It seemed utterly backward to me. How could Howie have been killed by a horse, when he was in the hospital, lying in a medically induced coma? Who had let him out of the hospital and near a horse? Also, I, who had the healthiest fear of horses of anyone I knew, could not in that moment imagine a horse-related death that did not involve riding one.

"When was he on a horse?" As I was saying the words, my mind caught up to what Cleo was telling me. Howie was dead. The beaming Santa Claus with the ironed shirts and the warm handshake had somehow been allowed to die. I thought of the nude painting out front and wondered if Cleo would take it down, as if its presence was suddenly impious. Our minds will rush to the nearest triviality, I swear.

"He was kicked," she said. Cleo seemed to be in that liminal space between reality and grief, where she could say the words without crying, in a kind of half comprehension. Widow, said my mind. I liked the dark, iron scroll of it. Cleo is a widow. The sentence could have been a stained-glass border, an ornamental crest above an old doorway. You are burning the croissants, was the next string of words that came through. I threw open the double doors of the oven and pulled out the tray using a dish towel. The croissants looked like they had been brushed with wood stain, their points like black fingertips.

"Uh-oh," said Cleo, still popping raspberries into her mouth. "We can label them diet croissants."

"You're not going to close the café?" I asked her.

"Over some burnt croissants?"

"Over the fact that your husband is dead." I didn't say *widow.* I was afraid it would open up the truth for her in a new, fearful way. That she would fall into it, and I would lose her.

"No. Once The People catch wind that your hours are unreliable, they give up on you. They're cold to the bone."

IN THE DAYS that followed, I watched Cleo's every movement, her shifts in tone, the quickening of eye moisture. In my mind, I was protecting her, pushing my body between hers and the needy People, answering the phone, telling her to sit down when she'd been standing in front of the oven for too long. All the check engine lights were blinking around her head at once. There were the funeral arrangements, the necessary phone calls, canceled plans and financial adjustments. There were also glaring social fluctuations—how the customers became hushed, their faces gaping expressions of sympathy, the way they folded their dollar bills before placing them into the tip jar, as if to say, *Every part of me has become delicate. Notice how sympathetic I am.* Cleo hated it.

"The People have become so *precious!*" she moaned,

pushing the bursting tip jar at me. She refused to profit from it. And that was how I was profiting from Howie's death: I had become Cleo's only confidante because I was the only person who was not putting on airs. I was the only one who could say *Howie* and *dead* in the same sentence without flinching, who did not look fearfully at Cleo as if her whole identity had been straightjacketed by tragedy. The space we shared behind the counter and in the kitchen took on a new atmosphere. We were off-grid. We were separated from the rest of the world—a new species altogether: our hair wild in the heat waves from the oven, our fingernails black with coffee grounds, our teeth aching from eating too much lemon-bar rope. When Cleo asked me if I would be her bodyguard at the funeral, I knew just what she meant, and it was a wonderful feeling. Being useful, just by being real.

I showed up in a black shift dress, black tights, and dark gray heels because those were the only articles of clothing I owned that could be made to look appropriate. The effect was doll-like. I felt that I was someone's strange stepchild entering a dinner party having just returned from French boarding school.

"Drew-Baby," Cleo said to me, slipping her arm into mine. I towered over her—she was a heartbroken nymph in red lipstick and subtle eye glitter, and I was a giant Wednesday Addams. What power we held that day: the widow and the widow's protégé.

AND SO, when the opportunity arose for me to become the widow's young housemate, it seemed a miracle and also a perfectly natural order of events. If it had happened any other way, I would have not believed my luck—and just when I felt that I could not survive another day in Nico's basement!—but all the pieces came together so tightly to push me out of one situation into the next that I could not question it. Life was a giant finger and thumb, and I was the slippery apple seed pressed between them. *Pop!* There I was, soaring into the next chapter of my life.

It happened like this: Four days after the funeral, I arrived at work to find Cleo staring into the oven.

"Don't do it," I said, halfheartedly. I hung my coat on the hook.

"What's that?"

I walked over to her. The heat from the oven was like a delicious, dangerous wall. It smelled like banana bread and made me want to take a nap. I laid my hand on Cleo's shoulder.

"You're not the head in the oven type. You'd do better in sunglasses and a headscarf, sailing a convertible off a cliff."

She looked at me blankly.

"You are a strange girl," she said. She closed the oven doors. You had to really slam them, or else they wouldn't lock properly, and the safety mechanism would turn the heat off, and everything would be ruined. There was a list of phone numbers on the table, almost half of them crossed off with black marker.

"I'm just stressed," she said, and explained to me that a neighbor had been caring for Howie's four horses since the accident, but it wasn't a permanent solution. She would have to find someone to adopt them, even though Howie would cartwheel in his grave if he knew that the herd was being separated. She tapped the list of numbers. So far, she had called his sister in Florida and his cousin in Rochester.

Neither could help. There was a riding school two hours north that had agreed to take one of the old mares, but that was only because Cleo had lied and said the horse was good-tempered and could jump a small crossrail.

"I know they're just animals," Cleo said. "But I hate them. You understand?" It's funny: If Cleo had been wailing and wringing her hands with grief all this time, it would have raised my suspicions. I would have questioned whether she truly loved Howie, if she wasn't secretly glad to be free of him. But this stony antiperformance struck me as real. Cleo was in the tattoo parlor of pain, gritting her teeth.

"I can take care of them," I said. I was measuring my words so carefully that it was making me lightheaded. Cleo looked confused.

"You have nowhere to keep them, Bug."

"I'll come to you," I said. I knew that I meant *I'll come* live *with you,* but I would hold steady and let her make the next move. Surely she understood that I had no transportation, that there was no way for me to ride the scooter to her house multiple times a day, in snow and cold weather, while also keeping the coffee shop hours. "I know horses. You wouldn't even have to look at them."

I could see her taking in the possibility while we both continued to stare at the list of numbers, as if it was going to provide the final judgment.

"They're bratty," she said.

"I'm brattier," I said.

"One of them is a murderer," she said.

"I can handle it. I promise."

I moved my belongings out of Nico's basement the day before she was expected to come home for Thanksgiving. It felt wonderful to leave like that, throwing my bags into Cleo's truck while Nico's parents watched from behind the vertical blinds in the living room. It was possible that, quantifiably, they had done more for me than any other person in my lifetime. But I loathed them. I hoped the sight of Cleo, with her no-bullshit sunglasses, her hippie scarves, and her leather jacket, baffled them. I hoped it whipped their assumptions about me into a dizzying froth. I bounced in my seat as we clipped the curb, watching the houses fall away, the neighborhood dogs running after us on their lines until they were bungeed backward.

"I hope you know what you are getting into," Cleo said. She fed a tape into the deck and it crunched into place. Lucinda Williams moaned about barbed wire and guitar strings, and about towns in Georgia that I could not picture. I had never been to Cleo's house, and I could not say that I knew what I was getting into. All I knew was that I believed this was where my life had always been headed. We drove to the outskirts of town, where the houses were mostly single trailers boxed in by sheds and four-wheelers and chain-link dog runs. I liked November in Vermont. It was an acquired taste, a ghost of a month that was too late for foliage and too early for skiing. The roads were quiet, and all the leaves had fallen except for some patches of gold on the mountains, which stood out like paint on a distressed picture frame. Meanwhile, Lucinda was prowling around for her joy because someone, presumably a man, had taken it. *I want it back*, she growled. I wondered if I was headed toward joy. I remembered listening to the *Amélie* soundtrack and feeling as though I had stumbled into someone else's version of joy, and how disturbing that was, knowing that I might not have the capacity for it. That joy was like the month of June—green and fragrant, and filled with people who knew how to plant flower beds and clean windows properly. Maybe my joy was November: It was the warmth beneath a soured pumpkin. A split in a floorboard. A clean moon. Shapes in the fog.

I saw the horses in the field before I saw the house. One of them—dark and mud spattered—was galloping in the same direction that we were driving. I thought it would crash into the fence, but it turned sharply, threw up its back end, arched its whole body in a heaving vertical leap. Sometimes I thought about how much heart it took to make a body that large lift off the ground. All that power packed away, until the signal came through to run, run, run. Cleo kept her eyes fixed on the road. She turned into a rutted driveway that extended about twenty feet before splitting into a circle. At the head of the circle, there was a long red barn, with a John Deere mower parked out front. Behind the barn was the field where I had seen the horses, but they were hidden now, and it all looked like choppy patches of grass and mud. Cleo stopped the truck before the split in the driveway and cut the engine. The house to our right was small and white, with a low porch in the front, a railing that looked to reach only knee-high. It was one of those houses that you could tell was old because of how many layers of paint it had on it. Mentally, you could bury a fingernail into the side of it. I liked the house instantly. Here was something with character, a far cry from the soulless white box that I had been living in for three years.

"There's still a lot of Howie in there," Cleo said, almost like an apology.

We rolled the Vespa down from the truck bed and stood it temporarily in the driveway. Cleo said that I could move it into the barn later and keep it there through winter. I suppose that was when I realized how serious she was about not going near the horses. I was impressed by her lucidity. I wished I knew exactly what to stay away from.

The front door opened into a narrow hallway where a couple of stacked crates held some work boots and a pair of men's house slippers. The floorboards were worn to a lighter shade down the middle, and a row of coats and flannels seemed to bow into the wall. To the left, there was a kitchen wallpapered in a pattern that looked like bluebells. Against it, a mid-century starburst clock. Rust-red cupboards. To the right, I could see partially into a living room, where the light was filtered through many houseplants. A shag rug. I did not get the impression that Cleo was a fastidious housekeeper, but I could sense that the house was kept orderly by way of a slow routine. Even the dust particles knew what to expect. I followed her past these rooms to a stairway that hugged the wall without a railing. The upstairs was small, with what looked like two bedrooms and a tiny wedge of a bathroom. In the bathroom, there was a radiator the size of a toaster and the simplest porcelain sink that made me want to cry. Did it remind me of a dollhouse that I had never owned? Something lost in the sun-bleached hallucination of childhood? We walked down another hallway, carpeted and lined with framed photographs of people with soft, private expressions. Cleo opened a doorway and led me into an office where a computer monitor sat on a cluttered desk. There was a dormer window with built-in bookshelves, which were crammed with books and folders at all angles and configurations. We crossed through to another door. I thought it would be a closet, but it opened into a long room with a peaked ceiling. It wasn't exactly an attic. If anything, the spareness of it reminded me of the inside of a toy suitcase that I had as a child. I'd loved the suitcase, loved the pattern of red roses on the inside, and liked to keep it empty. It felt tidier that way: a miniature room that I could lock up and store beneath my bed.

"We never knew what to do with this space," Cleo said. "It's not too claustrophobic, is it?"

I knew she was proposing that I take the room for myself, but for some reason, it seemed more polite to pretend that I did not understand.

"For what?" I asked.

"For you, dummy. Did you think you were going to sleep in the hayloft?"

"Is there a hayloft?"

"It's filled with feral cats."

I walked to the end of the room and bent down to look through the one window there. It faced the barn, and I could see the fields a little better: the simple lean-tos and the bumpy, black mud. I had seen the horses from the road, but they still seemed like phantoms to me. Would they be there, waiting at the gate, when feeding time came? Would they listen to me, or just turn away snickering?

I AM NOT sure if it was Cleo's hayloft remark that set me off, but that night I dreamed that I was climbing a ladder to what I thought was going to be a hayloft but turned out to be a stage. It was a crudely made stage, lit by candles. I felt as if I had been transported to the seventeenth century and I was about to perform Shakespeare. This was not a stage fright dream. I do not have those. I wasn't sure what I was supposed to do until I saw that Byron was in the audience, leaning forward with his hands clasped. For some reason, his presence signaled to me that I was a stripper, so I began to undress, twirling each item of clothing stupidly and tossing it. As they sailed through the air, I remembered the candles and feared that my clothes would land on the flames and start a fire, but I could not stop. I took off my pants and threw them, then my underwear. It was the underwear that was unlucky. It caught fire on one of the candles, exploding into a wall of flames that obscured the audience. Suddenly, Byron was beside me saying, *Look what you've done.* I lay down for him on the wooden stage and let him fuck me, his lips curled in an ugly, determined sneer, as if his own orgasm were a rabbit that he was chasing down. I was grateful for the curtain of fire, so that no one would see how much I was enjoying it.

4

DEAR BYRON,
Last night, I dreamed that I found semen in the wool of a lamb and woke up feeling very hungry. It's fine because I live with my boss now. She and I have a special garden out back where we grow long vegetables for sustenance and for pleasure. We never need to leave the house. What do you think of that?

Drew—
I assure you the vegetables will grow old and you and your lady boss will come running back into town.

Byron—
Your confidence is adorable. We are very good gardeners.

ALL OF HOWIE'S horses were rescue cases in some way or another. The roan mare was blind in one eye and came from a hoarding situation. The youngest gelding had been born literally in the wild. One had a racetrack injury rendering her unrideable. The other was just very old, as far as I knew. Two days after I had moved in with Cleo, I met the neighbor who had been caring for them. She brought me to the back of the barn, where one of the stalls had been converted into a feed room. She was an older lady with an endearing waddle and thick glasses that gave the illusion that she was gazing at everything in wonder. At first, it felt rude to not match her expression, but then it felt like I was mocking her, so I stopped. Her name was Lydia, and she explained to me that she had always been the one to take care of the horses when Howie went away, but she had lately developed an issue that made it difficult to be without a toilet nearby. This was fine, but from then on I felt like I needed to keep my questions and comments brief.

As it turned out, it wasn't Lydia who was going to teach me about Howie's horses; it was Howie himself. In the feed room, Lydia brought out a three-ring binder, blew the dust from it like it was an ancient book, and flopped it down on the splintery wooden table.

"This," she said, tapping her gloveless finger on the plastic cover, "deserves a Pulitzer."

It was a comprehensive book of horse care instructions that Howie had typed and assembled three years back, when he and Cleo had gone on a trip to Las Vegas. Its curled, molasses-stained pages covered everything, from the quantities of grain and medication that each horse received in the morning to each horse's particular phobia and superfluous nicknames. At the front, he had added a table of contents, the chapters organized by task, in order of appearance, followed by a separate chapter for each horse—a sad strikethrough on one chapter to indicate that that horse, Gremlin, had died sometime the year before. In the back, there were about a dozen phone numbers for emergencies, including the veterinarian, the emergency veterinarian, the farrier, a neighbor (not Lydia) who owned a horse trailer, and another neighbor (also not Lydia) who would come over to shoot something, if there was something that needed to be shot. I gave the pages a stunned flip-through and caught sentences like FRIDA: CYST IN LEFT EAR. DO NOT BEND. And QUEEN BISCUITS: HALF BLIND. DO NOT APPROACH FROM RIGHT SIDE, OR FROM BEHIND, OR AT ALL WITHOUT A WERTHER'S ORIGINAL. And THUNDER: GETS OATS FIRST, OR ELSE HELL.

Thunder was the young gelding I'd seen from the road. He had been born on a wild mustang conservancy in one of the Dakotas and had never been trained under saddle.

"Don't let Thunder intimidate you," Lydia said. "He's an entitled teenager, that's all." She stared at me with her falsely expectant eyes, and I wondered suddenly if she was trying to send me a silent message. Was Thunder the horse that had kicked Howie? Did she know something that no one else knew, or that no one else wanted to admit to knowing? I was about to ask, but soon realized that her glazed stare was the byproduct of acute intestinal distress.

"Oh no," she said in a soft, apocalyptic voice. I held her hand and rushed her into the house.

SOMETIMES, early in the morning when I was trudging up the driveway to the barn in Howie's unlaced and too-big winter boots, I made a point to feel some regret over Tristan. This was most likely to happen after dreaming of him—my four-thirty alarm never failed to bring the axe cleanly down upon some interesting or sultry storyline. I would stumble outside, my brain still blasted by the rudeness of being awake, and I would make a little clearing in my thoughts for Tristan, who was always trying to fuck me in my dreams but somehow never once succeeded. The obstacles to our lust were plentiful and absurd—once it was because Tristan was being wheeled away for brain surgery. Another time, we were defeated by a dress that I was wearing made entirely of safety pins. It was as if my mind had become a private hell for this version of Tristan, he, an eternally erect Sisyphus, doomed to be cock-blocked by my alarm every morning. My dream-self, on the contrary, was having loads of dream-sex with everyone except Tristan. Amos's dream-cock had made many appearances already, stubbornly normal sized but coming with the force of a fire extinguisher. Dream-Byron masturbated in the corner like a sleep paralysis demon. Dream-Howie (may he rest in peace) had a fearfully large member that he wielded shyly but then couldn't climax until I shouted, "It doesn't fit!" And then there was Dream-Cleo: always in the wings, never corporeal, as if my subconscious were too humble and groveling to cast her full likeness. The acts that we carried out in my dreams went beyond physics, the depths of intimacy that we reached were fevered and strange; fingers dipped in secret recipes, hairlines salty, eyes signaling darkness—sweeping and tragic like the eyes of horses. A belly button. A pointed canine. A wondrous and agonizing tease.

I suppose it was easier to hold space for Tristan, to blame my fantasies on the sexual tension between us that had never been fully excised, than to ask myself questions like, *Are you obsessed with sex, or are you obsessed with depravity?* I suspected it was the latter but had no idea what to do with that information. If I turned my thoughts off during the day, my dreams became a hundred times worse. So, I continued about my business, breaking the ice in the water troughs, fumbling to tie a knot while wearing Howie's old gloves, and dodging nips from a half-blind horse named Queen Biscuits while thinking, I'll show you a Queen Biscuit, for no reason at all, other than I could not stop myself.

It did not help that my "lady boss" actively encouraged this kind of behavior. When the cucumbers for the gazpacho finally arrived, she made a show of slowly inspecting them, squeezing some gently so that her hand just slipped over the tip, bouncing her arm a little as if to demonstrate heft. When she left to carry the crate into the kitchen, the sandy-haired delivery guy turned to me.

"Did her husband really die?" His entire boxer-thick neck was flushed.

"Don't sound so hopeful," I said. "The only way to get to her is to perform a series of herculean tasks, each one harder than the last."

"I grew up on a dairy farm," he said, in a hushed voice.

"So?"

"So? I'm tough." He did a little flex with his fist that made the muscles in his arm jump. I took a deep breath. Maybe I could be one of those herculean tasks, I thought. Instead of suggesting this, however, I looked at him smugly.

"I'll let her know you're interested when I'm done with her," I said. My whole body had become one taut and thrumming nerve. I was intentionally turning down something that might actually happen for a sex fantasy that I did not even know how to approach. One I had explored at length in my mind while lying alone in Cleo's spare room, rolling it around like a powerful cough drop until the world melted away and only the thrumming, menthol-hot nerve was left. Lusting after a woman was terrifying. It was novelistic, all-consuming. Psychologically drenched. With men, there were all these physically embarrassing steps to take, so much coaxing and reassurances of virility. You could keep track of your dimensions with men, check boxes, wipe up their evidence with a rag. With a woman? Oh God. I feared that if I tread too closely, I'd be sucked in, obliterated. So, I spent my days in a constant state of arousal like a guy who's sworn off jerking it for a month. I teased The People with my eyes, undressed them all in my dreams, and meanwhile tried to be a good little worker girl.

I don't know how I was able to stay on my feet from four-thirty to six at night, but it felt as though my body were falling in step with Cleo's own superhuman ability to be constantly busy. Some cohabiting women get drawn into each other's menstrual cycles, so why couldn't I ride the wave of Cleo's boundless energy? I was fucking half the town in my dreams, following Howie's hypergraphia like it was a religious text. I was constantly bouncing ideas with Cleo in the kitchen, then playing "good cop/bad cop" with her whenever a customer needed to be placated. (Cleo was always the bad cop.) After all of this, we would go home, where Cleo would somehow still have the motivation to cook us supper while I brought the horses in for the night and fed them their grain. We'd drink wine and eat crostini and stir-fry and review our day at Buster's: Which member of the insufferable People had felt it his duty to tell us that light roast coffee has the most caffeine. What about the guy who went to Italy as a college student and was now qualified to insult the potency of our espresso? And the hordes of people pioneering a new horizon of rudeness by continuing to talk on their cell phones while they ordered at the counter? Cleo and I vowed to never own a cell phone. It still seemed possible back then, like when you told the fifth-grade D.A.R.E. officer that you would never smoke pot. We did that too! We smoked with Amos and Cleo's painter friend, who I learned was named Farid, who spoke about everything with a discerning glimmer like a raven hoping for a puzzle. I found Farid to be a little exhausting, which was my own fault. When someone looks at the world as if they expect it to be interesting, I always feel obligated to live up to the task. Sometimes Lydia and her partner, Beth, joined us, although only Beth partook in the drugs and alcohol, while Lydia, with her upset tummy and feigned amazement, was more adept at talking trash. All these guests had known Cleo for far longer than I had, and yet, when they were at the house, they regarded me with a subtle reverence, as if I had always lived there. As if Howie had generously moved aside for my sake. Sometimes, when we were a bottle or two deep, sitting around the woodstove in Cleo's living room, Cleo would excuse herself to refresh her drink, then come back into the room and settle in beside me on the floor a few inches closer than how she had left me. Even though we spent nearly every waking hour together, this gesture always felt as new and alive as holding a wild bird in your hands. The idea that Cleo had chosen me—again!—when she could have had anyone in the world drove me crazy with pride and the fear that someday she might choose to sidle up to someone else.

There were questions that I might have asked myself, had I not been so busy and so terrified of accidentally spoiling the alchemy of our friendship. Most of them were some version of *why.* Why was a forty-year-old woman, who had her shit together, choosing to spend her time with someone like me? It was not difficult to see what made us good coworkers. There were also the unforeseen circumstances that had nudged us closer, and we could not be blamed for those. But there was an element that lay just out of reach, a border that evaded scrutiny, like a receding wave. Tristan had had the advantage of having sex with her while she was married, which threw him into an undeniable category. He was the affair. You could wear all sorts of hats under the title of "Affair Partner." I felt somehow that I did not have the same privilege, and it was not simply because I was a girl. It might have been because, on paper, I was a straight girl, and so was Cleo, and two straight women deciding to have an affair seemed more like potent witchcraft than love or lust. It would seem, especially in those days, like an inside joke ridden to the edge of mania. Like obsession. Like addiction.

If it was an addiction, it was an ambidextrous one. One side pining for Cleo, staring at her nude portrait like it was a mind-bending riddle, while the other side couldn't get enough of *not* having her. Living on the cusp of getting what I wanted preserved me in a way that made me feel invincible.

"Hey, Dairy Boy," I said when the weekly produce delivery rolled in. He perked up, looked around as if to make sure that it was just me calling him over. I stood behind the counter, at the coffee grinder, and beckoned him to lean in so he could hear me over the roar.

"I have a tough guy job for you."

I did, in fact, need help back at Howie's barn. Part of the fence had been pulled down when a herd of deer ripped through it in the night. Also, Thunder had kicked a hole in his stall because I had not adhered to Howie's manual, and, in a rush one morning, fed the horses in order of convenience instead of herd hierarchy. Thunder lost his mind when he saw Frida receive her anti-inflammatory-laced breakfast before him. Afterward, I, with a newfound respect for the manual, tried something that I had read in a section of the binder called "Tips and Tricks." LET THE HORSES KNOW YOUR SCENT BY BLOWING INTO THEIR NOSTRIL. YOU'LL GET AN ANSWER RIGHT AWAY. I was all about sharing scents, so I tried it with Thunder. I placed my hands on either side of his big head and, standing a little to the side, blew a puff of air into his nose. He made a short, internal creaking sound, and then immediately puffed the air back at me. It was warm and humid, and it smelled like blackstrap molasses and oatmeal stout, like the whiff of someone's woodstove on a snowy day. I blew again and got my huff again, as if Thunder and I were two sides of the same giant lung. This time, he seemed to soften into my hands. Thunder was a tall, leggy horse with a long mane that looked like someone had worked on it with a crimping iron. Inside the barn, his mane appeared to be a dark slate gray, but when he was running in the fields, the strands would ignite in the sunlight, showing their hidden red hues. I knew, without needing to be told, that this was where he got his name, the rust in his mane bleeding through like a storm. A storm's indication. The distant suggestion of a storm, folded away in the clouds.

"Did you kill Howie?" I whispered to him, still holding his face like he was a big dog. Suddenly, I needed Thunder to be the killer, for reasons that I could not explain. All I knew was that Thunder would not have acted out of malice, or fear, or even stupidity. There was something wild in him—and I know how this sounds, I really do. Remember, though, that I was not and never had been a girlie taken in by these tropes. I was not Elizabeth Taylor in *National Velvet*, swooning over The Pie. Still, I can't deny what I felt then, that deep respect for the instrument of Thunder's body, this thing that was all intentional motion, that could not be stopped, even when there was someone standing in the way.

I gave the delivery guy Cleo's address and told him to come by after five. I told him to dress warmly. I gave him no indication that there was payment or reward in his doing me this favor. Obviously, I should have had a plan to pay him, but his eagerness to be helpful, and to be allowed direct access to our world, seemed at the time like an indication that I was the one being overly generous. I was not ignorant to the setup that I was creating—me, luring this strong boy in his mid-twenties into the sticks of Vermont to fix my fence—but I consoled myself that I was not being calculating. I *did* need someone to fix the fence and the hole in Thunder's stall and, now that I thought of it, there was an old steamer trunk that I wanted to move so I could tuck the Vespa into a dry corner of the barn. He said that he knew the road and would be there after his shift the next day. His body language seemed to let me know that he was taking the request at face value. For now, at least.

"I invited the produce guy to the house," I told Cleo. "He is going to do some . . . maintenance."

She gave me the sly eyebrow.

"Am I going to have to cook him supper?"

I wanted to say, *Only if I don't scare him away first*, but there was the requirement for suggestive banter to be upheld at all times, so I said: "Only if he is a good boy."

We were interrupted by a young man with a septum piercing who approached the counter holding a camcorder. Cleo spun around to face him, her teeth set in an expression that looked a little vicious, but one that I recognized to be her serious scheming face. She and the septum boy started whispering over by the biscotti jars, while I was left to tend to Buttload Guy, who happened to be next in line. It was fine. I knew that Cleo had cast the net of her secession plan even wider. There was talk about making a fake documentary, possibly screening it covertly at the small theater on the college campus, which Septum Boy—a film student—had the keys to. The other day, on the way to work, Cleo and I were passed by a Jetta with a bumper sticker on the back windshield: a green square with a circle of blue stars.

"Is that what I think it is?" I asked Cleo. She reached over and squeezed my knee.

"That's just the free will of The People," she said.

Buttload Guy wanted to know what was in the Buzz Brownies. They were new. Cleo and I had just introduced them after about a week of perfecting the recipe. I shifted my eyes to convey secrecy.

"Half have weed in them, and the rest are chock-full of espresso beans."

Buttload Guy leaned in, eyes wide.

"For real?"

"It's brownie roulette," I said, holding his gaze. "Which kind of buzz will you get? Only one way to find out."

"That can't be legal," he said, scandalized, but no less intrigued. Who was this man? Someone's dad? Could it be that my Buttload Guy was someone else's Papa? Some woman's Bill or David? There was, of course, no weed in the Buzz Brownies. Just loads of caffeine. Cleo and I had made our first batch so strong that neither of us could fall asleep after sampling them. We had stayed up late watching romantic comedies, debating whether Hugh Grant's expression was a guilty fart face or a bad touch face. We were delirious, and I cannot remember what either of these things meant or what side I was on. I wanted Buttload Guy to say something annoying, so I could go about my business without worrying that this conversation was the only positive interaction he would have all day. Maybe he just needed someone to share useless knowledge with because there was no one else. I was falling into a slump. I needed another coffee.

"Well, you know," he said, wagging the brownie at me in emphasis. "You can't really bake espresso into a pastry. Espresso is just a brewing method. So, when you say *espresso bean*, you really mean *coffee bean*."

There it was. How dare he school me about my beans?

"Are you going to buy the thing, or just manhandle it?" I asked.

"Sure, what the heck." He tossed the brownie gamely onto the counter and pulled out his wallet. In my periphery, I caught Cleo handing something to the film student in a waxed sandwich bag.

THE PRODUCE GUY pulled into Cleo's driveway the next evening in the actual delivery truck. On the side of it, an anthropomorphic cucumber held hands with an anthropomorphic strawberry, as if swing dancing. I did not appreciate how the bottom tip of the cucumber formed a fat and ungainly crotch at half-mast. It seemed too middle school, too much like a gag.

"You drove the company truck?" I said, walking out to meet him. He had his hands stuffed into his pockets and his shoulders up by his ears. At six o'clock, it was dark already, and very cold. I worried briefly that he hadn't worn a coat because he thought that the barn work was a front for a threesome. It wasn't. And if it were, it would be far more endearing for him to feign ignorance, right up to the point where Cleo and I plied him with wine and took turns pulling off his boots.

"It's my uncle's business," he said, shivering. I gave him Howie's coat, which was too loose on his short, compact frame. He was not unlike Tristan in stature, but his face was different. Where Tristan was soulful and hopeless in a romantic way, this boy was scruffy and straight up guileless. I didn't know if I wanted to spank him or pinch his cheek.

"This is a converted cow farm," he said, taking in the barn's interior.

"Is that bad?" I asked.

He shrugged and stuffed his hands back into the pockets of Howie's coat. I showed him the hole in the wall and told him that one of the horses was a murderer, only no one knew which one because Howie had been alone at the time of the accident. He crouched to examine the damage, unconcerned, it seemed, by what I had just said. Maybe he came from a line of farmers who were used to that kind of thing.

The fence was the more pressing issue, so I followed him outside with the flashlight, while he searched for the broken ends of the electric fence wire and spliced them together. It was miserable work. I regretted the whole plan, and just wanted to be inside, warming my hands by the woodstove. When the delivery boy was finished, we went back into the barn, where it was a few degrees warmer, and stood stomping the blood back into our toes without speaking. Finally, I told him that I needed to feed the horses before I could go inside. I didn't say before *we* could go inside, because I did not know if I had the energy to watch him salivate over Cleo while she served him rosemary potatoes and arugula salad. The cold had knocked all the mischief out of me.

"Can I keep you company?" he asked. This surprised me, but I wasn't going to tell him no, so I let him follow me to the feed room, where I showed him Howie's manual. I pointed to a bullet in "Tips and Tricks" that said IF YOU FIND YOURSELF NEEDING TO ASSERT DOMINANCE OVER THE HERD, WAVE YOUR HANDS AND SHOUT "WICHITA!" IT IS IMPOSSIBLE TO SHOUT "WICHITA" AND NOT SOUND LIKE YOU MEAN IT.

"Crazy, right?" I asked.

But the delivery boy didn't answer. Instead, he said, "Do you think she loved him?" He looked soberly at the page.

"Yeah. I think she must have," I said. The conversation suddenly felt too familiar, like I was back at Grandview Stable listening to Tristan muse about Cleo. In a way, it was comforting but also exhausting, like spending time with a friend who only wants to talk about *Star Wars* or the lore behind a specific *X-Files* episode. He was standing very close to me, and I realized that I did not know his name. It's not like I was calling him "Delivery Boy" in my head whenever I looked at him. It was just him, with his broad, hopeful face.

"Can I call you Delivery Boy?" I asked, turning to face him. I didn't know yet if I was flirting or just looking for a flirty introduction, since we had both come this far without calling each other anything.

"Okay?" he said. His breath came out in a cloud, and I could smell the long day on it.

"You like her, don't you?" I moved closer, which put us at a proximity that could not be interpreted as anything other than me making a move. I knew that there was an opportunity here, but my body was still wary. It was so cold, and we both had so many layers on. What would I do? Give him a hand job inside the sleeve of my coat?

Yes, actually. That is exactly what happened.

He answered my question with a breathy "Yeah," and I said, "I like her too."

And he said, "Do you also like—men?"

And I said, "I like men who like her."

It was almost pathetic how true this had become. I kissed him and quickly undid his pants because I did not want there to be any awkward decision-making. I did not want to interpret anything or hear any other words spoken. His dick was stocky and the perfect weight. I didn't examine it. I just started tugging and thankfully he liked that approach. He shifted his footing and sighed generously in my ear. How had I managed it? Delivery Boy was now a stand-in for Tristan, who I had wanted only because I, myself, was a stand-in. Meanwhile, all three of us wanted Cleo but were just making the best of what we had. I wondered if I would ever be turned on by normal circumstances again. Maybe I was ruining myself and all my future relationships. These words played out in my mind just as the delivery boy pressed his darling face into my neck, and the inside of my sleeve became warm and wet. Fuck it, I thought. Let me like what I like.

He was more interested in the manual after that and flipped through it while I crushed the horses' supplements with the handle of a knife. I mixed the pill dust with oats and molasses and scraped the sticky mixture into the horses' feed buckets. As we were walking toward the house, the delivery boy said, "Do you think there might be a clue in that book?" I stopped with my hand on the doorknob. He continued.

"Like, in those murder mysteries? Where the victim writes the name of their killer on the wall in blood?"

"Don't you think if Howie had been able to walk back into the barn and scrawl an encrypted note, he would have called for help instead?" I kept my voice low.

"Right, right," said the delivery boy, a little chastened. We went inside and Cleo was there in her apron, which she called her "wifey apron," setting bowls on the table. She met us with a friendly, straightforward face, as if she had never entertained a sly or filthy thought in her life.

"Ah!" she said. "Our handyman!" The delivery boy gave a short, embarrassed laugh. He did not know what to do with his hands, and I felt immensely protective of him. Was that all it took to hook me? A warm penis going off in my palm? I went to the sink to wash up while I was thinking of it.

"I'm George," I heard the delivery boy say to Cleo. George! I thought. He's been George all this time.

We sat around the table and ate a penne dish in a spicy cream sauce. It warmed my insides and made me drink more wine than I normally would have, to blanket the heat in my mouth. Soon, I was drunk, and I could see Cleo slipping into a mood. Sometimes, she would become smug, rosy cheeked, and withholding. She listened to George as he told her about how he had had problems in school, which led him to drop out, but then his uncle—the one who owned the farm where the big squashes and lovely striped eggplants came from—helped him turn his life around.

"You don't strike me as a bad boy, George," Cleo said, without a hint of irony. Still, George blushed. I could tell by the way his lips receded when he sipped his wine that he was not a wine drinker, but he was doing his best to appear at ease. So many questions slopped around my mind that evening, such as: Did George remind Cleo of Tristan? Would that be upsetting for her, or comforting, like it had been comforting for me? Did Cleo know what we had done in the feed room, and if so, did she disapprove? Had I missed the point of all the sexual banter? Was the point to *not* follow through with cute hand jobs, but to always taunt and allude and threaten to kiss each other? Aside from the action that my coat sleeve had received, everything that evening seemed upright and normal—polite, even. Why did that make me so uneasy? Where were the schemes? The innuendos?

There was cheesecake for dessert. Cleo explained that it was made by the nuns up the road. They were very successful nuns, who had been on *Oprah*, and we should all learn from their business model. George ate his slice quickly and then said that he had to get the truck home and go to bed. His delivery route began very early in the morning. I eyed Cleo to see if she was going to try to convince him to stay. He was not drunk. Not like I was. She collected his dishes and thanked him for fixing the fence and patching the hole.

"We only got to the fence," I said. "It was cold and—"

"Well, that gives you an excuse to come back," she said with snipped cheeriness. It was possible that Cleo's attitude was not to be taken personally, that it was just the implication of the hole, having been made by a horse hoof, was a sore subject. I might have made a blunder by dressing George in Howie's coat. Yes, I reasoned, that must be it. It had only been a month since her husband's death. Of course Cleo would be moody and sensitive.

I walked with George to the driveway.

"I really appreciate you coming out," I said, too formally. I wondered if I should kiss him goodbye, but there was a strange lag between us, and I only patted his shoulder, limply. Hand jobs were not a good place to start when getting to know someone, I decided. The hand job rulebook was questionable at best. You could give a hand job to a stranger in a club bathroom. They were often distributed as a kind of pity offering. It was like lending someone your toothbrush and telling them to keep it.

"Oh, sure," he said. I watched him climb into the truck and wanted to tell him that I liked him, and I was sorry for taunting him about his large vegetables, but that I would probably do it again because I had no self-control. But I just waved awkwardly and jogged back into the house.

5

HE SHOWED UP at the café one afternoon wearing black jeans and an aviator jacket. When he got to the counter, he let one of his shoulders hang lower than the other—not a sloucher's slouch but a well-educated peruser's slouch—and ordered a breve. I immediately disliked the way he looked at me—and, besides, I mistrusted anyone who drank breves. There is something grimy about steamed half-and-half; it does not foam well and floats like the product of someone's cough on top of the espresso shot. His gaze wasn't just predatory. It was as if he were a tiger and I were a scrawny lamb, too easy a catch to bother with. I labeled him the Smarmy Man in my mind, and watched him take a stool by the window, where he stirred his breve with the air of someone who is consciously not in a rush while the rest of the world hurries around foolishly. To his credit, it was the week before Christmas, which was the most foolish time of year. Emotions were heightened, and The People were fussier than ever. If I gave someone the wrong-sized latte, I became the scapegoat for why the world was out to get them.

"This is why corporations are taking over," one woman hissed when I forgot the whipped cream on her hot chocolate. Everyone's blood sugar was low. Everyone wanted a sandwich. The Eggy Pie Lady, who I hadn't seen for weeks, wandered in out of nowhere, stared at the menu for a long time, and then turned around and left. How was it that she was living a life without the one thing she wanted? Was there no one that would give her a quiche?

That day, Cleo was trying to fulfill a last-minute cookie order and was confined to the kitchen. I barely saw her, except for the moments I ran back there with a bottle of seltzer and a straw, urging her to stay hydrated. Cleo waved the seltzer away.

"I don't have time to be peeing every five minutes, Buggy," she said. She was rolling out a mound of stiff cookie dough and paused to brush her hair out of her face with the back of her wrist. I reached over and coiled the runaway strand around my finger, tucking it back into her hair scarf. The health inspector was getting on our case about not wearing hats, but Cleo said she would rather shave her head than look like a Wendy's employee (even though I argued that we would look striking in matching uniforms). She closed her eyes and smiled a tired, little smile.

"There's a smarmy man out there," I said. "He's really terrible."

"Smarmy, you say?" She opened her eyes again. "That's a good word."

"I have a feeling this man is going to give it a revival."

When I went out front again, he was at the counter with his empty cup, the little spoon balanced over the top, crusted in dried froth. I hated the sight of it.

"Another, please," he said in a strange monotone. I could not tell if he had an accent. It was as if his words were American, but his cadence could not shake a mysterious asymmetry. I lifted his used cup, leaving the spoon and saucer on the counter.

"You're going to use the dirty cup." It was half accusation, half question. Again, he spoke in that obnoxious monotone, as if I was not worth the effort of inflection. I looked at him. He was tall and jaggedly handsome, with black hair flecked gray at the temples. His face had the chronic shadow of a man who needs to shave often. His eyelashes were thick and beautiful in a way that was clearly unfair to every woman in the world who wanted full eyelashes. I dropped the cup into the sink, almost breaking it, and reached for another. I made sure to show him that I was not smiling, and not because I was uptight, but because I found him boring. When I slid the fresh breve toward him, on a new saucer with a clean spoon, he took the old, crusted spoon and stuck it into the steamed half-and-half, as if measuring the thickness of the foam. I wished Cleo were out front with me. She would find a fitting way to torment him. She could always match an ego.

Business picked up again as the downtown shoppers staggered in for one more coffee to get them home or sat alone with a cocoa, surrounded by gift bags, warming their hands and looking traumatized. I was thankful not to have a list of people to shop for. I didn't even have a list of people to impress. When the café cleared out once again, I saw that the Smarmy Man was gone, his second empty cup left on the edge of the counter. I must not have seen him. Good, I thought.

On Christmas Day, I drove Cleo's truck into town to visit my mother. Cleo had insisted that I borrow it, saying that all she wanted to do on her day off was sit in one spot and read a book.

"Take your time," she said. "And take this." She handed me a tin of cookies.

"I thought these were for an order," I said, embarrassed that I had not thought of bringing anything like a gift. I did not know what my mother had or did not have in her house these days, or what she liked. At one time, she had been very fond of almond extract, coffee-flavored ice cream, and black licorice. I thanked Cleo and told her I would be back before dark. I did not want to leave her alone all day, although I could not tell if this was for her own sake or if the thought of not seeing her for any significant length of time made me feel anxious. At this point, I had known her as a widow for as long as I had known her as a married woman. It all felt very tender and cracked open. I thought about how I had used the word *resurrection* that day at Grandview Stables to describe Cleo's emergence, as if she were back on the scene, no longer theoretical. In a way, this was how it still felt to me. I was still worried that Cleo would somehow become formless and inaccessible again.

The pickup felt eerily spacious from my place in the driver's seat. Lucinda was still in the tape deck, this time wondering if she would ever get over a sexy man with crooked teeth. The guitar reverberated too painfully, like a dilated pupil. Like heartbreak when it's still wet with hope. I turned it off. It was snowing lightly. The truck bounced over frozen tire ruts in the dirt. I appreciated how the sun sharpened the dry thistles along the road, how the cold seemed to turn the land to resin. I need this stillness, I thought, and I tried to quiet my mind, as if preparing to cross a border. It had been months since I had spoken to my mother for more than five minutes. Our phone calls had become strained, mainly because my life was getting more difficult to explain—not necessarily the places where I had been or the people who I had met, but my motivations behind all of it. When you reach your twenties, there is a pressure to contextualize your actions so that they can be understood within a larger plan. I was certainly not doing *nothing*, but what could I say it was for? I might say: *With much effort, I've become a part of Cleo's inner circle. By day, we encourage casual conspiracy theories and drink too much coffee. By night, we encourage casual conspiracy theories and drink too much wine.* It sounded like a cult.

I decided to park on the street instead of the driveway, reasoning that my mother might be thrown off by the truck: It might be too visceral. It might vibrate the windowpanes and blow hot exhaust. Even after so many years, I was still prepared to make strange and unanticipated accommodations. She answered the door, distracted and happy, backing away as I entered and quickly carrying the tin of cookies into the kitchen as if they were in danger of melting.

"It's Christmas again," she said, coming back into the living room. I knew what she meant. It wasn't that time was passing quickly, but that today was a day that we could not get away with treating arbitrarily. We were in its snare, together again. The inside of the house was tidy and sparsely furnished. There was a lamp with a base like a crystal water glass that gave the whole room a dignified luster without any extra flourishes. The couch was tastefully firm but not antique. The whole interior gave off a sense of prohibition, as if the introduction of any unvetted object might tip it into a binge or an all-night bender. The shine on the hardwood floor was a held breath.

I sat on the edge of the couch and clasped my hands together. My mother took the armchair across from me. I would have never dreamed of any such piece of furniture occupying this house, but here it was, with right angles and tapered legs, upholstered in blue-and-gray paisley. Behind it, the lace curtains hung straight down.

"It looks really nice in here," I said. My mother gave an obligatory head turn, as if she was too modest to have noticed.

"Oh," she said. "The lamp is new. Well, not new, but new to here. New to me." She looked young and almost stylish, like an actress playing a plain role without makeup. Her hair was cut bluntly at the chin and she was wearing one of those cocoon sweaters. She must have only been in her mid-forties then. I wish I could have seen her as fresh as she really was, but to me she was the *Mona Lisa*: undisputable, with a thin rind. I was afraid I might break her.

"So, how have you been?" I said.

"I'm working an administrative job at the college," she said. "I can't remember if I told you that."

She had told me, but I said, "That's wonderful. And the library?"

"Still on the weekends."

I said that I was living on a farm, working mornings at a new coffee place in town. Had she seen it? No. My mother could hold down a job—had always been able to work, surprisingly—but she was avoidant of almost all other signals of sociability, even something as simple as grabbing a coffee.

"You could move back in, if that would be more convenient," she said, then added: "More convenient than a farm, that is." She probably assumed that no one would live on a farm if it weren't a last resort.

Once, when I was in the fourth grade, there was a kindergartener who developed a crush on me. A little boy named Daniel, who would run up to me in the hallways, throw his arms around my legs, and ask me to marry him. It was embarrassing for me on many levels, but mainly because there was no right way to react, except for overdone laughter that was not meant to be cruel but felt cruel all the same. Daniel was not deterred. I remember how sincere he was in his declarations of love, and yet, even then, I knew that he was expressing himself imperfectly, drawing from the little understanding that he had of the world. Trying to dress his big emotion in what he thought was correct.

I sensed a similar sincerity in my mother whenever she asked me to come home. Despite her flaws, she was a mother and she had motherly instincts. She knew that it was part of the backbone of motherhood to offer your children food and shelter whenever possible. I looked around the living room again, trying to place myself in the same spot five years ago. Ten years ago. Fifteen. None of the same feelings remained. The aura of the place was scrubbed and air-dried.

My parents bought the bungalow house in the mid-eighties, but divorced when I was six. If it was traumatic for me, I don't remember. My dad moved back to Tennessee, where he had lived as a college student, but his mother—my grandmother—stuck around and remained a rigid, but at least stable presence in my life. She came in with her spray bottles and her silent outrage whenever my mother went away, and I would spend the next week or two under her care, viciously defending all the dust and grime as if it were an art project that she was trying to throw away.

"It wasn't like this when your father was here," she once snapped at me when I tried to fight her over a ball of hardened Play-Doh. And she was right. It was only after the divorce that my mother's world began to fall apart. I'm almost certain it wasn't heartbreak that caused it, but rather the stark realization that she was in this life alone and no one was watching her, except for me, the one person she wasn't supposed to fuck up. It was too much pressure. One night, the smoke detector malfunctioned because it had gotten dusty, and my mother could not reach it to take out the batteries. It shrieked and shrieked, and she had no ladder and no one to call at that hour, so she panicked, and then just as quickly gave up. She zipped me into a sleeping bag and wrapped a pillow around my ears, and we slept on the basement floor, lightly rocking each other. She had tremendous endurance when it came to loving me, but none whatsoever for managing regular life. She seemed to suffer from a kind of practical amnesia, which became more and more difficult to hide. The halfway house provided her a break because she was not a crazy person who needed to be institutionalized, but a strange gray area of a person, who seemed outwardly functional only up to the point where it was evident that she had not been functional for quite some time. While she was at the halfway house, my grandmother—her ex-mother-in-law—threw away all the junk in our house and paid the overdue bills. My mother came back to a clean kitchen and a daughter with a new haircut, and for a while, everything seemed to run smoothly again.

Before I left, I told my mother about Tristan galloping after the runaway Haflinger, because it was a good story and I wanted us both to feel like we'd had a proper conversation. I know it sounds sad, but it did not feel that way. It felt more like an important and highly delicate job that we were tasked with. Her duty was to be on the verge of an epic apology—for the things she had done wrong when I was a child—and my duty was to divert her at all costs. She offered her home to me, and I kindly refused. We then both gave each other enough information about our lives so that we would know which questions to ask next time. With these moves in place, we were stabilized for another six months. It was this way because we loved each other.

CLEO HAD THE records out when I got back. They were scattered on the living room floor, some with the inserts removed. Behind her on the couch, I spotted what looked like a photo album. She gave me a glassy look.

"Oh, no," I said. "I know what this is." She was obviously on the precipice of a Howie spiral.

"Hi, Buggy," she said. She was seated on the floor in front of the woodstove. "How was your mama's house?"

I got down on her level. The stove's heat felt nice, but it warmed only the surfaces of my body that were facing it. I felt one cheek start to roast, along with the plane of my shin and my forearm. Cleo's face was pink. I reached for one of the records.

"*Harvest Moon*?" I gasped, dropping it back on the floor. "By yourself? With sharp objects in reach?"

She dropped her head into her hands and groaned.

"I think I got it out of my system."

"Thank God I was only gone for a few hours."

We sat silently, only adjusting our positions when we became too cooked on one side. The sun was getting low, and it shone briefly through the window onto a glass doorknob across the room. The cut of the glass scattered the light into a golden mesh that traveled slowly along the wall. It seemed too fantastic to be happening so quietly in the background like that. Sometimes my intentions felt like an exquisite golden mesh, only I had no projector for them. I could not unravel the feeling in my heart and turn it into words. I always thought that my inability to say the right thing to comfort people was unique to me, and never once suspected that the problem lay within grief itself. Grief was a black hole. It was as if Cleo could read my mind.

"You think I am grief-stricken," she said.

"I mean . . ." I gestured to Neil Young and Paul Simon.

She leaned back on her elbows and seemed to take in the mess around her. I could sense that she wanted to say something but possibly did not know whether to commit to saying it. Cleo's usual spot for confessions was the kitchen, where she could talk openly while chopping vegetables or kneading dough. She was a talented articulator—which was not something I would have ever thought to label someone until I met her. Sentences were punctuated by a swift blade stroke, anecdotes gained momentum with the speed of a wooden spoon.

"I'm not the kind of person that's surprised by death," she began. "Remember, both my parents are dead, my older brother died of meningitis at eighteen. As far as I know, death is the only thing I can count on anyone to do."

"I agree," I said, even though I did not know anyone who had died, except for Howie and a girl at my school who committed suicide. But she had already transferred to a school for troubled teens when it happened, and that, I am ashamed to say, made her death seem too far removed and foreshadowed to be shocking.

"Let's go to the kitchen," Cleo said. I followed her, tickled with affection for her predictabilities: She could not discuss certain things without her utensils in hand. I pulled up a chair and Cleo began chopping an onion at the table, which was a task that always sent tears streaming down her face. An involuntary reaction that still managed to seem like beautiful theater.

"Do you mind if it's just omelets tonight?" she asked me, wiping her cheek with the back of her wrist. I wanted to tell her that, yes, of course omelets were fine. I had no right to complain about anything that she prepared. I was spoiled. I would eat her boiled shoe if she served it to me.

Instead, I said: "Can we call them eggy pocketbooks?"

Cleo shuddered. She pushed the chopped onions to the side with the blade of her knife and started to towel off some mushrooms.

"Howie was a prude," she said. I shook my head subtly, trying to convey sympathy. "He was incapable of talking about sex, so when he wanted it, he would send desperate little signals, hoping I would catch on." She moved on to chopping the mushrooms. "I got so sick of it that I started to pretend I didn't understand. I'd say, 'Howie, you're all red, did you forget your blood pressure pills today?' He'd get even redder and more flustered, trying to touch me—casually, you know? Always so casual, like a guilty person." She brought her hands up in clawed irritation as if Howie were there with us, pawing at her.

I wondered if this was leading to a confession about the affair, and was suddenly fearful that my reaction—or suspicious lack thereof—would give me away. At the same time, the prospect of hearing about Tristan from Cleo's perspective was so juicy that I had to stop myself from smiling in anticipation. Would their stories snap satisfyingly into place, or would there be inconsistencies? If Cleo's version of Tristan was unattractive, whose side would I be on? Cleo began to sauté the mushrooms and onions.

"I must have thought that if I played dumb for long enough, he'd break into a blind rage, take me right there, over the kitchen table," she said. "But whatever was building up in there—whatever wild energy I thought I could coax out of him—died when he did." She cracked an egg into the mixing bowl with this statement, and I realized that she was not going to talk about Tristan or anything so predictable. I felt that it was my turn to offer something to the conversation, but I was utterly lost. I did not know where she was going with this, or what kind of signals of solidarity she was hoping to get. I did not even have a stupid joke to throw in.

"For years, I have been fattening Howie like a goose that I was never going to eat," she said. I felt sad in a desolate way. I can see now that it was not the specifics of her story that mattered, but the concept: You could love a person and still be disappointed by them. And the death of hope was sometimes the realization that the hope itself was ill-conceived.

I placed my hand on her arm and said, in my purposefully insensitive way, "I think I understood, like, two words of that."

It was the right thing. Cleo did not want sympathy from me; it would have been too distorted, like a reflection in a fun-house mirror, or a child's drawing of your own sadness. She pivoted and put her arms around me. From my place on the chair, my head was aligned for a moment with her chest, my ear between her collarbone and her throat. Her heart was so fast and insistent that it felt like an accident to have heard it. She smelled like garlic and lemons, with undertones of something that might have been incense or patchouli, which were two things that I had never come across in the house. I wanted to burrow into her to get to the bottom of it. I imagined what Tristan might do in this same situation: folding Cleo into his arms while she was weepy and vulnerable, placing his lips on the part in her hair. Becoming just aroused enough to show that he was invested. But I could not do the same. I had too much to lose.

We ate our omelets and Cleo turned the talk back to the latest schemes. The septum-pierced film student had gained some traction with the fake documentary, having convinced his advisor that there was real investigating to be done concerning an underground movement called Project Ethan Allen, or PEA. I had learned that there was no use asking Cleo about her objectives in any of this. She lived in the moment. If she was destined for world domination, it would be the product of many isolated moments of chaos. She would avoid the role of mastermind at all costs until it looped around and chose her.

Buster's was a mess the day after Christmas. It was as if the break in routine had caused The People to lose all sense of themselves. They required so much coffee. They had been pulverized by family gatherings and needed to take out their aggression on a barista somewhere, and that barista was me. I hurled it back, and there was catharsis on both sides, I think. Amos was morose. He walked in with his beard chopped short, wearing what appeared to be a homemade sweater. It was not a good look for him. Whoever had knitted the sweater had seemingly overcompensated—possibly in a panic—for his size and added a candy cane of thick stripes toward the bottom.

"What happened to you?" I asked.

He looked down at himself.

"I have seasonal affective disorder," he said.

I asked him if he was too depressed for tea. He said no.

"How was your Christmas?" he asked when I slid the pot across the counter.

"Cleo hugged me last night and I could have touched her boobs, but I chickened out," I said. I had not planned on saying this, of course, but Amos was even more comforting in his sad sweater.

He hummed thoughtfully.

"I keep wondering what would have happened if I wasn't a coward," I added, shocked again at my own words.

"I could watch the register if you want to give it another go?" He nodded toward the kitchen. Cleo had been out back all morning. She had a theory that if she doubled the butter in the croissant recipe and labeled them "more butter croissants," then The People would not be able to resist. She would wait a month, then make another batch called "even more butter croissants," and keep going until we were serving straight butter molded into a crescent moon. Low-fat and low-carb diets were at war back then, making both sides quick to judge what others put into their mouths. Cleo said that it was overly puritan. She wanted to feed the masses grease and sugar until they were round and glistening.

I shook my head, maybe too solemnly.

"The moment is gone," I sighed. "I'll have to wait until next Christmas."

Amos nodded, taking on my secret with generous calm. Someone walked out of the kitchen then, and Amos and I both turned our heads, expecting to see Cleo. It was the Smarmy Man, hands high in his jacket, a smug, devilish look on his face.

"The restroom is that way," I said to him, pointing rigidly. How did he get back there without anyone noticing? He smirked at me, cocking his head toward the table by the window where he had been seated the other day.

"I'll take my breve whenever you get a chance," he said.

"Excuse me?" I looked at Amos to confirm that he had also witnessed this act of brazen entitlement. He did a silent whistle and took his teapot to the opposite side of the room.

I marched into the kitchen where Cleo was slicing a stick of frozen butter.

"The Smarmy Man—" I started to say but stopped. Cleo turned toward me, and I saw that her face was rosy. One of her necklaces was slung backward.

"Drew-Baby," she said, too brightly. I heard it not as my name, but as a verbal rebound. I didn't like it.

"What is happening?" I hissed. She reached out an arm, beckoning me to step into a side hug. I submitted. It was hot in the kitchen, the air practically wavy with melted butter from the batch of croissants already in the oven. I could smell Cleo's powdery deodorant and see the texture of sweat along her hairline.

"Are you okay?" I asked her, even though my mind was piecing everything together with the fluency of a suspicious spouse. Of course, Cleo was now a widow and had no one to be unfaithful to in that sense. But in another world—the world where she and I were bound together against the Smarmies, and the Bitches, and the Mansplainers—Cleo had broken my trust. I could feel it, even though I still did not know the details of what had happened. All I knew was that a man, who was possibly the worst man ever, had strutted out of the kitchen and here was Cleo, looking like a high-school girl who'd just done something filthy in a movie theater. And even as my mind threw the evidence together, it settled on a survival plan: I would support Cleo in any decision she made because I was familiar with the long-term loyalty game. I had a high level of tolerance for other people's mistakes.

"What about this Smarmy Man, Bug?" Cleo was nuzzling me. She had become a purring kitten.

"I feel like I should be asking *you* about him," I said.

"Oh no," she said, pushing herself away from me, her face filling with wicked epiphany. "My Jean-Remy is your Smarmy Man!"

I could not believe what I was hearing.

"*That's* his name?"

THEY HAD MET in a chat room, which was information that I could not process right away. I wondered, how had Cleo made the time to meet men in chat rooms when she was busy grieving her husband, running a business, and, most importantly, being my friend? The answer was that she had been talking to him for the last two years, only, because he lived in Quebec, they had not had an opportunity to meet in person until now. He was driving down to Boston for a conference and had stopped in Vermont to surprise Cleo at work. At the time, I was most concerned with the conference aspect of the story—what kind of conference was it, exactly?—and also fixated on the possibility that Cleo might have been juggling more than just the affair with Tristan. Did Tristan know? In all this speculating, I missed a puzzling detail. I had seen Jean-Remy the week before Christmas when I had made him that first breve. He had been there for hours, sitting smugly by the window without announcing himself. Why hadn't he chosen that day to make his surprise entrance?

"So is he going to be your boyfriend now?" I asked Cleo.

"Boyfriend?" she laughed. "My husband just died!" She gave me a light shove, as if to remind me of the etiquette of the situation. But I was never schooled in such etiquette. Which parts of this weren't I supposed to label? Which parts weren't I to voice? Were there things that I was altogether expected to ignore?

I had reluctantly prepared the breve for Jean-Remy. As a peace offering, I had even attempted to foam the half-and-half, but it coughed around the steamer wand, then died, swimming flatly on top of the espresso. When I brought it to his table, he thanked me and looked at me with a slightly censuring expression.

"You're Drew," he said, extending his hand. I took it because my sense of self-interest has always been higher than my standards. Also, I was pleased that he knew my name, because it meant that Cleo had talked about me.

"That's me," I said. "Who are you?" I certainly wasn't going to admit that Cleo had talked about *him*.

He took his hand from mine and placed it on his heart.

"Jean-Remy," he said. "Very pleased to meet you." Now that I was hearing him again, he did sound Canadian, and I suppose that comforted me. It was possible that I had overreacted, misinterpreted his flippant humor for rudeness. Whatever mix of emotions I was feeling, I knew, in that moment, that I did not have the endurance or the tact to make this guy my enemy.

"I'm going to sit here for a while and respond to some emails," he said. "If that's all right." He opened a leather satchel and pulled out a laptop. At the counter, we had a miniature chalkboard with the Wi-Fi password written on it. I nearly floated across the room to place it at his side. He looked at it and sniffed a laugh.

"Keaton123?"

"My vote was for 'Go Fuck Yourself,' but I guess this was more on brand."

Jean-Remy really laughed this time.

"Easy there, Champ," he said. He sipped his drink and gave me the A-OK with his long fingers. I returned to the counter, feeling placated against my will.

IT'S FUNNY HOW easy it is to forget the landscape of old technology. I can remember the exact placement of my grandmother's jewelry dish on her dresser, each gold-dolloped earring and gaudy pink gem. I remember the pattern of marigolds that my first-grade class planted outside the school in the spring of 1993. But I cannot tell you what an early 2000s chat room looked like, or the sounds that it made, or what a person would type into a search bar to find such a thing. What did search bars look like? In my mind, they are lines of Wite-Out, part of a collage of little boxes and blinking text slapped together to resemble a screen. More of an after-school art project than a real memory.

In middle school, some of my friends liked to visit chat rooms to talk dirty to older men. I understood the appeal—it was a space that was practically begging for our presence. If there were no actual underage girls, then there were sure to be men pretending to be underage girls. We felt that we were the target audience, and therefore we were immune to rejection, which was far scarier than the prospect of being kidnapped or stalked or murdered. Tiff, the orgasm face girl whose father was a detective, turned out to be the most avid chat room offender. She bragged to us about all the men she was leading on at once, pitting against each other. The problem that I had with it wasn't the danger or the dishonesty, but that it was like a game of chance, requiring very little skill. Just as I could not revel in the achievement of winning at a coin flip, I could not seem to understand the triumph of seducing a faceless man by flashing just the standard age/sex/location. Honestly, I think for Tiff it was more about the thrill of doing something so obviously unwise right under her father's nose than it was ever about the content of the chats themselves. I wonder what became of her, and whether these elements are still things she craves. Do we ever truly outgrow our first dirty little game?

We did not see Jean-Remy for another week. Buster's clientele fell back into its pre-holiday rhythm, with the exception of the skiers, who, decked in formfitting athletic attire, wanted to camp out with their children for hours. The skiers always started out speaking to me as if I knew about skiing—what was the quickest way to such-and-such peak?—but quickly withdrew when I made it clear to them that I understood nothing of their world.

"But you live in Vermont?" one sleek, bendy mother asked, not meanly, but maybe aggressively confused.

"Vermont is not for Vermonters," I told her. It was an exaggeration, but sometimes it felt like the truth.

IN A VERY Vermont fashion, there was heavy snow that week, followed by a thaw, and then rain. One morning, I trudged outside to find that the nearest paddock had flooded. The water had breached the side entrance of the barn and was spreading steadily toward the stalls. I dragged some hay bales away from the puddle and then just stood there, wondering what to do. Outside, I heard Cleo start her truck.

"I don't think I can come into work today," I told her, standing at the driver's side window. "I need to dig a trench?" It came out as a question because I was sure there was more to it than that. There was mud to deal with, which, if left alone, could lead to sprained ankles. Moisture itself, I assumed, carried a list of hazards. Moldy hay, damaged equipment. I had heard about something called foot rot in horses, which was enough to paralyze me with dread.

Cleo seemed to be studying her rearview mirror. I hoped that she would not allow me to stay behind, that she would call someone to take care of the problem while she and I continued our manic coffee slinging and vegetable ogling. I hoped this for more than one reason. One, because the flooding had opened my eyes to the enormity of my responsibility at Howie's barn; four horses was a big job, and I felt that I was not doing it justice. My second reason was selfish: The arrival of Jean-Remy had made me more insecure than ever about leaving Cleo to her own devices. I worried that she would give some other girl a cute nickname. She might start wearing a hat without consulting me. Make a low-fat brownie. For all I knew, my position as sidekick was on a rotation, and I was in danger of being thrown off the edge, as if Cleo's whims were a crazed carousel.

It was a Sunday, however, which was the day that Buster's was least busy, so Cleo gave me the go-ahead. She placed her warm hand on my cold one through the truck window.

"Thank you, Bug-Bug," she said. "I'd be lost without you."

I watched her back down the driveway, hearing the marshy thudding of music inside the truck become more distant. I had never been alone out there, and now I was alone with a monumental task that I did not know how to begin. Inside the barn, the horses kicked their stalls, demanding oats. I had no other source of guidance, so I went to them, slopping up the center aisle through the growing puddle. As I crushed the pills, mixing the dust with molasses, I eyed Howie's manual and remembered what George had said about there being clues inside. I had not yet read the whole binder front to back. It was overwhelming, in the way that reading the instructions to a serious board game is overwhelming. It was also sad, because I could see how much Howie had cared for each creature, how tenderly he wrote about their quirks and their preferences. For example, Gomer, the gray geezer of the four, liked you to massage his gums after dinner. Howie had left detailed instructions, outlining the proper gum-rubbing technique. USE ONLY AS MUCH PRESSURE AS YOU WOULD MOLDING A STIFF CLAY. I was often too hungry and too tired to commit to anything beyond the essential feeding and cleaning. But who was I to say that gum rubbing wasn't essential? These horses were living their whole lives right here. They weren't waiting for their number to be called for another, more important existence. I thought about Thunder as a lanky and wild foal, learning to run on a windy plain. Now, he was under my care, and he was going to be standing in cold water if I did not figure out what to do. After I distributed the grain mixtures, I grabbed a shovel and went to the side door, where I began to dig along the side of the barn, hoping to divert the water toward the paddock fence. At first, I had some success, as the stream of melt coming off the hill filled the indent that I had made, but this new vein began to soak the flat area of the paddock around the water trough, glistening beneath the hay spread over the dirt. All around, the ground was black and pocked with watery holes, some deep enough to sink a horse up to its knee. I was still a rookie horse girl, but I knew enough to know that I needed help.

I dialed Grandview Stable, and a girl answered.

"Hi," I said to her, and for a moment I did not know how to explain myself. "There was a man who worked there—Tristan? I'm wondering if . . ." It did not make sense to say that I was a friend, because a friend would not need to call an old employer for information.

"Drew?" the girl said.

"Diane?" I am not sure why I was surprised. I had not left the stable that long ago. I suppose I was used to the kind of workplaces that were caught in a constant ebb and flow of fresh hires, where your name was forgotten as soon as it was erased from the payroll.

"Oh my God," Diane said. For some reason, she sounded delighted. "I'll put him on."

I stood in Cleo's kitchen with the phone in my hand, stunned. I could hear murmuring on the line, like when you call for takeout and the ambient noises rush in and out in the background. I could not picture what was happening. I imagined the old stable to be a cavernous, echoey place where I no longer belonged.

"Hello?" Tristan had the phone. I must have expected to never speak to him again, out of shame. After all, Tristan had given me the memory of Cleo to keep safe, and I had exploited it.

"I have a horse problem," I told him. "I'm sorry. I didn't know who else to call."

I explained to him that I had taken a second job as a farmhand but was once again in over my head.

"The paddock is muddy and full of water, and it's just going to get worse when the rest of the snow melts."

"Can you use another paddock for the time being?" His voice was focused and faintly curious. It was clear that he was capable of separating this conversation in his mind from any hurt that I had caused him. I wanted to tell him that he should be a police officer or a first responder. He should be the guy that gets called to an emergency just to walk around putting his hand on people's shoulders to make them feel grounded.

"Yes, but you have to walk through the flooded one to get to the non-flooded one," I said. The non-flooded paddock was a section of rocky hill that I had not yet ventured into because it was where Howie had been discovered. The driver of a passing car had spotted him lying face down in the grass. The driver said that he might not have stopped if Howie had been face up, because he had seen people doing weirder things out in fields. Even though Howie had not died on the spot, it felt somehow too personal to be stomping around up there. What if Cleo saw me through the window? I would feel the same humiliation as if she had caught me in her bedroom, trying on her lipstick in front of the mirror. I had no business being on that ground. It felt like tourism. Tristan was quiet on the line.

"What happens when the ground freezes again and it's all choppy?" I asked. "What if the horses get foot rot?"

"I can come by and have a look later," he said. "Where are you at?"

No, I thought. It was enough that I was spending every day in Cleo's employ. Tristan did not need to know that I was also living with her. And furthermore, it would be a disaster for Cleo to come home and find him there, spreading cat litter just yards away from where her husband was fatally wounded. Did I just need to buy cat litter?

"Oh, I can't ask you to do that," I said. "Maybe I just need to buy some cat litter?"

"Cat litter? No," he said. "You'll probably need a gravel delivery, but I can't know unless I see the spot."

Fuck, I thought. The gears in Cleo's kitchen clock whirred above my head. Outside the window, water dripped so steadily from the gutters it looked like a silver garland.

"You're still there," I said to Tristan.

"I'm here," he said, reassuringly.

"No, I mean, at Grandview. You were supposed to move away."

"Oh, well. How many people do you know who have successfully left Vermont?"

I thought of everyone I knew from high school, how eager they'd all been to go *someplace real.* New York City. Los Angeles. Nico had only made it as far as Boston, but still. Boston had its own accent.

"Everyone left as soon as they could," I said.

"Give them a few more years."

I did not know where this left us in terms of the flooded paddock, and I started to question whether I had really called for advice, or if I just wanted the comfort of hearing Tristan's voice.

"Do you have a boss or someone? To help you?" I could tell that maybe Tristan was starting to wonder the same thing.

"They're on vacation," I said. "I didn't want to bother them." I asked him for a number to call for a gravel delivery. He gave me one. Then he gave me a second number.

"That's me," he said. "In case something else comes up." I thanked him, feeling that queasy gratitude when someone you've wronged is being kind to you.

"Oh," he said, right before we hung up. "It smells like rotten eggs."

"What?"

"Hoof rot," he said. "It looks like a yeast infection. Check your horses and get it treated."

I told him I would.

FIRST, I CALLED Cleo at the café and told her that I had assessed the problem and I was going to have to purchase some gravel. It was such a clean and practical solution, and I felt so knowledgeable, that it was easy to keep Tristan's name out of it.

"Thank you so much, Bug." She heaved the words in a sigh. "Seriously, I would not be able to deal with all of that."

"You can count on me, girlie," I said in a husky voice.

Next, I called the gravel and sand contractor, which was a job that I did not know existed until that day. The man on the phone told me that they'd send a truck around tomorrow and that I didn't even have to be there. All I had to do was tell him where to dump it. I liked the old-school honor system. I loved the phrasing.

Checking the horses' feet was a practice that I should have been doing from the beginning—horses can get stones and caked manure lodged in their shoes—but I had been intimidated. It takes confidence to pick up a horse's foot. You cannot do it by force alone. Tristan had taught me how to ask for a foot in one motion: Slide your hand down the horse's leg while pushing into her side with your shoulder. The idea is to gently upset her center of gravity, he explained.

"That's kind of romantic," I had said. "*Hey baby, you gently upset my center of gravity.*"

It worked on Howie's horses, and I found myself looking into some very dirty but not infected hooves, one after the other. When it was Thunder's turn, I tried to slow my breathing and make my arms loose, to show him how casual all this was meant to be. Still, I was thrilled inside. What if he kicked me in the head and I blacked out? Would Cleo brave the barn to save me? Even more exciting was the prospect that Thunder would take to me, relaxing in my presence, because he could sense something in me that was unique and edgy. I know that it sounds absurd, but something about my fascination with Thunder reminded me of those women who write to violent inmates. There is validation in being accepted by the other side, by turning your back on the standards of good behavior that are expected of you. I remembered how wonderful it had been to reject my therapist's cozy cottage fantasy, and the satisfaction I found in defending my mother's filth against my grandmother's broom. Couldn't these people see that I was a girl of complex needs, who could not be bought with pretty things and heartwarming scenarios?

I went into Thunder's stall and attached myself to his side. When he shrank against the wall, I stuck to him. When he turned in circles, I turned with him. This way I was not hounding him, but rather sending the message that I could play the game all day and it was up to him when we ended it. Once he stopped spinning, I pushed against his side, offsetting his balance just enough to grab his first foot. He allowed this, but unlike the other horses, he leaned his weight stubbornly into my hand, reminding me that he was still in charge. I brushed the manure from inside his hoof with my bare fingers. No bad smell. No curdled infection. We repeated the spinning game for each foot, and when I reached the last one—his back left leg—Thunder pulled it sharply away and held it, as if winding it up.

"Ho, buddy," I told him. I glued myself to his side again and caught him by the ankle just as he was kicking out, wrestling to hold him still enough to brush away the compressed mud. Underneath, the center of the hoof did not look any different than the rest, but there was something that I had failed to notice about Thunder's hooves in general. He was the only horse there that did not have shoes. This struck me as significant in some way, only I could not guess why. Thunder stamped the floor, and I got out of there.

WHEN CLEO'S TRUCK pulled up, I was in the living room, transfixed once again by the golden webbing that the glass doorknob cast against the wall. It seemed that it was more than just a reflection; it was as if some secret inside the glass was being revealed—an unspooling of what was, at all other times, incomprehensible. I heard the snapping gravel and the throbbing of the truck's stereo, and there was something else, as if a sixth sense was telling me that Cleo was not alone, and that I should ready myself. I hurried upstairs, to the dormer window in Howie's office, so I could look down at the driveway. The bass cut out, and the driver's side door opened. I could hear the dinging, signaling that the keys were still in the ignition. Next, the passenger side door opened, but no one emerged. I leaned my forehead against the cold glass. Who was going to be our visitor tonight? Two days ago, Lydia and Beth had been over, and Beth had gotten very drunk and told us a story about a man who, knowing that she was a lesbian, had asked her if she would allow him to eat her pussy. She began the story, leaning forward and holding her wine glass loosely, as if it were going to be very funny, but it turns out that her funny-story lead-up was almost identical to her incredibly-fucked-up-story lead-up.

"He was a close friend, and I wasn't really seeing anyone at the time," Beth said, "So I thought what the heck. He got to business, and it just wasn't happening, like not at all." She looked into her wine glass with a kind of jaded amusement. It was obvious that Lydia had heard the story before and that she did not like it, and I felt uncomfortable for her. She still had that thick-eyeglasses innocence, and it made her seem defenseless to Beth's words, like someone had left her lid open.

"So, I tap him on the shoulder, like, your ten minutes are up, sir. But he won't quit. He won't quit"—Here, her voice got louder, as if she were trying to talk over herself—"because if he can't make me come, then, in his mind, he's not as good at eating pussy as a woman."

"If you faked it for him, I'm not talking to you anymore," Cleo said. She was reclining on the couch, with her legs resting on my lap.

"No, I didn't fake it for him," Beth said, her voice lower now.

"Men think that all orgasms are good orgasms," Cleo said angrily, like she wanted to start a parade about it. She was derailing the conversation, maybe because she, too, could sense Lydia's discomfort. Without Beth having to say it directly, we all knew that this was a rape story, and not because the man had penetrated or physically harmed her, but because he was driven by ego. Because he had not seen Beth as a friend, but as a challenge, something to brag about to straight women afterward. There was more to it that I couldn't shake, as if Beth's story wanted to stir up something ugly within myself, but by then I was too drunk. I felt the thought drop away like a crumb onto the shag rug. Cleo's legs over mine suddenly felt too hot, her little feet in their heavy-duty winter socks seemed too intimate—or maybe it was that they appeared very mortal—making me aware of my own body beneath her in a way that I did not like. I am not trying to infer anything profound from this. Again, I was drunk, and drunkenness, after a certain point, floods me with shame, the coals of it lodged in my stomach with no way to douse them other than sleep.

Finally, Cleo emerged from the passenger side of the truck, holding a cardboard box in her gloved hands, which was filled with groceries or packages, I couldn't tell. She was laughing, and she kicked the door shut behind her. The interior dinging stopped, and Jean-Remy emerged from behind the wheel, wearing a long scarf wrapped many times around his neck. He tossed Cleo's keys and caught them like he owned them. The dread that I felt upon seeing him was not completely centered on my dislike for him. It was a more selfish awareness: Instead of relaxing this evening, I would have to actively manage my dislike, keep it from charging into the foreground. My limbs became heavy. My forehead went flat and numb against the window. I backed away, took a breath, and prepared myself mentally to walk downstairs to meet them.

"Ah, there's our Bug." It was Jean-Remy. He was in the front hallway, bent over to remove his boots. I could see, even from where I stood, that they were expensive boots, which made me suddenly aware of my own ratty sweater, my pilled, mismatched socks. He straightened himself and looked at me.

"You've hurt yourself," he said with a mix of concern and interest. This confused me, until he brought his hand to his forehead, and I realized that my window spying must have left an indent.

"Oh," I said, rubbing the spot. "That's personal."

Cleo came into the hallway from the kitchen.

"Is she being strange again?" She wrapped me in a hug.

"She was being very strange, yes," Jean-Remy said. He, like Cleo, seemed playful and affectionate.

Cleo held me at arm's length and called me a hero. She told me that they were going to cook a special dinner that night to thank me for my help with the murderous horses.

"I barely did anything," I stammered. "I called a gravel guy."

"We don't just mean for today," Cleo said. *We.* Here was the Smarmy Man, in his socks, whirling Cleo's keys around his index finger. He was calling me Bug. He knew where I lived and how disheveled I looked on my days off.

They told me to sit on the couch, and Jean-Remy delivered me a glass of wine. It tasted smooth and did not sear the roof of my mouth with acid.

"This isn't Two Buck Chuck," I said. Jean-Remy smiled and put his hand on his heart, which seemed to be his thing. I could not tell if I trusted it or not, but the wine was excellent, so I allowed myself to take another full sip. From the kitchen, Cleo called out, "I can tell you were cleaning in here, Bug!" And I, locking eyes with Jean-Remy, called back, "It's because I missed you." He kept my gaze for a long time, his eyes appraising me. When he finally joined Cleo in the kitchen, I was left with the sense that he had seen too much, and I vowed to be more opaque from then on—a vow that I had probably made hundreds of times already in my life. I drank more of the wine, which tasted like what I imagined wine from a tapestry to taste like. It flooded my body with heat, beginning with my thighs and moving up through my pelvis. So, I thought, this is going to be a horny drunk. Not a giggle drunk or a sob drunk. I finished the glass much too quickly.

The wine was a pinot noir that was supposed to be impressive because Jean-Remy knew the guy who owned the vineyard. I was not as impressed as I was scandalized that Cleo had made a curry to go with it, which I assumed meant that she was about to break her nearly thirty-year streak of vegetarianism—and all for some guy with pretty eyelashes who she'd met on the internet. I sat at the table and allowed Jean-Remy to fill my glass again while Cleo spooned steaming rice onto my plate.

"So," I said, attempting to swirl my glass, "were you really at a conference, Jean-Remy, or did you make that up?"

I could see him stiffen in my periphery, just for an instant, before setting the bottle back on the counter.

"Such distrust!" said Cleo. "Where did she learn that?"

"Maybe she's just being protective," Jean-Remy said, and he winked at me. "I think it's sweet." He sat at the table and whipped his napkin onto his lap.

How could I convey to them that it was neither? I had been around too many men like Jean-Remy, by which I mean men who have never been second-guessed about anything. Men who get what they want and wink obnoxiously when they don't, as if they'd choreographed the entire thing. Someone in the room had to hold him accountable.

"Why don't you take it down a notch, Bug?" Cleo was spreading the curry over my rice, and I saw that there was no meat in it at all, just cubes of soft, sauce-laden tofu. The sight made me remorseful.

"I'm sorry," I said, and I meant it. Suddenly I could not

remember what was so terrible about Jean-Remy. He obviously wanted to make Cleo happy. And Cleo was buoyant that evening. The tip of her nose was pink. The wine on her teeth gave her smile a siren-like quality: beautiful, eager, maybe a little bloodthirsty.

"I have low blood sugar," I tried to explain.

"That's all right," Jean-Remy said. He had gotten up again to light a trio of mismatched pillar candles in the center of the table. "You're the hero of the day, after all." This time, his wink seemed more involuntary. A nervous tic. He turned off the lights.

I don't think I had ever eaten by candlelight before. In theory, it seemed cliché, something to take for granted, like sliding down a banister as a child, or taking a bubble bath, but I had not had the privilege of experiencing those things either. I looked over at Cleo and saw that she was practically supernatural. Her beauty was not the beauty of contours, or angles, or any carefully designed mood. Her beauty was that of the horizon before a waterfall: always on the precipice of itself. And in the swell of the candle flame, this kinetic quality was even more intoxicating. Once again, I was being obvious in my adoration, and Jean-Remy said, "Isn't our Cleo lovely?" *Our Cleo. Our Bug.* Everything was softened and familiar. I felt myself being lulled, for when had I ever had a dinner like this—and not just with candles, but a dinner where everything was done correctly? Where I was gazed upon so affectionately, as though I truly belonged?

"Yes, she is," I said without shyness or humor. I was growing tired of always hiding behind an innuendo or an attitude, and Jean-Remy, sitting powerfully across from me, with his forearms on the table, gave me confidence. I almost felt that I could tell Cleo everything through Jean-Remy. As if male approval were the missing ingredient to my adoration. I could say, "She's not just lovely. She's sexy too. I want to touch her, but I want to do it slowly, as in, I want to touch her over the course of weeks, months—a year. I want to watch terrible Hugh Grant movies with her while, under a blanket, we move closer, centimeter by centimeter, feeling the wonderful ache of the slowness, as if it might kill us. When we finally kiss, I want only our eyelashes to touch, and I want that moment to be a novel in itself. In that novel there is no word for lips, because each stage is its own, blissfully ignorant universe. And during all this, this drawn out, deliciously painful coming together, I want the security of knowing that no one else is going to swoop in and take her away."

But I wasn't that drunk, so all I said was, "You met in a chat room?"

Over the lick of the candle flame, something behind Jean-Remy's eyes seemed to turn like the spinning lock to a safe.

"You really told her everything, didn't you, Cleo?" He sat back in his chair, beaming across the table. It was hard to tell which one of us he was looking at.

"I'm not judging you," I said. "It's not that strange to meet people online these days."

"Ah," he said, still addressing Cleo. "I see you didn't tell her what kind of chat room."

Cleo bit the rim of her cup, smiling. "I'm the girl's boss," she said. "We have boundaries."

"That's the first I've ever heard of them," I said.

We were having a good time. All of this back and forth was tastefully self-conscious, and it felt like it was leading somewhere emotionally important. I could feel the ties between us pulling taut. I could see the three of us seared into a Polaroid, clipped beneath the sun visor in Cleo's truck. We were having "that dinner," our conversation the bellows to an era.

It was a BDSM forum. Cleo said she had been visiting it on and off, noncommittally, for about two years, and that it wasn't so much the kinky subject matter that kept her logging in, but the fact that the BDSM community consisted of the most well-spoken group of people she had ever encountered.

"It's all about consent and communication, right?" She took a bite of food and chewed it carefully before continuing. "The result was a population of men who knew what they wanted, knew how to talk about it, and would not tolerate ambiguity. What more could you ask for?" She darted a look at Jean-Remy and took another quick bite. I wondered how many well-spoken men she had been in contact with during her connection with him.

"And you two . . ." I made a gesture between them.

"We found out that we shared similar interests," Jean-Remy said. I knew he meant fantasies, but the way that they were being so relaxed about it made it seem like they were two people who had inadvertently wandered into a nudist colony and formed a bond as outsiders. He saw me placing my fork and napkin on my plate and jumped up.

"Oh no, no, Bug," he said, taking my plate and then stacking Cleo's on top of it. He seemed to enjoy using my nickname, like a new pair of boots that he wanted to break in as quickly as possible. I couldn't help but like it. I liked any kind of enthusiasm directed my way. With Jean-Remy at the sink with his back to us, Cleo placed her hand on the table next to mine.

"I never met anyone from the chat room," she said to me. "Until now." I could see that she wanted to reassure me of something, either that she was not one to make unsafe decisions, or that she was not a cheater—not a prolific cheater, anyway. This softened me. I wanted to tell her that I would never judge her. I understood that she was lonely with Howie. Anyone could see that her very life force was of a greater caliber than the rest of the world's. Even a Canadian bad boy with beautiful eyelashes and an undisclosed kink would most likely run out of steam long before she did. At least, that was what I was hoping.

The room seemed to list slightly, as if beneath a shifting layer of transparency, which meant that I had reached a new degree of drunkenness and the candles were making things complicated. I remembered then that I still had to let the horses inside for the night. I groaned.

"I have to go do my chores," I said.

"Bug?" Jean-Remy turned around to face us, holding the dripping plate that he had started washing. He grabbed a hand towel and began to dry it in slow, thoughtful circles.

"Yeah, J. R.?"

"Ew," Cleo shook her head. "Never call him that again."

Jean-Remy made another circle with the towel and looked soulfully at me.

"I'd like your permission to spend the night."

"What?" I laughed sharply.

"It's important to me that you are comfortable with me being here. With Cleo."

"It's Cleo's house," I said, shrugging. Maybe consent was a big deal for whatever they were doing, but I did not want every part of my comfort zone touched and examined. I definitely did not want to be the *yea* or *nay* between whatever was going to make Cleo happy. He must have known this.

"But this is your home also."

I moved closer to the door.

"Do you want me to sign a waiver?" I asked him.

He laughed and, standing behind Cleo's chair, placed his hand on her shoulder. Her eyes were half closed, wine dozing. Blissful.

"At least give us a nod."

He was serious about this. I lifted my face to the ceiling and then slowly rolled my head on my neck in the most exaggerated head flop I could muster. I heard slow clapping behind me as I went to put on Howie's boots.

"Brava!" Jean-Remy shouted after me.

Sometimes I wondered what Howie might have thought while he was lying in the field, post-kick. If he had been conscious at all. I did not believe that he would have been angry at his assailant. If anything, he might have cursed himself for lowering his guard or cutting corners. Whatever sting of betrayal that he might have felt would have instantly been cooled by forgiveness, the tall grass combed through by it, the hills hushed by it. Maybe there had been time to dream out in his field, with the world knocked off course and the big canvas sky rolling over him like a set change.

I'd like to think that Howie and I had this in common: our big betrayals being interchangeable with our big moments of forgiveness. I was seventeen when I first left home for a significant amount of time. An essay that I had written awarded me a scholarship to a young writers' conference at a university upstate. It was a two-week affair in summertime, so the young writers could be housed in the dorms while the university students were not occupying them. I did not want to be a writer, but my English teacher was an overly passionate woman, hell-bent on convincing me that I was talented, probably because she had watched too many movies about reluctant working-class savants who are discovered by passionate professors. I had stupidly promised her that, should the essay win the contest, I would attend the conference, assuming, of course, that there was no chance it would happen.

Anyway, I squandered the experience by showing up late to my workshops, laughing at a boy's poem about suicidal ideation that was not, as I had assumed, intentionally funny, and then turning in a subpar essay centered around an onion metaphor. I'm not proud. What's worse is that my English teacher herself drove me the two hours to campus, and then brought me home when it was over.

When I returned to my mother's house, it was no longer the dusky, poorly ventilated bungalow that I had left two weeks earlier. At first, I thought that my mother had gone to the halfway house again. I expected to find my grandmother in a state of stooped fervor, pitching take-out cartons into the trash can. What I found instead was my mother at her typewriter, bathed in light from the open window. No dust motes. No clots of hair, or balled-up bills, or unexplained heaps of wool blankets stuffed into the corners to "deaden the emptiness." My mother turned as I walked through the door, grasping the back of her wooden chair.

"Drew," she said.

"Mary," I said, because I did not know, in that moment, what else to call her. She had never liked the name Mary; she said it was a name that tarnished too easily, like a silver cup gifted to a baby. Marys, in her eyes, were always someone's dead relative, a portrait hung at the end of an upstairs hallway. To her, this was too much pressure. But my mother had never been more of a Mary in her life as she was in that moment: classical, clean, and writing letters by the window! Somehow, in the two weeks that I was away at the conference, she had figured out how to live. I understood instantly: My mother thrived when I was not there. And I forgave her instantly because it was so obviously not her choice.

Later that week, I cried in Nico's bed while I explained to her this strange twist that had taken place in my life, but the crying was not genuine. The tears were real, but they felt more like a lubricant for the truth, so that Nico could fully understand the unique circumstance. Somehow, I knew that it was important to feel devastated by such a discovery or else risk being seen as heartless. But, while it was painful, I found at the center of it such a clear crystal of relief that there was ecstasy as well, a pinnacle of human understanding. A separation of familial expectations and real love. I could love my mother by leaving her. Nothing in my life had ever felt so thrillingly mature. Nico, unable to bear my distress, jumped into action, and by the end of the weekend, she had convinced her parents that I was in desperate need of a place to live. I went home to my mother and said to her that the young writers' conference had given me a taste of freedom. I wanted to move out. No one pointed out that living in my friend's middle-class basement was no more of a step toward freedom than chaining myself to a wall. My mother was not stupid. She said, "You're welcome back any time."

The rain had stopped, but it was still humid for January. The horses trotted in from the marshy paddock, blackened nearly to their bellies in mud. While they munched their oats, I tidied up the feed room and brushed the dust guiltily from the cover of Howie's manual. Maybe the reason that I had not spent more time reading it was because it was always so cold in the barn. I could bring it inside and study from the warmth of my bed. But not tonight, I comforted myself, because tonight I was drunk.

The downstairs was dark when I returned to the house, but I could smell the char of recently extinguished candles, so I guessed that Cleo and Jean-Remy had only just gone upstairs. I hung up my coat and carefully aligned my boots with the others. Jean-Remy's boots were smaller than Howie's, and prettier. He was probably the kind of man who used products in his hair with names that I could not pronounce, who knew how to smoke a cigar without looking like a doofus. Did he feel a sense of superiority in our modest little country home? Was that a turn-on for him? I went upstairs, stepping as quietly as I could. The second floor was split down the middle by a narrow hallway, with Cleo's bedroom on one side and Howie's office on the other, my little annex as far removed from Cleo's side as you could get. I walked past her door, careful not to linger in case the shadow of my feet was visible through the small gap—not that I imagined that Cleo and Jean-Remy would be watching the small gap. I heard their low voices. Jean-Remy's tone was coaxing and somewhat affected, like someone having a one-sided conversation with an animal, or a dentist asking you questions when your mouth is filled with metal tools. I do not know why I had such a clear impression, but that was what it was, unquestioningly, in my mind. Maybe it was because Cleo's responses were monosyllabic, more like small mewls, or whimpers of affirmation, than words. It was fascinating to hear her this way, even just in passing. In Howie's office, I could still hear them, but once I was in my room—even with the door open—there was too much space, and the wind against the side of the house created a kind of ambient confusion so I could no longer decipher what was human, what was nature, and what was my own mind playing tricks. There were a few times that I was sure I heard moaning, but when I darted out into the office, it was silent. Did I want to hear them having sex? The answer was a definitive *yes.* But I did not want to be caught doing so, and also I was not sure how to comfortably accomplish such a feat. The wall was ice cold when I put my ear to it, so I scooted toward the door, allowing it to swing, unlatched, just a sliver, and I crouched beside it, listening into the hallway for whatever sounds wanted to travel toward me. At first, I heard very little. Jean-Remy's voice arched a few times in an authoritative question, followed by Cleo's one-note response. I wondered why she was not speaking, and then it occurred to me that she might be wearing a gag. But was that too stereotypical? Just because they had met on a BDSM forum did not mean that they had to conform so accordingly. Surely Cleo would want to be the one in charge—not full dominatrix, but maybe something close, something psychologically bullying. She bullied the customers at Buster's all day, and they kept coming back because any kind of attention from Cleo felt like a gift. She could scold you, strip your opinions bare, and then hand you a warm drink, and you would feel cared for in a deep, cleaned-out way. But now that the image had presented itself, I could not shake it: Cleo hog-tied with her face turned sideways, her mouth a tight grimace around the scarf that she wore in her hair. Jean-Remy kneeling behind her on the bed, asking her questions that she could not answer. Giving commands that she could not fulfill. I felt guilty for picturing these things, and had decided that I would go back to my room and stay there when I heard Jean-Remy make an explosive sound of surprise. Cleo whimpered.

Shut up, I heard Jean-Remy say, his voice not angry, but wicked. He moaned again, louder, as if the same act had startled him a second time.

I HAD BEEN living in Nico's basement for three months when she started dating the wrestler. His name was Mitchel, and he would frequently starve himself so that he could qualify for a lower weight class. It made him irritable. He'd stop eating salt and would not drink any water starting the afternoon before weigh-ins. This was not uncommon among the wrestlers, and somehow their ugly behavior during these "cuts" were tolerated because the school's athletic director held a lot of power, and also wrestling seemed to be the only sport that our high school was any good at. It had to be protected at all costs. Nico made a lot of excuses for Mitchel, saying that being on the team was more stressful than I could imagine, and that Mitchel was not a total meathead; he felt pressured to act that way in front of the other guys. Sure, sure. I had heard similar claims before. One night, however, Nico came home late. She wanted to use my shower instead of the one upstairs. I said okay and fell asleep on the futon in front of the television. When I woke up, Nico was sitting next to me, wrapped in a towel. She looked confused, and I wondered if I had done something wrong.

"What?" I said.

She wrinkled her nose. "I think something bad happened to me."

"You think?" I sat up. I wished that Nico had clothes on. I could sense that she needed me to comfort her about something, but with her bare shoulders and her wet hair dripping down her arms, the task seemed impossible, unpleasant even.

"Do you want my hoodie?" I asked, handing it to her.

"Uh, yeah," she said, and she dropped the towel to pull the hoodie over her head. I saw her breasts before I could look away. They were not like mine at all. Mine were small and immovable like a Barbie doll's, with no life of their own. My nipples were a structural deviation, always in the same location, pointing toward the same horizon. Nico's breasts were each their own separate idea. Not perfectly round, or oval. Structure was not a concern, and neither was symmetry. They lifted as she put her arms through the sleeves and, for a beautiful instant, her nipples pointed toward the ceiling. She pulled the hood over her wet hair and wrapped the towel tighter around her waist. I shoved the blanket toward her, and she packed it around her legs.

She told me that she had been at Mitchel's house that evening, fooling around on his bed. He was sleepy and restless at the same time, probably starving himself, but sometimes it was hard to tell. He asked for a blow job, and she complied, kneeling on the floor while he sat at the edge of the mattress.

"I had my hair in pigtails," she said. "And he was kind of holding onto them. I didn't mind. At first, it made me feel kind of cute?" She looked sheepishly at me, as if hoping I would get it. I did.

"I could feel that he was getting close, because his balls kept jumping into his body. I was starting to pull back a little because I don't like to taste it. Mitch knows this. He's never had a problem with that."

She paused to take a breath and packed the blanket even tighter around her body.

"Well, he just grabbed my hair—like I was a pair of handlebars or something, and he . . . And it actually hurt!" She had her hands up like fists, to show me how tightly he'd held on. She did not need to explain the rest. I saw it unfold in my mind.

"What an actual pig," I said. She sniffed, but she was not crying. I could tell the whole experience had been confusing for her. Back then, we were not taught about the nuances of consent, so Mitchel's sudden aggression presented itself as a riddle. What to call such an act? How to feel about it?

"You think it's bad?" she asked me. That's what she wanted: a decree. She was not asking for advice beyond that. I nodded.

"It's definitely not good," I said.

I was angry at Mitchel. I felt that I understood the situation better than Nico did, but that it wasn't my place—or even possible—to explain to her the list of violations that had occurred. But I could not stop myself from thinking about them, or rather, thinking about the event. Mitchel and Nico were inconsequential. Mitchel and Nico were what made the event distasteful, so I got rid of them and put other people in their places. It did not matter who. And when I imagined the scene, I saw it through the eyes of the boy, his fingers tangled in the girl's pigtails, twisting them tighter like reins, pulling her mouth deeper. So deep that she snorted and gagged. Sometimes, in this fantasy, the boy came so forcefully it dribbled out her nose.

This was why, when I heard Jean-Remy say *Shut up* and when I heard him say *Bitch, you little bitch,* I could not peel myself away from the open door. Because there was something wrong inside me that did not want it to end. There were no alarms sounding in my gut. Just the twisting of fascination, twisting like a rope until it burned. I opened the door wider and felt the cool draft from the hallway. Jean-Remy moaned again, this time a grunt, like he had been struck on the back. I loved to hear him like this: this man, so careful with his image, coming undone, making noises that were involuntary. If he was hurting Cleo, then it was also destroying something in him, something rigidly upheld that wanted to be broken. I leaned my back against the wall next to the door and I made myself come, holding the image of Cleo with her gag and her hands bound behind her back. In this scene, Cleo was Cleo, Jean-Remy was Jean-Remy. No, *I* was Jean-Remy. Yes. That was it, and it was over too quickly. I tried again: This time Cleo was in pigtails, Jean-Remy pulling them so hard her eyes watered. From outside the door, I heard Jean-Remy say, *Take it.* Or maybe I was so deep into my own imagining that I was conflating what was real and what I wanted to be real. I came a second and third time until it was no longer pleasurable and felt more like a gut punch than an orgasm.

Afterward, I crawled into bed, sore from the long day digging in the mud and nauseated now that my buzz was thinning. I could feel the shame of what I had just done seeping in around the edges. With my eyes closed and the room wobbling, I imagined myself on my mattress, floating on a dark lake, the water pulling slowly at the sheets. The water was my shame. I had to fall asleep before it soaked me through.

6

THE NEXT MORNING, the three of us rode into town in Cleo's truck. Cleo was driving and Jean-Remy was riding shotgun, which left me crammed between them. The fields around us had turned damp and tawny with the warmer weather, and the woods were threaded with mist. Whenever we turned eastward, the sun would spike over the mountain, and I could feel that we all wanted to put up our hands to shield our eyes but were collectively too embarrassed to do so. What a strange and intimate thing to hold between us, I thought. I had forgotten to brush my teeth, so I was hoping that no one would ask me anything. I was afraid that if I opened my mouth, the cab would be filled with my stink. I already felt filthy, in need of a hot shower. Thick strands of greasy hair had escaped my ponytail and were tickling my neck. Beside me, Jean-Remy turned his head from the sharp sunlight and seemed to study the landscape through the side window. His face was dark with stubble and his eyes were lush and black. I wondered if he knew that I had heard them the night before, and whether that was something he cared about or had possibly intended. I did not dare look at Cleo's face from where I sat. Everything was too close up.

I had been relieved to see her that morning unharmed, although I told myself that I was never truly worried for her well-being. She was a grown woman, after all, and how awful would it have been if I'd run into the bedroom in a panic to make sure that she was not being murdered? Jean-Remy would have remained cool, smirking at me. He would have made no attempts to hide his nakedness. My intrusion would have confirmed what I suspected he had seen in me all along: that I was a prude. On the outside I was all talk, but inside I was as soft and flinching as a grub.

Oh, Bug, he might have said. *Oh, darling. We did not mean to frighten you.*

That morning, Cleo had burst into my bedroom, yelping when she saw me tangled in my sweaty blankets, still asleep.

"Drew-Baby, you're not up!" She stood over my mattress, her curls dark and wet from the shower. The sky through the window was a stony-blue color. I winced. I don't think I was hungover as much as exhausted, and now the events of the previous night were hitting me head-on as if no time had passed since I'd crawled shamefully into bed, jeans twisted and unbuttoned, hair matted around an elastic. I looked across the floor at the clothes and dishes strewn about—not just from the one night, but from many tired evenings when I could not find the strength to clean up. I was mortified that Cleo was walking into my mess. That there was sunlight at all to see meant that it was late. I had slept in.

"We thought you were out in the barn," Cleo said. She pulled my blankets away and my knees jerked to my chest. I groaned, and to my absolute horror, Jean-Remy appeared in the doorway behind her.

"The truck is all warmed up," he said to Cleo. Then to me, "Wake up, sleepyhead!" I growled at him like a raccoon.

BY THE TIME we reached the café, we were already more than an hour behind schedule. Cleo set the oven to preheat and began prepping a quick batch of muffins, scones, and frozen turnovers. The People would have to survive on a whittled-down menu today. Out front, I warmed the carafes with hot water and began brewing pots of coffee. Jean-Remy made himself at home, flipping on the espresso machine and preparing himself a triple espresso topped with hot water.

"I'm off," he said, and gave me a gentle squeeze on the shoulder. He left through Cleo's office, where his car was parked out back. I did not realize at the time that his good-bye was a real one, and that he was driving all the way back to Quebec that morning.

Most of the baked goods were still in the oven when I put the flag outside. A woman with tired lines down her face was on the step, waiting to come in. She seemed somewhat familiar, but by then everyone in town had been through our doors at least once. I could not go anywhere without recognizing The People. If they had so far evaded being assigned a cruel nickname, then I would refer to them in the privacy of my mind, or aloud to Cleo, by their drink order.

"There's Double Decaf Skim at the intersection," I might say.

Cleo would say, "Why bother?" And I would pout, and she would say, "No, I mean, *Why Bother*." Because that was her name for a double decaf latte with skim.

The woman pushed her way inside before I had a chance to take the keys out of the door. I followed her to where she was already leaning against the counter, her gloved fingers spread out across the glass surface. She was wearing a fake fur coat that ended at her calves. Salt-stained flats over stockings.

"One plain bagel, scooped and toasted," she said to me. I stopped and stared at her. Here was the infamous Scoops—my first sighting!—and she had found me on the only day that we did not have bagels.

"I'm so sorry," I said to her. "Our bagels aren't—There are no bagels today."

She leaned forward as if looking for Cleo on the floor behind me.

"Where's that other woman?" she asked. "She'll know what to get me."

I tried to explain to her that it wasn't a matter of knowing or not knowing, but a matter of supply—there was no way I was going to admit that the real problem was that we'd all drunk too much fancy wine and slept in. But it was as if she did not understand the words that I was speaking. More customers began filtering in behind her, and I felt the adrenaline click on at the base of my neck. Scoops slammed her fist onto the glass counter, rattling the displays and shaking loose the topmost blueberry muffin of a muffin pyramid. It bounced onto the floor.

"What the fuck? Are you psychotic?" I was already shouting, which seemed odd. I didn't usually like to shout; it was too much of an admission. My limbs loosened and my solar plexus took a hit of helium. Was this what it felt like to go into fight mode? Was I about to experience my first real rage over a woman addicted to gutted bagels? Yes, I thought. I picked up the muffin from the floor. I thought: This is a totally appropriate moment to lose my mind. But I felt Cleo's hand on my wrist, as if she were trying to stop me from throwing the muffin across the counter. I could not believe that she thought I was going to throw it.

"Drew—" Cleo said. "Why don't you go to the office and sit down." It was not a question. I glanced at Scoops, who was lowering her arms slowly, as if she had been shielding her face.

"Oh, relax," I said to her.

"Drew."

Cleo's eyes were such a bright hazel that they appeared yellow in the sunlight coming in from the big windows. Her complexion was flawless, and in that same light, I could see the fine dusting of powder on her nose. The glitter on the apples of her cheeks. There were precious, little lines forming at the edges of her lips, the only indication that this small, fierce woman was nearly twenty years my senior. Maybe I had forgotten my place. Maybe I was becoming a horrible brat. I bit the top of the floor muffin in defiance and left Cleo at the counter. As I was walking through the office's beaded curtain, I heard her placating Scoops, offering to pull a frozen bagel from the back.

"I'll zap it and toast it up for you," she said. "You won't know the difference."

The office was a small, carpeted cubby with a love seat that had probably been there since the building was erected. Its cushions were as dead as bags of grain and faded to threads. I fell onto it face down, my throat hot with tears of embarrassment. I did not understand why Cleo was siding so readily with Scoops. It was her job, I knew, but there had been no shred of irony, no indication that she and I were on the same team. It wasn't just that I had been scolded, but that Cleo had looked as if she did not know me, her eyes filled with a sharp incredulity that

I did not deserve. I still had the muffin in my mouth, but I could not swallow. I rolled off the love seat and pulled the wire wastebasket from beneath Cleo's desk, letting the chewed, slick mush slide out. I coughed and then vomited for real. A thin, straight line. The beads in the doorway tinkled, and I slumped onto the floor as a reflex. Let Cleo see how wrecked I was. I did not care anymore.

"I heard there might be bagels back here?"

I rolled onto my back, with my hands folded over my stomach, and saw Amos towering in the doorway, holding the beads aside. He was wearing a jean jacket over a black T-shirt and some kind of necklace on a leather string. He looked less depressed than the last time I'd seen him, and even gently concerned. I felt like a dog in full submission mode.

"Hi, Amos," I said. The tears were here now, running from my eyes into my ears. Amos reached down to help me up. His giant hand nearly snapped my wrist, but it was a wonderful, light feeling to be lifted like that. I wanted him to throw me over his shoulder and escape with me through the back door. We sat on the hard love seat, and Amos offered his jacket sleeve for me to wipe the snot and puke dribble from my face—his actual sleeve, still on his body. I used my apron instead.

"Cleo is having weird sex with the Smarmy Man," I told him.

He was silent for a moment, then said: "Which part don't you like? The sex part, the weird part, or the smarmy part?" He seemed to consider another angle. "Or the man part?"

I wondered if this was his way of asking me if I was gay. And if so, if that was because he was feeling out his options. This idea—that Amos could possibly be interested in me—struck me like the lowest note on a piano. A vibration that I had not considered, that required a certain stretch and courage. I became so wrapped up in this new feeling that I forgot what he was really asking. Could I sleep with Amos? Yes, I thought. Did I want to? I would want to when I got there. It would be like jumping into the ocean. I put my hand on his knee, which felt like my first real risk of the day, though I should have perhaps given more consideration to how I nearly threw a blueberry muffin at a woman's face. I put all of that out of my mind and looked up at him. His eyes were on my hand. If he did not say or do anything in the next ten seconds, I resolved, then I would take my hand away, and walk swiftly out the back door. He placed his hand on mine, lightly. It was a cautious gesture, and I recognized it as kindness. Not lust. Not even hopeful interest.

"Drew," he said.

I slid my hand away and held it as if cradling a burn.

"I know," I said. The tears had stopped.

"What do you know?"

"Either I'm disgusting and pathetic, or you're . . ." I hesitated. "Gay?" It suddenly felt so shallow to be allowing him these options, as if his level of desire for me was the only indication of who he was.

Amos laughed. It was such a deep sound that I could feel it shifting in his body.

"I'm afraid it's a lot less scandalous than either of those things." He patted my knee but held it a beat so that I would understand something. And for a moment, I saw myself outside the few markers of worth that I had been led to believe were available to me. It was terrifying.

I RETURNED TO the counter, my fight instincts burned up like rubbing alcohol, and tended to The People with a new, hardened attitude. They could not hurt me, but in return, they were going to receive no humor, no dimple of tenderness. No "Careful, it's hot" or "Hold the bag from the bottom so it doesn't break!" Let them figure life out for themselves, I thought. Let the world worry the back of its teeth with a burnt tongue. Amos had left without ordering. Either he was more embarrassed by our backroom conversation than he'd let on, or he had floated into Buster's on an instinct, there for the sole purpose of rescuing me from my funk. As absurd as it sounds, I wholeheartedly believed it was the latter.

Cleo worked in the kitchen until lunchtime, when she came out carrying a large tub, her gaze sidelong with some new triumph.

"Today is the day, my dear," she said to me. I looked into the tub and saw a reddish slurry.

"Salsa?"

She pulled it back.

"It's gazpacho," she hissed, and set it on the back counter by the soup warmers. I could feel her lightened mood. It fell on me like cashmere, like one of those head tinglers. When it came to Cleo's shifts of direction, I was her wind sock. And I welcomed it. I wanted to be whipped around. I wanted to work harder, to make secret vows within myself, inside my most brittle places, as if to test them.

"There's something else," she said to me, and crooked her finger. I followed her into the kitchen, where a rising bread loaf lay on the table under a towel.

"I found this at the bottom of the crate." She plucked the towel away, and I saw that it was not a loaf, but the largest cucumber I had ever seen. It was as long as my forearm, and at least four inches in diameter.

"King Cucumber," Cleo said.

We found a glass display stand, and Cleo placed a doily over the top of it.

"You never told me we had doilies," I said.

"Nothing has warranted one until now."

We brought the stand to the front and cleared a place for it by the register, then set the King Cucumber upon it. The ends stuck out, splendidly curved and thick. I wondered if George had laid it there at the bottom of the crate with us in mind. Where was George? I remembered the way he had gasped into my neck, the hot trickle in my palm. I felt as though he and I had not reached our full potential, that we could do better than a cold, sober tug session. I reminded myself to make a list of more possible barn chores, in case the opportunity arose again.

The door opened and our policemen strutted in. They walked as if they had just come from a dinner where they'd eaten too much. One had a shiny bald head working double duty as a shelf for his sunglasses. I kept looking at the head, as if it were its own person.

"What's this?" asked the other one. He was somewhat fleshy, like a gelatin mold of masculinity, the square jaw and looming forehead an illusion that you could put your finger through.

"Our latest," said Cleo, patting the cucumber. "From the Lonely Girl's Vegetable Patch."

Dead stares.

"Tell us you like it," I said. Cleo brushed her mouth with the back of her hand, covering her smile. The cops exchanged a look between them. The fleshy one stepped forward.

"It's very nice," he said, and pushed two dollars across the countertop. I noticed that the cops did not like handing money over. It was always a slide or a coin drop. "Can I get my usual?"

"What part of it is nice?" I asked him. His partner laughed a loud *ha*. The sunglasses stayed strong, as if pressed into clay.

"Come on now, Bug," said Cleo, pulling a paper cup from the top of the stack. "Don't tease the law."

I put my hand on the cucumber and looked at the Sunglasses Cop.

"And what do you want?" I asked. He shook his head, recusing himself from my game. It was fine. All I wanted was for them to see that there was a game, and that it was fixed, like those laser trip wires in spy movies. They could dodge them all they wanted, but in doing so, they were still playing.

Cleo and I spent the rest of the day showing off our prized cucumber and telling customers that the soup was cold. We amassed great chaos and confusion, as well as some bitter disappointment. The only person who did not complain about the gazpacho was Quad Bitch, who ordered a pint of it to go, and then a second pint when Cleo told her that there were only forty calories per cup. Her eyes widened. I could see the calculations churning inside her brain. She could eat the whole batch, and it would hardly count as a real meal. Maybe she could splurge and only cut her brownie into thirds. When we showed her our big cucumber, I could see her making a meal of it also. Some people were so painfully unfun I wondered what, if anything, they were trying to win at.

"That woman needs a good spanking," Cleo said to me as Quad Bitch was walking out the door. She said it loud enough that a man stirring his coffee at the self-serve station perked up. He walked toward us, his head cocked sideways.

"Can I ask you something?"

"Shoot," Cleo said. She was standing next to me, her arm around my shoulder. The man studied us. He had a narrow face and a mustache that I can only describe as appearing to be poorly attached. I expected him to make a perverted crack at us. After all, we'd been asking for it all day: petting a vegetable that looked like a jacked up hard-on, punishing the masses with bad soup, flirting until we practically foamed at the mouth. The man leaned in.

"I'm wondering if you ever feel . . . affected. By all the ground coffee in the air." He had a weird, street magician manner of speaking that I did not find comforting. "Do you smell it in the shower when you wash your hair? Do you see it in your tissue when you blow your nose?"

We stared at the man, waiting for him to arrive at his point, but he just straightened his shoulders, his posture conveying that his questioning was finished.

"Yes," I told him, truthfully. "I smell the coffee when I shower. I smell horse manure too, and hay and a strange burnt toast smell that seems like the accumulation of all of it: the people and the grime and the grit from the street."

Cleo pinched my side, probably wondering why I was humoring this guy when he was obviously a serial killer. The man nodded slowly. He was indeed killer-ish, in that he looked anemic and gaunt, and his eyes, small and direct behind wire-frame glasses, were too intense for the situation. This was only a coffee shop, not a hostage exchange. He looked into his coffee, nodded again, then walked to the trash can and poured the entire steaming contents of the cup into it. He looked back at us, then turned toward Cleo's painting on the wall, and then at us again, as if caught in a dilemma. Finally, he crushed the empty cup in his hand and carried it out the door. Cleo pulled me to her side, and for a moment, I could see that what we thought was our superiority, our cleverness and beauty, was merely luck. Our confidence was strong as a rope above a flame.

IT HAD BEEN a day. As afternoon hit and business waned, we wrapped the leftover pastries in plastic and poured out all but one of the carafes. Cleo dipped a spoon into the gazpacho and slurped.

"Ugh!" she spat. "It tastes like straight Tabasco." She picked up the tub and poured it into the garbage, smothering the coffee that the creepy man had dumped earlier. Then she hefted the bag and spun it shut, a swift gesture that seemed to bring everything to an end: Jean-Remy, the Scoops Woman, Amos, the King Cucumber, the cops, and the serial killer, who we decided to name Stabby Stan.

Back at the house, I forced myself to clean my room. I had brought three empty wooden crates from the vegetable deliveries, two of which I stacked by the window to make a shelf. A third I upended as a kind of bedside table to place my laptop on. I had been feeling lately that things were becoming too condensed. So much had happened, and I had not processed any of it. Clearing the floor of my mess and arranging my small belongings on the crates was satisfying. I imagined that life could be spare and lovely with one small window and a square of winter light on the floor. Wooden crates for furniture. The tiredness in my arms and the tight hinge in my back could be considered stabilizing. And if I could go to sleep more often without the murk and turbulence of alcohol in my bloodstream, then maybe my dreams would not be so frantic and sex crazed. My mind would have time to stitch itself back together. I opened my laptop to try out my new crate table, and I saw that I was already logged into my email, a new message in bold on the screen. It was from Byron. The subject line read RE: TONIGHT. That was strange, but he had done stranger things. I clicked it and read something that I did not comprehend at first, until I did, suddenly, understand. Sometime last night, in my wine-drunk torment, I had written to Byron. *I* had written to *him*, completely unprompted.

> *Hi. How are you. Tonight, my Lady Boss and I lured a man into our house. He is very pretty and wears expensive boots. We made him do the dishes and then tied him up.*

To this, Byron had responded, sometime around two in the morning:

> *Drew,*
> *What is the application process for such a position?*
> *Your servant,*
> *Byron*

This had to stop. I had no recollection of writing these words, only the swimmy memory of listening to Jean-Remy's pained moans, imagining him gagging Cleo, binding her, holding tight to her hair. Was it a coincidence that all these actions had to do with keeping Cleo in place, not letting her get away? I got up. Outside, it was almost dark. I hated how winter sucked the sun out of the sky, how the night was hard as slate. Sometimes the wooden fence posts and the metal buckets glittered in the cold, but this was only pretty in an apocalyptic sort of way, never inspiring. I prepared myself to do my chores. It was good to have all this work, I decided, because otherwise I was idle and desperate. I thought about what had happened with Amos earlier, and squeezed my eyes shut to try to force the memory elsewhere—packed into my teeth or my appendix. Why did all these blunders, in the moment, feel like noble risks? What was the point of doing anything if I was just going to regret it later?

IN FRONT OF the barn, I discovered a pile of gravel. On one hand, it was satisfying to see that a small action I had taken had resulted in something tangible. Like the crates in my bedroom, it prompted the same sense of clearheaded subsistence. On the other hand, it presented a literal mountain of work, a time-sensitive chore that would not get done if I did not deal with every part of it. The space between my eyes crept into the deep chambers of a stress headache, like a hand reaching into a glove. My actions lately—the fugue state email to Byron, the pervy eavesdropping, the fact that I had, indeed, been planning on hurling a muffin at a customer—made me feel like an unruly person who required a stricter schedule and a more optimistic set of goals. I could not just pant nervously at the heels of my boss. I needed a purpose.

I breathed in the smells of the barn, and my head pounded with the dust and the sweet mold of the bales. There was the chocolaty oats and the gasoline stink of manure. Here, I thought, was the answer to my troubles. Horses had always been the answer since the days of the therapeutic riding center, where I had felt the purpose of each footstep, where the miles went nowhere but added up to immeasurable joy. I got to work mucking the stalls. The sun was setting, and the interior lightbulbs stuck out sideways along the aisle, burning warmly and without pretense. I took care not to rush as I sifted through the pine shavings, hunting for the smallest clumps of poop. Here in the barn, there lingered a mystery, a restlessness. As I worked, I thought about the things that I knew about Howie's accident, which was not much. The information was already becoming confused with another story that I had heard about a man who had fallen off a bull in a rodeo and was gored in the stomach on his way to the ground. He walked out of the arena and drove himself home, not knowing that the damage had already been done and his organs were shutting down. He would be dead in the morning. I wondered if anyone had thought to inspect Howie's kick site to see whether a horseshoe mark had been left, or if it was just a horse hoof. If there was any way to tell.

When the stalls were clean and fluffed with new shavings, I opened the side door and let the horses walk in. Frida, Gomer, Queen Biscuits, and Thunder. *My Thunder*, I thought, perhaps a little experimentally. He pivoted in his stall and dropped his head into the oats bucket.

I stood by him and watched the working of his jaw. It was a serious apparatus. Humans did not eat with such full-body commitment. We were always trying to look at something else, think of something else. I placed my hand on Thunder's neck and felt the vibration of his teeth grinding. I placed my hand on his chest and felt it there as well. He raised his head, probably wondering what I was doing. I blew into his nostril. *Did you kill Howie?* He blew back. His breath smelled like cereal, like a deep, sweaty sleep. Like the damp bridge of my underwear at the end of the day. Of all smells in the world, that last one was my favorite.

Before I went inside, I checked the manual, thinking I was going to study the section that Howie had devoted to Thunder, but instead my eyes fell on a divider near the end that had a list of dates on it. It took me a moment, but I came to understand that it was a schedule for when each horse needed to see the farrier. From the dates recorded, I gathered that the horses' appointments tended to be staggered, with Gomer and Queen Biscuits needing an appointment every six weeks, and Thunder and Frida requiring every eight weeks. It seemed that everyone was overdue. I closed the binder, feeling my headache reach through me again. It was so much to keep track of, so many numbers to call and questions to ask. The more I thought about it, the smaller and weaker I felt. I wanted to put my hands up around the sides of my face like blinders, just as my mother would have done in this situation—hand blinders and loud humming to block out the looming, impossible tasks. Sometimes she wore an extra pair of socks, to keep her feet from freezing to the spot like a fly on glue. It was most likely this comparison that stopped me from going to Cleo and telling her that I was overwhelmed, from calling Tristan again and begging him for guidance. I was not ready to become my mother.

WITH FEBRUARY APPROACHING, Buster's hit its slow season, and Cleo decided that it would be best if I took Sundays off until business picked up again. Even Cleo could not scheme abundantly enough to keep us busy on those long, dead afternoons. She had lost some traction with the fake secession when her film student had a nervous breakdown (unrelated to their project, Cleo insisted) and had to miss a semester of school, and her fervor for tormenting the city people, the sandwich seekers, and the fad dieters had reached a certain equilibrium. It would not have been correct to say that Cleo was slowing down. Instead, it seemed to me that she was easing naturally into her new life as a charismatic widow. This calmed me, and I found that it was easier for me to stay behind on those Sundays, as I was less fearful of Cleo burning too brightly without me.

As for Jean-Remy, he was not totally out of the picture. There had been no rift, no dramatic separation, but, as far as I knew, there had not been any further plans made. I was hopeful that Cleo had gotten him out of her system, although I could not deny that there had been something comforting in having him at the house. After occupying the space so prominently—calling me Bug and having the audacity to moan loudly on his first night—he had inadvertently left an absence behind. I could not figure out the shape of it, whether it was just the absence of maleness or if it was specific to him.

On my first Sunday at the house, I slept so late that I woke up nauseated, my stomach unaccustomed to the extra hours without sugar or caffeine. I was almost frightened by how luxurious it felt to get up, to stretch even, and to totter my way to the kitchen, pawing around for a coffee filter, a spoon. How was it that normal people made coffee in the morning? The horses were angry at me for making them wait, and the two mares had taken care to hold in their urine until the moment I walked through the barn door. They let their torrents drop in tandem, boring steaming holes into the bedding. The smell had a foul, medicinal quality.

By then, the flooding in the paddock had been remedied by the gravel and then further aided by changing weather conditions that firmed up the ground. I decided that it was time to do a walking inspection of the upper paddock, to check for broken places in the fence. Yes, I would look at the spot of the incident. Yes, I would stand there and imagine that I was seeing what Howie had seen before the lights went out for good. I was also not ruling out the possibility that there would be a clue—something from that day, preserved miraculously in ice, or wedged beneath a stone. The upper paddock covered a greater area than the lower paddock, and included a long strip of field, like a runway, along the road. Farther from the road, at the tree line, there was another flat and grassy area, but the only way to reach it was by scaling a rocky incline. This was where Howie had been found and why he had been spotted so easily, laid out at an angle, as if on display. I took my hand out of my glove and touched the rock. I cannot express just how little sentimentality I felt out there, and how alone I was with my head wrapped in the wind. It was obvious that there was nothing there, that nature had no intention of preserving a man's last moments, because in nature there is no special treatment. I did wonder, however, what Howie was doing on the hill. He must have come to catch one of the horses when it did not return to the barn of its own accord. And then I wondered why he would want to catch a horse in the middle of the day, between mealtimes, when none of them could be ridden. As I walked back down, I decided that I would use my extra time on Sundays to observe the horses more closely. I would take note of who liked to walk on the incline. Who was the most stubborn about coming when called. But even the manual had stated plainly that it was Thunder that required the most caution.

THUNDER: GETS OATS FIRST, OR ELSE HELL.
THUNDER: MUST BE LED WITH SLACK—A LOT OF SLACK.
THUNDER: DOES NOT APPRECIATE COWBOY HATS OR EXTRAVAGANT TRAILING SCARVES.

It struck me how similar Howie's written account of the horses was to Tristan's stories of Cleo. Both seemed to be compulsive manifestations of love, delivered in bursts, catalogued according to mood. Tristan's words in my mind had been like the graffiti on an endless passing train: hypnotic, vivid, and sparingly informative. Knowing Cleo as I did now, I, like Tristan, would have difficulty forming a complete picture if asked to describe her. *She's fastidious about the elasticity of socks,* I might say. *Men would pay to watch her pipe custard into an éclair. She has seventeen rings in her ears: eight on one side and nine on the other.*

It was a Sunday afternoon in early February when Jean-Remy came back. I had been in the barn—I was only ever in the barn, my bedroom, or behind the counter at Buster's—filling water buckets with the hose. I had to pee, and because the weather was warmer than usual, and because I did not want the bother of turning off the hose until I was finished with my task, I decided to drop my pants and use the farthermost stall as a toilet. Horse girls do it all the time. They change their tampons in horse stalls, they take pregnancy tests. I looped the hose through the upper bars of the stall so that it was pointed into the bucket, and challenged myself to finish peeing before the water reached the fill line. I was pushing through the point of no return, when the barn door screeched open. This was not something that I was prepared for. No one ever showed up to the house—much less the barn—when Cleo was not there. I forced myself empty and stood, yanking my jeans up in the same motion, and saw Jean-Remy, already halfway up the aisle. He stopped short, and I could tell that I had startled him.

"Ah," he said, raising his eyebrows in a question that seemed also to be a sign of approval, as if whatever I had been doing with my pants down was a mark in my favor. There was something different about him, although I could not say what. It was possible that he had put on weight in the weeks that he had been away.

"What are you doing here?" I asked. I felt as though I were the one in the wrong, or that I, in being caught off guard, should be embarrassed. It reminded me of why I had disliked Jean-Remy in the first place: He shouldered his way into other people's spaces without an inkling of modesty. He placed his hand on his chest.

"Bug, I apologize. I did not know that you would be here."

"How does that make this any better?"

I had the sensation of pushing against a current, like a problematic woman who insists on taking the unpopular opinion.

"I was only searching for something," he said, his hand still on his heart. "Perhaps you can help me find it."

I took a step forward, but realized that, in pulling up my jeans, I had neglected my underwear. They remained halfway down my thighs, hobbling me. There was no way around it. I unbuttoned and shoved my hand down my pants, watching Jean-Remy watch me with mild interest.

"Where's Cleo?" I asked, sucking in to button myself once more. Jean-Remy thrust his chin forward, as if to indicate something.

"I think you—" he started to say.

"Does she even know you're here?"

"It looks like—" He walked forward, looking beyond me. There was something not quite steady about him, like he was searching for the right words to say, but could not find them. He pointed again with his chin. "You're spilling," he said. I had forgotten about my hose, and now the water was dribbling over the sides of the bucket. I quickly pinched the flow. Jean-Remy watched with amusement as I dragged the hose to the front of the barn to shut off the pump, lifting his feet exaggeratedly as the hose passed under them. It set him off-balance. He grabbed hold of a supporting beam to keep himself from falling over, while still looking at me as if the awkwardness of my task were a product of my own silliness. He was drunk.

Outside, I closed the pump and detached the hose,

shaking out the excess water so that it would not freeze inside the tube when the temperature dropped again. I took my time, wondering what, if anything, I was supposed to do. Cleo's truck was not in the driveway. Only a small, dark sedan—a Mustang that reminded me of a Matchbox car—was parked there. I coiled the hose and went back inside, where I found Jean-Remy standing where I had left him.

"Cleo doesn't know you're here," I said. He shrugged.

"I wanted to surprise her," he said. This did not make sense. Didn't he know that she never set foot in the barn? He seemed to know what I was thinking and said, "It's good that you are here. You can help me find it."

"Find what?"

He let go of the beam.

"That's the thing. I don't know what to call it." He held his hands out about two feet apart, as if demonstrating length. "If I wanted to correct a large animal, without being too cruel. If I wanted to send a message." He smiled at me. He was darker beneath the eyes, which was not ugly, but tantalizing, in a Disney villain kind of way. Still, I hated him. I wanted to hate him, and I flexed the core of myself tighter in an effort to keep hold of that hatred.

"You want a whip?" I asked. His smile broadened. I squeezed harder within myself, trying to extinguish the pleasure that his approval brought me. I went to the dusty corner behind the stacks of hay, where my shrouded Vespa was parked, and produced a long dressage whip, shaking off the cobwebs that it had collected. It wasn't for hitting the horses. The idea was to strike invisible pressure points in the air, or to tap the horse lightly, to show him where and with what speed to move. I knew, through the manual, that Howie had used it to break up quarrels between the horses, they being less afraid of the bite of the whip itself and more wary of the spatial anarchy that it created when waved about. I gave it to Jean-Remy, who straightened like a lion tamer the instant it was in his hand. He stared down the length of it and shook his head.

"Nope," he said. "I'm looking for a closer correction."

We both liked the sound of that.

"I'd better call Cleo," I told him. "It's weird that you're here."

Jean-Remy came toward me, still holding the whip. I knew that flinching or moving backward would tell him something. Standing my ground would tell him something too. I inhaled sharply and took one step back. I did this almost involuntarily, because it was the choice that I thought was more flattering to him. Despite the ball of hatred inside me, I wanted him to like me.

"Oh, Bug," he said. He dropped the whip. "I forget sometimes how young you are."

Did he know that this would anger me? Yes, he knew.

"You should call her," he said. "If that makes you feel better."

JEAN-REMY FOLLOWED ME into Cleo's kitchen, where I dialed the café. I watched him lean against the sink, inspecting his nails.

"Buster's," Cleo said brightly.

I tried to explain the situation, which was awkward with Jean-Remy right there, holding himself calmly—almost proudly—like a tough boy who had been called to the principal's office. He had not removed his boots. They had left gleaming little half-moons on the linoleum.

"Oh, Drew-Baby," Cleo cooed. I did not like her sudden softness. "I'm so sorry. I should have explained it to you better."

"So, you knew he was here?" It was awful to admit to my confusion, but I had no choice at that point but to get the facts.

"Well, no," she said. I could hear the café sounds behind her, and wondered if there was a line of people watching her, if she and I were both choosing our words carefully in front of an audience. It was perhaps the first time I had ever considered the pros of having a cell phone.

"I didn't know that he would show up there. Or today, even. I should have told him not to scare you."

"I'm not scared."

Jean-Remy took the phone. He tucked the receiver between his cheek and his shoulder and stood so close I could smell him. He was a cologne man. Beneath that, there was the smell of his pores, airing the alcohol in his bloodstream. It was like the sweet, slimy water beneath cut flowers.

"Hey-o," he said into the phone. "I was just making a pit stop." He jumped his eyebrows at me. "I didn't know our little Bug would be here."

After a moment, he pushed the phone back at me.

"She wants to talk to you," he said. This time, he left the kitchen.

"Drew-Hunny," Cleo said. "Jean-Remy and I have an agreement. What might seem like an intrusion to you is—well, more like a contract. I never meant to bring you into it."

"You don't have to be so patronizing. It's not a big deal." I didn't want to talk about it anymore. It was clear now that I had overreacted and that, in calling Cleo, I had been ratting myself out, not Jean-Remy. Whatever they were doing was beyond the scope of my stunted imagination. They couldn't have made it more obvious.

"Don't pout, Bug." Jean-Remy came back into the kitchen after I had hung up on Cleo. He placed his hand on my shoulder and squeezed. I knew that if I shook him off, then it would further confirm that I was bitter. If I let him rub me, then it would confirm that I had no backbone. For a minute I was truly miserable.

"What did she say?" he asked.

"She said you can stay till she gets back." I pulled away and pointed to a cabinet. "There's wine in there. I'm going to take a shower."

I left him in the kitchen and went upstairs to the bathroom. Something didn't feel right, but I figured it was because I had looked foolish in the end, and not, as I had hoped, loyal. I had wanted Cleo to see that I would tell her anything, alert her to any problem, suspicion, or act of sneakiness, like a lapdog. But, like a lapdog, I could not tell the difference between a burglar and a regular guy looking for a riding crop to fulfil his spanking kink. The shower spurted a weak stream, which grew stronger as I adjusted the temperature. The rules of the shower were this: If I wanted it to be scalding hot, I had to give up the joys of water pressure. If I wanted a steady jet, then I had to give up the pleasure of nearly burning my skin off. That day, I needed a molten rebirth, so I stepped under the trickle and danced around so that it covered the whole of my body. I thought: Cleo is immersed in something that does not involve me, where there are strange rules that she does not want to burden me with. It felt like a cold room in my heart. A walk-in freezer. *STOP. YOU ARE NOT*

LOCKED IN. Yes, actually, I wanted to say, *I am.* I had a cavernous capacity for loneliness, it seemed, and a staggering inability to form close bonds. *A poor design,* my mother would say. I could see her sweeping crumbs into the crack between the counter and the stove. That crack was more fulfilled than I would ever be.

JEAN-REMY PREPARED DINNER that night, but even with the candles lit, it failed to achieve the same hominess as the last meal we'd had together. Cleo squirmed with sympathy for me, checking in with her eyes across the table and reacting overenthusiastically to anything that I said. She talked for most of the dinner about the fake secession. It had gained momentum again, after the owner of a souvenir store downtown had agreed to sell pins depicting the green-and-blue flag (Who made the pins? Cleo wouldn't say, but I guessed that it was one of her art student followers). A local guy who fancied himself a kind of guerilla journalist had purchased one and written about the conspiracy on his personal webpage, which, until then, had been mostly dedicated to protecting gun rights in Vermont (where they had never been in peril). The page had somehow gotten so much traffic that it crashed.

"He sounds unhinged," I said. "Is that the kind of crowd you want to arouse? Militia dudes?"

Cleo sniffed. It was obviously not her business if things got out of hand.

"Cleo arouses everyone," Jean-Remy said. "She can't help it."

I rolled my eyes like a teenager. Cleo and Jean-Remy made me feel infantilized, which led me to react in ways that were immature, which led to further infantilization. It was a frustrating pattern. Cleo continued on about work, dropping nicknames of regulars that I was sure Jean-Remy had never heard of, but he nodded and chuckled all the same, as if in on every joke. I watched their faces in the hammered gold of the candlelight. It was all an act, I understood, for my benefit. Behind the façade, I could sense their disappointment; whatever plans they had laid that had led Jean-Remy into the barn that afternoon had been dashed for reasons that I did not quite understand. All I knew was that I was somehow to blame for it.

That night, the alcohol seemed to have a less exuberant effect. Jean-Remy slowly developed a lazy eye that I had not noticed before, and Cleo let out a series of long sighs that I could not interpret. I guessed that they wanted to be left alone, so I offered to clear the table and started to wash the dishes, trying to convey permission, not rudeness, through my turned back. I heard them move into the living room, the aural pinprick of a record being dropped, and then I turned on the faucet, willing my curiosity away.

Lately, I had been up to something that even I would deem questionable, but it seemed to be holding me accountable, in a way, for something that I could not even describe. I had been emailing Byron on purpose.

Byron,
I confess, I am not a very good detective. All this time I have been trying to gather clues, but then I forget them right away. Maybe you can help me collect my thoughts. Here is what I know:

Time between accident and death: 72 hours
Cause of death: internal bleeding and a bruised heart. A bruised heart!

Visible marks on the body: unknown (by me, at least)

Length of time between incident and hospitalization: estimated 30 minutes to an hour.

Name of 911 caller: Reuben Woodstock Jr., a landscaper/handyman.

Horse that seems the guiltiest: Gomer, but that's only because he poops in his water bucket and then gets remorseful.

Thanks for caring,
Drew

Dearest Drew,
It's so good to hear from you. I remember, when you first started working for me, how you would sometimes stop in front of the glass cabinet where we kept (and still keep) the rare books. You tried not to be obvious, but I could see how your eyes wandered to your own reflection, checking out your profile as you walked past, stack of books in hand. There was a fluency to it that I still think about. A flash of approval, of insecurity, and surprise. Delicious.
Your eager servant,
B

Hey there Champ,
I'm wondering if it would make me seem like a psycho if I asked the farrier to examine the horses' feet the next time he is here. I know that's his job, but maybe there's something he can see due to his expertise, a physical clue that would suggest minor trauma to the hoof. Surely kicking a man hard enough to kill him would leave a trace?

I remember some girl from high school telling me that a dentist can tell if you've recently had a dick in your mouth, because it bruises the back of your throat. I've been seeing the same dentist since I was five. Did he know the day would come that I would break his heart in this way?
Thanks for nothing,
D

The wonderful thing about Byron was that he was so delusionally self-centered that I could write anything and he would receive it without argument. And I was so delusionally self-centered that I found his enthusiasm and quick response time encouraging. It was like telling your troubles to a dog hell-bent on humping your leg; the love was misguided, but it was still, in a primitive way, companionship. So far, I had not received another unsolicited email attachment, but I suspected that it was only a matter of time.

BETWEEN THE SOUNDS of the running sink and the jazz playing on the stereo, I did not hear Cleo come up behind me. She placed her hand on the small of my back, and I could feel the warmth of her body next to mine. I scrubbed the plate in my hand.

"People want the same thing every day," she said into my ear. "They line up and look for the same thing." Something about the quiet pitch of her voice made me drop the clean plate back into the dirty dishwater. I held my breath as her hand found its way around my waist, her cheek lowering to my shoulder.

"What I want is a real surprise, but no one around here has any imagination at all."

"And Jean-Remy?" I asked.

"At least he's got ideas."

"Like a riding crop?" I couldn't hide the skepticism in my voice.

"No, Drew-Baby. Not a riding crop."

"But you won't tell me. You think I'm a child." I was suddenly angry at her for treating me so delicately. She never had before. Not at Buster's. Not when we had guests at the house. I got drunk and stoned and talked shit as much as anyone. My frustration rose through my chest. I felt suffocated by Cleo's body so close to mine, and I thought that I was going to push her off me. It was almost the same fight instinct that had gripped me in my altercation with the Scoops Woman. I saw my arms lift, shoving Cleo's hand away, grasping it with my still-wet and soapy hand. At the same time, I knew Jean-Remy was in the next room and that he would inevitably be spending the night. This thought was comforting, because it meant that there would be no aftermath of my actions; Cleo would have to pretend like it didn't happen. I had both of her wrists now, held tightly by her sides. I felt strong and masculine, and because Cleo was so much smaller and softer than I was, and because the candles had made the kitchen fibrous and dark, this illusion took hold of me completely. I kissed her on the mouth—not aggressively, but also not allowing her any room to reciprocate. Her response was not the point. When I pulled away, I looked at her, hard, making sure that she could see me and see that I was not a child. I could be surprising too. Then I released her.

Later, when they started making sounds in the bedroom, I listened without shame. I sat on my mattress with my back against the wall, the door beside me open to Howie's office, and the office door open to the hallway. I had a wine bottle with me that Jean-Remy had abandoned half full in the living room, and I drank straight from the mouth of it. Not to get drunk this time. Not to bury the remorse of the day—for in each day for the last month, there had been some slick pearl of remorse, so much so that they were losing their rarity—but as if to feed something that had been unleashed inside me that I did not want to lose track of, not just yet. Kissing Cleo had changed my chemistry. I had seen, in a flash, the answer to the riddle of how I was meant to want her. It was subtle as the sunlight threading itself through the glass doorknob, revealing its interior. I saw how it might be possible to have her without the world imploding in on itself. And then I lost it. The answer was gone as quickly as it had appeared.

Shut up, Jean-Remy said. The rest, even with both doors open, was consumed by the space between us, as if the air had chewed and muddled it. I wondered what Cleo had said and why Jean-Remy wanted her quiet. After I had kissed her, she'd looked over her shoulder toward the living room. When it was clear that we had not been seen, she'd turned back to me, eyes narrowed. I knew that she had no choice but to look at me like I was in trouble, although it told me nothing about whether she had liked the kiss, or if she would want another one. I wasn't offering, that much was clear. She rejoined Jean-Remy in the living room, and I did not see her again. They went upstairs shortly after. It was Jean-Remy who ducked into the kitchen to tell me goodnight, his lips stained, his beautiful face flushed.

"Make sure to blow the candles out," he told me.

What Cleo wanted was someone to flip the narrative on her for once. Jean-Remy would find her on a day that she was alone at the café, cleaning up after closing. He would sneak in through the back door, his approach concealed by Hank Williams or Patsy Cline—if this were a movie, the director would choose "Crazy" for the sultry juxtaposition. The rope would be real, the knots would be carefully practiced; bruises were permissible, but pinched nerves were not. The most important thing would be that he look and speak to her as if he were driven wild, wishing powerfully that he were not a monster, but being a monster nonetheless. That was what Jean-Remy had to offer: his ability to be kind and erratically gentle while still being the assailant. They did not use the word *rape.* Rape had no place in what they were doing, although it was the inspiration. I wondered what else in life followed this formula.

They had, in a sense, been planning the first encounter for years, but they did not succeed in making it happen until the beginning of March. Jean-Remy could not just show up the weekend after he'd walked in on me peeing in the barn, because that would be like a game of rock paper scissors, where you anticipate your opponent's move based on what they've just thrown down. Scissors comes after scissors to try to psyche you out. Rape fantasy comes after failed rape fantasy attempt. No, he would have to be smarter than that.

They had been through many scenarios already, by way of the chat room. Cleo, at first, had believed that their chats were all she needed. She liked how their stories could pan out over a course of a day or two, like a game of *Choose*

Your Own Adventure. Jean-Remy was a good writer with a knack for details:

> *JR: I tie your hands behind your back. Your ankles, too, but I am worried about your bare knees on the cement floor, so I bring you a folded towel.*
> *CBB: You're considerate. It makes me want to do something nice for you, against my better judgment.*
> *JR: What nice things do you have in mind?*
> *CBB: Showing you that I'm afraid. I can tell that's what you want.*

I don't actually know what was written, only that it went on and on. I imagine that it fed into Cleo's need to scheme, while also providing her an outlet for her frustrations with Howie. While her husband was in the barn with his rescue horses, she was in front of the computer, typing wildly, waiting for Jean-Remy's reply, thinking about what she would come up with next to drive him crazy. They did not send pictures. It could have been that they considered themselves above the game of genital peekaboo, like writers who would not deign to slip into a genre that they considered lowbrow. I could see Jean-Remy approaching cybersex pretentiously, maybe sipping brandy, wearing a robe. Would he touch himself? Would Cleo? I wondered what I would have done in her place, and decided that I would have written ten volumes' worth of smut before I masturbated in front of a computer screen.

I will never know whose idea it was to meet up in person, whether Cleo's or Jean-Remy's, just as I will never know the details of that first successful encounter in March. Cleo had warned me weeks earlier not to be worried if she did not come home one night.

"I can assure you that I will never be worried again," I told her. "I'm still trying to live down the last time."

"You're a good girl," she said sweetly. In this way, we continued to flirt with each other, without the danger of arriving anywhere. A treadmill of sexual banter. We did not talk about the kiss, but I could tell that it was still between us, something that neither of us knew how to cash in. That was fine with me.

Howdy Partner,
The farrier came by. He had nice arms and wore real leather chaps over his jeans. He brought a Lab mix named Porky that plopped down on the barn floor and ate the hoof trimmings. The dog made them look appetizing, like they were beef jerky. I asked the farrier if he knew Howie, and he said, "Sure." Have you noticed how men around here pronounce that word? As in—Sure do, ma'am! Like, they're both happy and annoyed that you asked??
Anyway, he said that Howie kept the horses on a tight schedule, and then looked up at me over the hoof that he was filing. I think the look was meant to imply that I was not doing as good a job as Howie. It cut me. It really did. I'm trying so hard to be good.
When I brought Thunder out for him, the farrier spent a while on his back hoof. He told me that Thunder would be ready for shoes again in a few weeks. He whistled for Porky, who was mopping up the hoof shavings like they were coconut flakes.
What do you think he meant by "ready for shoes"?

Oh, Darling,
I can see how good you are trying to be. Don't fall for a man in chaps. Don't whittle yourself into a cliché.
Patiently yours,
B

Byron—
I looked through the loose papers in the back of the manual, and there is a note that says THUNDER: HAS BEEN KNOWN TO THROW A SHOE. This is it, right? Proof that he is a kicker? What else could that mean?
PS—I also found a sticky note that said IF THE HORSES GET LONELY, PLAY THEM "HOWIE'S GRAPES." Wtf?
PPS—That stands for "what the fuck."

Cleo tattooed Howie's name on her wrist, above a simple line drawing of a skull. She'd taken a lunch break to get it done and walked back into the café afterward, ripping off the bandage in excitement.

"Check it out," she said to me, and held her hand up like she was swearing an oath, so the area of the tattoo was visible. Her skin looked like it was sweating blood, especially inside the pale circles that depicted the eyes of the skull. "How metal is that?" she asked. Then she turned to show the line of customers across the counter, one of whom was the health inspector, who took points off our grade and told us to get hats or else.

THAT EVENING, after settling the horses for the night, I walked into the house to find Cleo seated at the kitchen table. Her teeth were set to scheming mode, and in front of her, on the place setting, there was a plain baseball cap and an electric razor.

"Choose your poison," she said.

I approached the table. The temperature outside had dropped once again, and there had been days of bitter, sideways snow that never stuck anywhere, unless you counted the inside of your bones. I had my arms crossed around my body.

"Am I allowed to choose some hot tea first?" I asked.

"No."

I regarded the two objects. It was not difficult to see what kind of game this was, especially after our recent run-in with the health inspector.

"Which one are you choosing?" I asked. Cleo clucked and shook her head.

"You'll find out after."

"You seriously want me to shave my head?" My hand went up to grasp my hair. It had never been impressive—stylists never gasped in approval when I shook my braid loose for them to shampoo—but it had also never betrayed me. My hair was shoulder-length and just a little wavy. It became greasy within a predictable time frame and grew at a rate of about half an inch per month. I was grateful that my hair stayed behind my ears when I tucked it, and I had never considered doing anything differently with it—bangs, for example—for fear that it would become high-maintenance. I supposed that shaving it off would be zero-maintenance, but I had never thought about it. Plenty of women looked ferocious and high fashion with bald heads, but what if I looked scary? What if there were lumps? I picked up the clippers to see whether Cleo's face would reveal approval or disappointment, but she did not even blink.

"Is that your choice?" she asked. She shifted as if she were about to stand up.

"No—" I dropped the clippers. "I'm sorry," I said. "I don't think I can." Cleo shrugged and pushed the hat across the table toward me.

"There was only one hat anyway," she said. I watched her rise and go to the sink, where she began to take out her hoop earrings and place them in a line on the counter. She pulled the scarf off her head, and it fell in a loop onto the floor behind her. Her only mirror was the window above the sink, which cast her dark reflection. I watched Cleo watch me through the dark world of the window while she hacked through thick sections of hair with a sharp pair of kitchen shears. I knew it was too late to change my mind, so I watched, allowing her the triumph. Later, when Cleo had gone upstairs to shower, I parsed through the scattered clumps on the floor and selected a lock of ringlets, tying it together with a piece of string and putting it in my pocket. I would wear my stupid hat tomorrow, pert ponytail strung through the back like a flag of cowardice.

BUT THE NEXT day was a Sunday, so I stayed behind while Cleo debuted her new avant-garde look to The People. She was lovelier than ever—I already could not remember what she had looked like with hair. Long-haired Cleo was outdated, like a heavy, old couch. New Cleo was fresh and clever, with eyes big and round enough to soak up the world.

I called her right before lunch.

"Who has fainted, and who has proposed marriage?" I asked her.

"Neither, but there's been a conjunction," she whispered into the receiver. "Buttload Guy and Shoot Your Wad Guy are here at the same time again. It's like a planetary alignment."

"It's good luck, for sure."

AND MAYBE FOR Cleo it was, because that was the day Jean-Remy chose to ambush her after closing. When she did not come home, I wondered what Jean-Remy's reaction to Cleo's baldness would be, if it was a deterrent to predatory men—even pretend predatory men—when a woman did not have hair to grab. I felt for my own thick ponytail and tugged at it, remorseful once again for my inability to part with it. Was it vanity? I wondered. Or did my insecurities run deeper? I decided that the worst thing to do would be to wait around anxiously for Cleo to come home, so I made myself a box of mac and cheese, reveling in the sodium high that I was so rarely permitted to have those days. When I was done, I asked myself: What does a young woman do when she is alone? It had been so long since the solitary days of Nico's basement, the meandering scooter rides, all those hopeful novels with dignified covers that I might have finished if I were a different type of person. When left to her own devices, my mother became practically baroque with good taste and self-discipline. I imagined her dancing in her living room, record spinning, arms weightless, her neck a timeless symbol of grace. I, too, could live my moments clean,

I thought, and I picked through Cleo's record collection, searching for the music that fit me like Lucinda Williams fit Cleo, like the *Amélie* soundtrack fit adorable girls who bought flowers and never looked in the mirror. The collection was more eclectic than I had expected, reaching from the lush, existential emergency that was Bach to Frank Zappa. Maybe I was *Hot Rats.* Maybe that was me. A hallucinogenic hotel lobby. The stretch of bubblegum on the bottom of a platform hooker boot. I nudged the needle to "Willie the Pimp" and sunk into the couch, letting the mess seep into me like liquid chaos, like being licked by a Picasso painting.

CLEO WAS BACK the next morning. The whine of the shower woke me right before my alarm. I was surprised to see that Jean-Remy was not with her. There were no traces of him in Cleo's bedroom, just the bare triangle of sheet where her little body had hopped in and hopped back out sometime during the early hours before dawn.

We rode together in the truck, Cleo's mouth stretching in one endless yawn.

"Get the coffee into me," she said.

I studied her arms pushing against the steering wheel, searching between the shapes of her tattoos for evidence that she had been consensually victimized. I could find nothing. She leaned toward me, eyes still on the road ahead.

"Go on, I can see you staring," she said.

"What do you mean?" I was jumpy, thinking that she had read my mind.

"I know you want to rub it."

I put my hand on her head and scratched the bottom of my palm with her stubble. She was right. It was better than sand between your toes. Better than that first sip of coffee.

"You can stop now," she said, and I laughed, as if nothing bothered me. As if I knew how to stop any of this.

7

OF ALL MONTHS, March is the emotional abuser. It promises sweet, warm sunrays and flashes spring crocuses at you as fresh and slick as newborn bunnies, then it snatches it all away. It gives you twelve-inch-deep potholes full of slush, winds that could skin a bull. Getting through March as a child with wet sneakers, and as a scantily dressed high school student who liked to sneak outside for a smoke, was one thing. I had never endured this time of year as a farm girl. It was enough to make me want to reevaluate my entire life plan. I had skipped college for *this*? Freezing my fingers off to pick burrs out of a horse's butt crack? Fishing dead rats out of an icy trough? I was starting to sympathize with the autumn girls at Grandview Stable, who were known for their cute sweaters and intolerance to harsh weather. Maybe what we had deemed weakness was really sanity all along.

The People seemed to be suffering the most, even though many of them were lifelong New Englanders who had seen more Marches than I had. One would think that this would toughen a person, but their reserves were low and all they wanted was meat. Their new ringleader was a woman in her thirties who we called, very simply, the Carnivore. She seemed to think that she could break us by ordering a chicken sandwich every day, when no such sandwich existed. Her attitude was aggressively chummy; she was the kind of woman who grabs hold of your arm the first time you meet her and scream-whispers into your ear, "We're friends now!" She looked like Katy Perry, if Katy Perry were infected with a virus that made her want to bite through people's throats.

"Cleo, I'm ready for that chicken sandwich!" she sang. "I know you want to make it for me." The Carnivore had unnaturally straight teeth that clicked when she smiled. She wore blush on her cheeks that made her look like she had been sprinting. I held my hand to my neck.

"We don't serve animal flesh here, ma'am," I said. She laughed, unruffled, and ordered a tall latte to go.

"So, a large?" I asked her. This was my own stubborn game: refusing to convert Starbucks sizes—refusing to even acknowledge that Starbucks existed. It drove the city people wild. They thought they had landed in Amish country. The Carnivore tilted her head and said the first truly mean thing to me: "You know, someday you won't be young and cute anymore, and you'll actually have to think before you speak."

I mouthed a silent *What the fuck* at Cleo as the Carnivore was leaving, but Cleo had bigger things to worry about.

"I'm thinking of taking you off Mondays," she said, carrying her ledger, as if she'd just been running numbers.

"That's fine," I said. "Mondays blow."

"In addition to Sundays."

"Oh," I said. I had not known business was that bad. I wondered what I would do with two days off, stranded at the house. March was still too icy and cold to get the scooter running, and Cleo would need the truck, unless I drove her into town and picked her up. Would I be forced to get a hobby? Cleo sensed my distress and assured me that by May the café would be hopping again.

"Maybe you could look into online classes," she suggested. "Or you could come into town with me, drink free coffee and—"

"Just watch you work?"

She sighed. Her hair had already sprouted into a dark, spiky crown. Not long enough to be a pixie cut, but not quite G. I. Jane anymore. She must have known that I would have watched her work all day without compensation. I wondered if she finally knew me well enough to pity me.

"I'll figure it out," I said. I would be twenty-two in July, and I hadn't even thought about the possibility of furthering my education. I knew it was what was expected of me—we couldn't all have uncles to take us under their wing like George. The problem was not so much the money anymore, but that my days behind the counter had split the world in half. On one side there were the Workers—the Drews and Cleos and Tristans—and on the other, The People. The People tended to be educated, but more often than not, they had no perception of how they appeared, no self-awareness whatsoever. Soon enough, they all morphed into the same giant face, peering grotesquely into the canary cage of the "uneducated," spraying us with their spit. I lost sight of why I was supposed to want what they had.

Cleo saw that she had depressed me, so she brought me toasted banana bread with peanut butter and told me to sit down. I did as I was told, taking the armchair by the front window, from which I had a clear view of the sidewalk where a woman wearing a Dolphins puffer coat over a nightie was hunting for cigarette butts. I wanted to give her a bouquet of cigarettes—or better yet, a Frankenstein cigarette, stitched together so that it was three feet long. I imagined what someone like Quad Bitch would say about that, she who had probably never allowed herself the pleasure of something foul and obscene and perfectly absurd.

I was still sitting by the window when four o'clock rolled around. We had not seen a customer since two-thirty, so Cleo brought the flag in and locked the door. When I stood to start packing up the pastry case, she motioned for me to sit and took the armchair opposite mine. I expected Cleo to pick up the conversation where we had left off, but she just looked at her hands, folded on her lap, and was silent. Outside, the street was deserted, except for a few parked cars and a high school cross-country team running up the center of the road. The boys had floppy haircuts and ran with a casual, protective air. The girls stared ahead with knifelike determination.

"I need something in my hands," Cleo said, laughing at herself. Later, I would not understand why she chose to make the proposition there, framed in the picture window, when she could have waited until the warm lighting of home, after we were both good and drunk. Perhaps she wanted to catch me while I was still sober or in a setting that was technically public, where I would feel less pressured. She came back with a small mug of tea, her hands wrapped snugly around it, and asked me if I would be willing to try something a little crazy.

Cleo assured me that I would be the one with all the control. That was the beauty of it. As she continued to explain, and as it became more evident that I was not going to get up and run (where would I go?), her voice loosened. The nervousness that I had detected in the beginning of our conversation was replaced by the faintest stirring of excitement. She reminded me of a woman voicing a long-held dream aloud for the first time, experiencing the snowballing sensation of *this might really happen* mixed with practiced caution. There were details that I would have never thought to consider. The quality of rope, my own fitness level—how long could I kneel on the floor?—and the acts that I would permit myself to witness. Lastly, a safe word, which we would agree on later. When she was finished, she asked me if I had any questions.

"Do I need my mom's written permission?" I asked. I didn't mean to sound skeptical, but I couldn't figure out how any of it was supposed to be exciting after all the boxes were checked, each section signed and dated.

"Think of it like a roller coaster. You're not having any fun if you don't know, with one hundred percent certainty, that every piece of it is bolted together."

Cleo had a point.

"Okay," I said, but she put her hand up to shush me.

"I want you to think about it. Really think about it." She stood. "Let's get this shop wrapped up and go home."

THE NEXT DAY was Sunday, and I was left at the house to make my decision—although Cleo would never have pressured me like that, and I am certain there was no expectation for me to have an answer for her by the time she came home. But that was, of course, how I saw things.

And the fact that I had already made up my mind did not mean that there were not many angles to consider. There were so many angles to consider, beginning with the question that I probably should have started and ended with, but chose instead to treat as though it were irrelevant: Did I want to do it? The question of wanting struck me as foreign. It was like asking myself whether I wanted to be alive. I suppose that I did—want to be alive, that is—but I was not thrilled with many aspects of it, some of which downright terrified me.

I woke to the sound of sleet on the roof. There is nothing easy or exciting about sleet, except that it is rare enough to spark wonder in the meagerest way. It's also somewhat unrealistic—this stuff like glass beads pouring from the sky. You can hold it. It doesn't melt in your hand. It bites. I laced up Howie's big boots and walked through the sleet to the barn, the whole world stirred up like the inside of a maraca. I thought: The problem with being horny in winter is that it's cold. As if that statement could sum up my life. As if that was the one design flaw in all of this.

It was even louder inside the barn than outside, and I was grateful for the white noise of the sleet falling on the tin roof, the staccato kicking of hooves against wood, the bucket pouring of the mares, who still held their piss for me on Sundays. Was it love, or was it resentment? All the lines were blurred. What worried me the most was that all aspects of my life were beginning to feel inevitable, and wasn't I too young for that? At the same time, everything seemed like a contradiction. If, for example, I said no to Cleo, then wasn't I just clinging to the illusion of having control? If I said yes, then wouldn't I be flirting with the same illusion? I don't think Cleo meant to leave me on the verge of an existential abyss, but there I was.

After feeding the horses, I went into the paddock to break the ice on the water trough, but found that the surface of the water was a lovely, stiff slush. I made the mistake of stirring it with my bare hand, carving a path as if my hand were a small ship navigating the Arctic. My hand became numb almost immediately, and no amount of breathing on it or banging it against my leg seemed to help. I slipped into Thunder's stall and warmed myself in the crease where his front leg met his belly. He quivered, but allowed it. I had always appreciated the way horses can control the surface area of their bodies by the square inch. More experienced riders, I knew, had a sophisticated understanding of a horse's anatomy, their aim being not to merely sit on the horse without falling off, but to bring all parts of the animal into balance. When I thought about this—the prospect of not only being commanded, but of also being held firmly together—I found that some of my fear dissolved. I walked back into the house and picked up the kitchen phone.

"I want to do it," I said.

To which Cleo said, "Let's talk about it when I get home."

WE DID NOT talk about it. Cleo arrived late, after a harrowing drive over the slick roads. She fell in a heap in front of the woodstove, exhausted, and I brought a blanket to her, wrapping it around her shoulders as if she were too weak to do it herself.

"Some guy tried to teach me the etymology of *bunghole*," she whimpered.

"Shh," I said, hugging her from behind. "You're safe now."

THE SAFE WORD was "tower." I came up with it myself, and was pleased to see Jean-Remy nod with approval. *Tower* was strong but modest, like the name of a rock band that you are proud to know. The three of us sat around the kitchen table while Jean-Remy showed me the rope that he would use, demonstrating how the knots would feel secure, but they would all have a quick-release. I understood from working with horses the concept of quick-release knots, so I nodded astutely. He was wearing a black sweater over black corduroy pants, accented by a long white scarf. He looked very attractive, but it was possible that nothing about him had changed and I was seeing him in a different light. It was the light of having been newly accepted. *Chosen.* It's true that I felt chosen by Cleo and Jean-Remy, even though I knew that their options for a third party were slim to nonexistent. During this strangely formal tutorial, Cleo was quiet. It could have been that she felt, finally, that someone else was doing the scheming. Maybe that was part of the appeal for her: She needed someone to take charge, but, because she was Cleo, she required higher stakes, intricate planning, and an aspect of danger. The danger part was what I was having trouble understanding. How were we going to uphold the illusion of risk when Jean-Remy was there in his scarf and corduroys, rubbing a swatch of rope on my arm to show me how soft it was? I didn't dare ask. I decided this was further confirmation that there was something unnatural about me; I was frustrated by all the precautions. It was like being forced to watch a corny sex-ed video before the act itself, rendering everything sterile as if under the inspection of a chaperone. My favorite kind of sex was the kind where I was least present. The best sex of my young life was when I felt as though I were watching myself from the other side of a screen door. So when Jean-Remy asked me how I felt about words like *cock* and *pussy*, I wanted to tell him that my opinion was really none of my business. I did say that, in fact:

"My opinion is really none of my business."

He touched my chin.

"You would prefer I stick to the correct anatomical terms?"

I ducked my head away from his hand, glancing sideways at Cleo. Did she mind that Jean-Remy had touched me? But she didn't mind, because she was the one who had asked me to be part of this in the first place. I had to keep reminding myself that I was part of it now, and to be grateful for that. When I did not answer him right away, Jean-Remy continued: "Penis and vagina? Anus?"

"Whose anus?"

"Not your anus, Bug," Cleo said gently.

"No," I said. "No, I don't like those words."

Jean-Remy opened his hands as if to say *See? You do have opinions.*

When it was time for him to leave, he gave us each a stiff hug. It was my first time being that close to him, and I felt my body, where it was pressed to his, doing a quick and involuntary scan. *Yes*, said the results of the scan, *okay.* Whatever scent he was wearing had a layered quality to it. Lofty and animalistic at the same time: if celestial beings had BO. Sometimes even now, although very rarely, I will pass a stranger wearing something similar, and my body will light up like a map, alerting me to all the points where the screws are still rattling.

Observing the horses wasn't going as I had planned. I couldn't see them well enough from inside the house, and if I stood by the gate, they lined up along the fence, expecting that I was there to feed them carrot stubs. I suspected that I liked the idea of observation much better than its reality. Horses were beautiful, but they spent a lot of time standing still, munching hay, grouping together for warmth. What, I wondered, had I been expecting to see? Was I waiting for one of them to visit the scene of the crime like a serial killer? I decided to busy myself in Howie's office, which had been gathering dust for the last few months and was beginning to feel like a graveyard whenever I walked through it. It was a bardo of outdated technology, yellow notepads, and file cabinets. The books were mostly about business, which I found to be a depressing subject. No doubt these books had helped Cleo get Buster's up and running, but there were inside details about the café that I did not want to think about. Sure, I was privy to her cult-worthy French onion soup recipe, but I did not want to know how much a bulk order of plastic coffee lids cost. I wanted to be completely ignorant of matters of inventory. That kind of knowledge threatened to turn me fully Buddhist. I stacked the business books neatly on the shelves beneath the dormer window, every now and then checking outside to see if the horses had moved from their pile of hay in the lower paddock. So far, they had not. There were dead stink bugs and some husks of yellowjackets around the window frame that I brushed into my hand and brought to the garbage can. Next, I tidied up Howie's desk. It revealed little about him, except that he struggled with carpal tunnel (as evidenced by a wristband in the top drawer) and that he either had a cocaine habit or liked to drink Alka-Seltzer at the keyboard. I told myself that I wasn't snooping, because I did not care about what I saw. A snoop, in my opinion, is someone who searches, and I was merely dusting, stacking, and letting my eyeballs land where they wanted to, naturally. My engagement with Howie's belongings only became active when I found the tape. A brown cassette with a handwritten label: HOWIE'S GRAPES.

"What on earth?" I actually said this aloud. There was no way that I was going to slide this back in the drawer and forget about it. Aside from the tape deck in Cleo's truck, the only other option was an ancient, dust-choked portable radio out in the barn. It had metal buttons and a long, retractable antenna. I went to find it right away.

There had been a similar radio—although sleeker—at Grandview Stable that the summer girls had permanently tuned in to the country music station. No one, under any circumstance, was allowed to move it from its position on top of the hay, because that was the only place in the barn where the signal was clear. Even after the summer girls left, I did not touch it. And I did not let on to Diane and Aurora that music was even an option. I'd had enough of country. I found Howie's radio on a shelf in the feed room and wiped the dust away, hoping the batteries were still good and that the spatter of molasses over the plastic cassette window was only a cosmetic problem. The tape sunk in, the door clapped into place, and a quavering male voice filled the room like the voice of a poet. *In the roads where the teams moved, where the wheels milled the ground and the hooves of the horses beat the ground, the dirt crust broke and the dust formed.* I am not sure what I had been expecting, but it wasn't this. I listened further, feeling strangely out of my element and just as strangely transfixed. *Every moving thing lifted the dust into the air.* I had heard this before. Images of a bright green campus came to mind. A lawn rolled out to meet a brick building with slim, arrogant windows. Me, sweating behind my knees, clutching a bag of books as I ran toward the doorway, late again. *A gentle wind followed the rain clouds, driving them on northward, a wind that softly clashed the drying corn.* It was Steinbeck. And I hadn't read these words since those two weeks in summer at the young writers' conference, when I had been assigned *The Grapes of Wrath* to read in my sweltering dorm room. I had thought then: How am I, a stupid girl of seventeen, expected to say anything groundbreaking about this text? I did not understand that the expectation wasn't originality as much as it was a shared sense of worship. Unworthiness. Devotion. Suddenly there was a sound at the side door. I stopped the tape. Would Jean-Remy be here already? For a moment, I couldn't move. I hadn't expected to be so anxious, for my nervousness to feel so much like stage fright. The sound came again. Two knocks. I walked slowly down the aisle toward the wooden door. Maybe Cleo had a point about her roller coaster analogy: The body could still be thrilled, convinced—deceived—even when the brain knew better. But when I opened the door, I found all four of the horses standing there, looking expectantly at me.

"Oh, you poor things," I said, and reached out my hand to stroke them. For I understood then that it had been Howie's voice on the tape.

There were times when I wanted to ask Cleo when did she think it would happen. Would we be expected to snap into character immediately, or would there be time to prepare? What if I couldn't take any of it seriously? What if I laughed and ruined everything?

In this way, the situation was only real to me through my insecurities about it. For many days, I imagined how it would feel when Jean-Remy came for us—what he would look like, if he would speak differently—but it was as if my mind were incapable of holding focus. Therefore, it would not be right to say that I forgot about it, only that I forgot to believe in it, the same way I often forgot to believe in the arrival of spring.

Meanwhile, I became so accustomed to my role behind the counter at Buster's that I also forgot to believe that members of The People were more than the two-dimensional caricatures I had made them out to be. They fussed, they looked over my shoulder as I steamed their milk to make sure that I had selected the right fat percentage. They wanted to know if the pastries were homemade.

"How can they be homemade if we make them at work?" I asked.

"No respect," they muttered. Were people truly leaving the house assuming that they would be respected everywhere they went? It seemed like such a strange concept. As more time passed, the human race itself became less and less relatable, which left me, it seemed, with only Cleo and a scrappy crew of murderous horses. Every morning, I breathed into Thunder's wet nostril and received a blast of warmth in return. It smelled like the center of the earth. Like a bran muffin in the microwave. It was the only thing I could count on.

AND THEN, ONE morning I was at the coffee grinder, lost momentarily in the storm that it made, when I heard my name spoken. I turned, and there was a man standing at the counter. He was maybe in his late fifties, with unnaturally dark hair falling over his forehead. I knew the man. I felt, in fact, that I knew him intimately, but I was so out of touch that I could not remember who he was. There was a flash of something like love—a micro-speck of confusion, where I wondered if it was my father, if this was what he looked like now. The man smiled warmly.

"All this time, and you were just a block away," he said.

It was Byron. He had dyed his hair, and he was standing at the counter. A customer. A real person. It might have been that moment, of all the strange moments that would follow, that made me realize just how isolated I had allowed myself to become. So isolated that I had forgotten Byron had free will, that he even existed outside the back alleyway of our weird emails.

"It appears that way, doesn't it?" I said. It was the first time I had seen him in person since discovering what his dick looked like. Isn't that another realm that we all exist in between? The clothed and the unclothed? Whenever George rolled in with our produce delivery, the memory of him in the feed room seemed like a dream. I've held you in my hand, I thought, almost forcing the sensation back into my skin. Did it make me special, in a way? Was I closer to George than I had been, or was touching his penis no different than learning his name? More customers took their place in line behind Byron.

"What can I get for you?" I asked him.

"You can tell me when you get off work." He tossed his hair, and I understood that he had dyed it for my sake. He thought that our emails meant something. This was his grand entrance.

"I have plans," I said. Another inexplicable thing was happening—aside from Byron and my growing detachment: I was about to predict the future.

"All evening?" He flicked his hair again, and I wished that I had shaved mine when I had the chance. That would have really sent a message.

"Tonight I am going to be the victim of an attack," I said calmly. "Don't worry. I have been led to believe that the rope will be soft."

That evening, after feeding the horses, I decided that I had put it off for too long: Tonight would be the night that I would do as the manual had instructed. I went into Gomer's stall. He was an ancient, gray quarter horse with faint dappling and a pink nose. His eyes were rimmed in more-sensitive pink skin and seemed always to be squinting at the brightness and also the sheer effrontery of the world. I lifted his lip to reveal his long, bone-brown teeth and, with my other hand, I rubbed vigorously along the slick ridges of his gums. He grunted and farted and let out a long series of wheezes. I'm sorry, I thought. I'm sorry I made you wait so long.

IT WAS DARK inside the house when I got back. I hung up my coat, then stopped to listen. The record player had been left running, and the needle was grinding softly. It had an eerie effect, making the darkness woolly and pressed close. Still, my first reaction was annoyance: Had Cleo forgotten that I lived there? I stepped forward, hands out in caution, but also as a dramatic show of self-pity: *Look at me, wandering blindly.* And then it was happening. I'd become used to anticipating Jean-Remy. The ever-present, undefined threat of him was familiar as seeing his boots on the doormat. But now he was really here, the smell of his cologne filling the narrow hallway, and he was pressing his body against mine. He moved more like an assertive dance partner than an attacker, but there was so much power in it that I gasped—and in that gasp, I heard that I had already become her: Pretend Drew, the girl surprised in the night.

"I'm not here to hurt you," said my attacker. He was wearing a kind of modified ski mask, chopped off at the bottom so that it exposed his mouth and the thick stubble on his jaw. Somehow, this decision made him seem more vulnerable, like a man trying to pull off a serious hat. And yet, even this slight awkwardness had its place. It made me want to work harder in my role. It made me realize that this experience was going to be about a different sort of thrill than I had expected. Before I could consider this any longer, I became aware of a cold pressure at the base of my neck.

A knife! thought Pretend Drew.

A real *knife?* True Drew whispered from her seat in the audience. I tuned her out. Of course it was real.

My attacker pushed me into the living room. Cleo was there, lit softly by the glow of the woodstove. I could see that she was sitting strangely upright on the edge of the couch, her arms behind her back. Her wrists must have been tied together. She was wearing jeans, and her shirt was missing, as if it had been pulled off in a struggle, revealing a cream-colored bra. I recognized it as one of her "dowdy" bras, the kind she wore when all her better bras were air-drying, and I wondered if she was disappointed that all of this was going down on laundry day. As we walked closer, the knife still at my neck, Cleo looked up. Her scarf was tied tightly around her mouth, just as I had imagined that first night I heard her and Jean-Remy in the bedroom. Her eyes in the dark seemed to gape in recognition, and I found that I was self-conscious, standing in front of her with a knife pressed to my skin. I'm not sure why. I think it was because underneath it all, I was still her employee, and maybe I had it in my head that good worker girls don't let fake attackers poke them with real knives. From there, things started happening faster.

"Cleo," I said. I was dropped to my knees.

"It's not your turn to speak," said the ski mask, calmly. "Nod if you understand." I nodded. He'd pushed me down, shadowing me with the knifepoint. This maneuver felt considerably less amateur. I tried to check in with True Drew, wherever I had left her. Was she enjoying this? But then my attacker's voice came again.

"Can you follow directions?"

I nodded.

"Good." With this, the knife lifted slightly, and the mouth beneath the mask brushed my ear.

"I need you to go to your friend over there and take out her earrings. She can't do it herself."

I shuffled forward on my knees and climbed onto the couch next to Cleo. She looked straight ahead, and I could see where sweat had dragged her mascara down her face. I was glad she didn't turn. It was too risky. If our eyes met, who was to say that True Drew wouldn't do something out of line? Try to reach across the space between us and pass a note to True Cleo? It seemed that my willingness to play this game and the fragility of my belief in it were in a standoff.

"That's nice," said our attacker as I unhitched Cleo's silver loops. "You seem like a nice friend." He was still standing just behind me, and in that way, he seemed to be everywhere at once.

"You like your friend very much, don't you?" he said, now taking a step back so that he was facing the couch. I could see his black jeans and his belt. He was wearing a flannel shirt, which was not his style, but neither was the ski mask. I nodded again. It amazed me how Pretend Drew was right there when I needed her to be, as if Pretend Drew and Pretend Jean-Remy had been in cahoots all this time. Maybe I had sensed it from the beginning. Maybe I had stirred it into the breves I'd prepared for him, my subconscious already fawning over his.

"I can tell that you like her," he said. "So, you will do what I say? And she'll stay safe?"

"Yes," I whispered.

"Ah—" he made a sound of warning, and the knife jumped over to Cleo's cheek. Her eyes flashed at me, then back into space. It was the first time the knife had not been directed at me, and I could see its surface flipping a faint glow. Only, the handle wasn't a handle. Not a regular one, anyway.

"No talking, remember?"

I nodded. It wasn't a knife, but one of the blades from Cleo's pair of kitchen shears. The same shears she had used to chop her hair weeks ago.

"You don't have to." Cleo was speaking through the gag, her voice shaky but kind. I couldn't help but feel disappointed that she had broken what seemed to be, until then, an effective illusion. Our attacker snorted in amusement. He tucked the scissor blade into his back pocket.

"Can you help your friend with her sock?" he asked me. I looked down at Cleo's feet. They were tied together at the ankles with rope. It was one of the lead ropes from the barn—I could tell by the dirt caked into the seams. This struck me as a little strange—it wasn't the soft, white rope he'd been so careful about showing us ahead of time. No quick-release knots in sight. Also, there was nothing wrong with Cleo's sock, so I assumed that this was a new development, a ploy to get me to kneel. I got down on the floor—ready for what? I don't even want to know.

Our attacker wanted me to peel Cleo's sock off and hand it to him.

I did.

"Good girl," he said.

Cleo's bare toes curled against the rug. Tristan had told me how much she hated her feet touched, ever since she'd gotten a pedicure in her twenties and found that she could no longer walk barefoot outdoors. All her hard-earned calluses were gone, just like that. Or had Cleo told me this story herself? Sometimes it felt like I'd known her forever, like my first lessons in school had been about her. My life just a flour fingerprint on the fat recipe roster of hers. I remained on the floor as our attacker balled the sock in his hand and crammed it into Cleo's mouth, retying the scarf to keep it in place. To do this properly, he had to climb halfway onto the couch and pin her down with his knee. Her throat was making muffled sounds. It reminded me of the few times I'd tried to scream underwater. Scream in a dream. I focused back on Cleo's foot, her toes flexing. There were more underwater sounds from the couch and then just the sound of ragged breathing. It seemed to take ages for me to look up, and when I did, I saw Cleo slumped to the side, ribs heaving. Her bra had been pulled down and her breasts were out. I thought: The painter got them wrong. He'd painted her nipples like blue steel, but here they were, as soft and careful as my own. All this time, I had imagined that in a moment like this I'd want to touch her, crawl into her, but now that the moment had come, I wanted to wrap her in a blanket. I wanted to take off my own sock and cover her little toes.

I started to feel hot, then the heat turned to sickness. I brought my hand to my mouth, and discovered that my hand smelled fishy, which made me cough in disgust. Suddenly, I was remembering Gomer's pink gums and long, streaked teeth. The old horse had trembled with gratitude while I rubbed him, his lower lip flapping and shining wet, as if I were performing some kind of rare sex act. This somehow made me think of Byron, and whether he would have acted more or less the same, had I gone with him tonight instead of being here, lost in whatever this was. I tried to check in with True Drew, and then had the terrible thought: She wasn't here. She never had been.

"I want you to close your eyes," my blue-eyed therapist had said. He pulled out a small gong, about the size of a saucer. It seemed to me a kind of prop you might find in the gift section of a bookstore or an airport. He tapped it with a travel-sized mallet, to demonstrate. The sound was not unpleasant, but not exactly reverberant. "Now," said the therapist. "Whenever I strike the gong, I want you to take note of whatever is on your mind at that moment. Just notice. Don't pass judgment, don't try to redirect." I was thirteen then, a volatile age. Adults tend to mistake thirteen for a time of blossoming, when, in fact, it is a time of destruction. Thirteen-year-olds do not want to be nurtured, they want to be given a wax apple to sink their teeth into. They want to snap the glow stick of their parents' trust. "Close your eyes, and follow your thoughts," said the therapist. All I could think about was black licorice and cat scratches. Screaming smoke alarms. Filed teeth.

Gong.

"Now, whatever thought you land on, I want you to imagine yourself touching it, as lightly as a feather touches a balloon."

"As what as a *what*?" I opened my eyes and met his gaze, his floating spectacles like microscope slides. His eyes watery, magnified cells.

"As lightly as a feather touches a balloon," he repeated.

I had never touched anything as lightly as a feather touches a balloon. In fact, at age thirteen, I couldn't think of anything more scandalous. Bowls breaking, I thought. Chalk screeching. Didn't my therapist know better than to offer my mind a balloon? He had given me a cozy cottage and I had filled it with trash. He had given me a punching bag and I would have punched it straight through the fabric of time rather than admit defeat. I squeezed the balloon in my mind until I saw its surface strained, the color draining. It grew bigger and bigger.

And then I woke up on the floor, because I had been

holding my breath. Because I'd rather pass out than touch a balloon lightly. I'd rather die than entertain one pleasant thought.

"Are you sure you want to do this?" Jean-Remy asked me. "It's only just started."

I had expected the safe word to stop everything, like the lights going up in a haunted house at a carnival. And this was what had happened, more or less, except suddenly all eyes were on me. I felt like a passenger on a train who had pushed an emergency button and could not remember why. Jean-Remy was Jean-Remy again, his ski mask pushed up around his forehead. His face was clammy and a little too rosy. I wished he would roll the mask back down. Cleo was on the floor between the couch and the woodstove, on her knees. Her wrists were still tied behind her back, but the gag was hanging loose around her neck.

"I don't want you to hurt her," I said. My voice sounded meek and unconvincing. I was still trying to piece together what had happened. Who had done what.

"I'm not hurt, Buggy," Cleo said. "Why don't we take five?" She moved her gaze entreatingly between Jean-Remy and me. "Open that bottle in the kitchen?"

It was too weird for Cleo to be suggesting a little wine break while she was still on the floor with her boobs out. Even in the dim lighting, I could see where patches of rug burn had already bloomed on the side of her face, where her mascara was dragged down her cheeks.

"No," I said. "I don't want that."

"You have to speak up, if you want me to understand you." Jean-Remy sounded irritated. He had started to pace, and I knew the longer I took to make up my mind, the harder it would be to resume where we had left off.

What had happened was an accident. Cleo must have seen that I was feeling sick and, wanting to pause things, had tried to say the word. Only, she was really and truly gagged, with the sock nearly in her throat. I heard it—like a muffled siren—submerged in her before I understood what she was trying to say. Jean-Remy had told her to be quiet, but the siren persisted. Then he told her to shut up, really, truly shut up. I could hear in his voice that it was not our attacker barking the order, but Jean-Remy himself.

"I want to keep going," I said.

Jean-Remy shook his head. He was sweating. We were all sweating.

"Maybe this wasn't a good idea."

"We can always try another time," said Cleo. She seemed overly cheery, like she didn't want me to feel bad. I remembered how I'd felt the day Jean-Remy walked in while I was peeing in the barn. The awkward phone call with Cleo. The cold room in my stomach, like a walk-in freezer. I thought about how, back in October, Cleo had asked for advice about the painting. *I am asking you a* when *question.* Who asks a thing like that of a stranger? It was almost as if Cleo had been offering me a choice and I had one-eightied my life in her direction. I had kissed her—*I* had kissed *her.* I had agreed to all of it.

"You can tie me up," I said to Jean-Remy.

He threw his face toward the ceiling, smiling in frustration.

"I was going to do that anyway."

"No, wait—" I said. I stood and slipped the half-shears from Jean-Remy's back pocket.

"Drew!" I heard Cleo call, but I was already in the kitchen. I flicked on the light and the room buzzed back at me, fluorescent and unforgiving. There, beneath the clock on the wall, was Cleo's landline. Jean-Remy appeared in the doorway just as I was cutting the wire. I walked over to him and put the blade in his hand.

"Now it doesn't matter what I say."

WHAT NEEDED TO happen next was for the three of us to become our pretend selves again. I worried that this would be impossible, that I'd ruined the vibe. Jean-Remy could not just hop out the window and hop back in, surprising us for a second time. He was down on the floor with Cleo, saying something to her that I could not hear, touching her cheek where the rug burn was, like an apology. After he had shouted at her in his real voice, there had been a quick and awkward scuffle. Cleo had lost her balance and, without the use of her hands to break her fall, landed face-first on the floor. I had been prepared to witness many mild acts of violence, but the sight of Cleo falling over like that—the ugliness and vulnerability of it—shook me. I pulled the scarf from her mouth so she could say it, but then I heard it in my own voice.

"Tower."

JEAN-REMY MADE AS if to pull his mask back down, but then thought better of it.

"Get the light," he said to me. I did what I was told, and the living room, which had been sliced down the middle by the hard light from the kitchen, was dark again.

"Come here."

I went to him. His finger pointed toward the floor. I followed it, dropping to my knees next to Cleo.

"Drew, are you a child?"

I shook my head.

"Tell her." As he said this, he pulled the fabric of the mask down and nodded toward Cleo.

"I'm not a child," I said to Cleo. She gave me a weak smile, then looked back down at the rug. Jean-Remy left the room abruptly, then came back holding another length of rope—this one a closer match to the sample he'd showed me weeks before. He pulled my arms behind my back.

"What are you?" I felt the rope tighten and the muscles in the center of my back contract.

"I'm—"

"You're a good friend, aren't you?"

"Yes."

To Cleo he said, "Stop protecting her." His tone suggested that he had said this to her before. Maybe there had been a conversation—an argument—sometime in the recent past and somehow my being tied up was proving a point. I wondered if Cleo had doubted that I could handle this and Jean-Remy had convinced her that I could. On one hand, the thought made me furious and ashamed. On the other, the notion that Cleo would want to protect me stirred up a wonderful paradox: How to prove to her that I was brave, but worry her senseless at the same time? Again, I caught a glimpse of why we were here. The kind of thrill we were after. It put me in a better mood. Maybe I had not ruined things after all.

Jean-Remy was retying the gag around Cleo's head.

"I like you better like this," he said, which was probably too cliché, but then again, I also wanted her gagged. It provided a barrier that I needed if I was going to do a good job. I couldn't risk her suggesting that we all take five. I didn't want to hear her say my name.

WE FACED EACH other on the rug in front of the woodstove, looking like mirror images. Both of us kneeling, both with our hands behind our backs. The only differences were, (a) I could talk if I wanted to and Cleo could not, and (b) I was dressed in a tank top and jeans, and Cleo's breasts were still spilling out.

"Show me what a good friend you are," Jean-Remy said to me. He was seated on the couch, twirling the blade around his finger, like he knew I didn't need it shoved in my face. I had seen firsthand how sharp it was.

"What do you want me to do?" I asked. I heard Jean-Remy sigh. Since starting over, I could no longer believe in Jean-Remy as the attacker. I was not disappointed. It was not as if the attacker had been any more enigmatic. If anything, I had feared the attacker less, because I didn't care what he thought of me. I looked into Jean-Remy's masked face for long enough to understand that he was done giving directions. If I couldn't figure out this one request on my own, then I was not worthy of continuing. I turned my focus to Cleo. To her expressionless face, swollen from the sock in her mouth. I looked at her large breasts with the small, pink nipples. I had not seen many other naked women in my life. I expected them all to be different than me, inhabiting bodies that I would be incapable of inhabiting. But I was surprised by my own confidence, kneeling in front of her—not necessarily in myself, but in my sudden understanding of what needed to be done. I inched forward, carefully, so as not to lose my balance. I could sense Jean-Remy become slightly more alert from his position on the couch. The blade stopped spinning in his hand. So, I thought, this is going to be like a game of hot and cold. I would be able to tell if I was getting warmer by Jean-Remy's body language. At the same time, I was following another authority—or, maybe that's not the right word. Was it desire? It reminded me of that day with Tristan in the tack room; how I had begged for two things at once and gotten neither. How everything was perfect for those few minutes.

By today's standards it might seem strange, but at thirteen, I was expected to walk to my therapist's office by myself and then walk back home. Any distance under three miles was nonnegotiable. After my falling unconscious on his floor, however, the therapist would not allow me to go anywhere without supervision. He picked up the phone.

"Don't bother," I said, watching him clamp the receiver to his ear with his shoulder so he could check his watch.

"Your mom not home?" The eyes flicked over their glass panes.

"She's home," I said. "She just doesn't pick up the phone between three and five." I was furious at him for being shocked by my behavior. It felt like a violation that a man who was an expert on strange behavior would make an exception for a two-second-long fainting spell. He had wanted to know what was so upsetting about the gong that it threw me into a fit. Had there been other gongs in my life? Gongs that signaled trauma? Oh, I could see the dissertation touching down in his brain as he spoke. No, I had tried to explain. I just didn't like feathers, and I didn't like the idea of them touching balloons, because it made my skin feel funny. It made me want to break things, to stop the funny, squirmy feeling. But he had never heard of such a problem, so, in his mind, it did not exist. He was left with no other choice but to drive me home, which he insisted was highly unorthodox. My mother met us at the front door, but, as was her fashion, she would not let my therapist past the threshold. I remember her crossing her arms as he explained the situation. Her expression shifted into a tight smile.

"We've dealt with this before," she assured the therapist, but later, to me, she said, "This is what happens when the world finds out."

With my teeth, I began to fix Cleo's bra. I took the first strap, which had fallen loosely over her arm, and tugged it upward with small, careful movements so that I would not topple us both into the woodstove. I felt Cleo's skin react to my breath. I could smell her lemon herb soap and that unidentified hint of incense. I could smell the sex of damp spandex. My adrenaline began to spike, as if my cells had each popped open a glistening, reflective eye. A thousand stunned animals in a dark forest. From the periphery, Jean-Remy's shadow looked on.

Once the straps were up around her shoulders, I had the more complicated challenge of fixing Cleo's bra cups. This, of course, would require me to put my face directly in her breasts. The thought was agonizing. I could tell that it was also agonizing for Jean-Remy—that he and I were now on the same wavelength. When I lowered my head, I heard him make a soft gasp as if involuntarily. I moved slower, finding the edge of the bra cup without letting my lips touch her skin. It was like a game of Operation: my mouth the forceps, Cleo's flesh the electric metal rim.

And where was Cleo in all of this? I was so focused, so close to her, that there were moments where it felt like I had pressed pause on the whole world, and the world was Cleo. Like a genie had granted me access, with one condition: I couldn't use my hands. The bra cups were difficult to control, and by the time I had hiked them up, they were damp with spit, and my mouth had touched her far too many times.

I sensed that Jean-Remy was getting bored with this task, so I quickly thought about what else I could do. As if on cue, I heard him say: "I need you to be an even better friend." The blade resumed its spinning. By then my arms were aching, and I had lost feeling in my hands, which Jean-Remy had assured me was not supposed to happen—but how could I sound the alarm a second time? We'd barely edged ourselves back into the game. And now I needed to figure out how to take it even further. Once again, I was conscious of the skipping record, the rough hum and maddening click of it. I leaned in, closer to Cleo, willing my mind to think of something else to do, another act of devotion to perform. I had dressed her with my teeth, and I could not just undress her again. Jean-Remy's blade kept spinning. The fire next to us kept pumping heat. I was so close to Cleo that I could smell the waxy scent of her smeared mascara. Maybe that was it. I could clean her face with my tongue, like a mother cat. Smooth her hairline, catch the line of sweat between her breasts. Was that too deranged? Or not deranged enough? But just as I was thinking this, my face brushed against her lips, and I felt how dry and scaly they were from the gag. As if by instinct, I licked them because Cleo could not do it herself. She tasted like the low tide.

"Oh, Bug," I heard Jean-Remy say. "You are an artist."

And here was where I lost her—just when I might have had her. With Jean-Remy's praise, I became insatiable. I wanted to show him all that I would do. The things that I would endure. I felt that I understood it, finally: why we were doing this and why Jean-Remy needed to be in charge. It was important that I distrusted him, just as it was important that I disliked The People but chose to serve them anyway, every day.

People want the same thing . . . They line up and look for the same thing, Cleo had complained. *No one around here has any imagination at all.*

I stood, nearly losing my balance. My legs were stiff, all my hinges wanting to snap back to the position I'd been holding for so long. Around me the room seemed to vibrate with shadow. I wanted to bump the record needle off course, but I was afraid that if I did so, it would be too quiet, as if the sound of the record was insulating us, somehow. I stepped toward the couch. Jean-Remy lifted his face, and even with the mask over his eyes, I could see his amusement. The shears blade lay across his thigh. I knew what I wanted to happen, but I didn't know how to ask for it, so I said to him, "I want you to let her go."

"Not a chance," he said, his face still amused. I had expected this answer.

"Please," I said.

Jean-Remy cocked his head, slightly more interested now.

"No."

I moved closer. Jean-Remy studied me. Even through the mask, I could tell that he had stepped out of the game. We both had, and we were about to break the rules so we could settle this thing that had been between us. Maybe it was rivalry. Maybe it was that neither of us thought the other worthy of Cleo's attention. Or maybe it was the fact that we both knew, deep down, that she didn't truly love us. And we couldn't stand that.

8

I STARED AT the silver lump nestled in the shag of the rug. It looked like some kind of rectangular egg, tinted rose by the light of the coals. I knew it was a cell phone, the kind that you have to unfold to answer, but I was having trouble understanding why it was there. Cleo had left it for me. She had pulled it out of a drawer in the kitchen before she and Jean-Remy took off. But Cleo hated cell phones. We had a NO CELL PHONE sign on the counter at Buster's that Cleo liked to wave in front of customers who were yapping too loudly on theirs. Most of them just gaped, leaning their phone against their shoulder as if to mute it. Too stunned to put up a fight.

"Shoot me in the head," she used to say to me, and I had always assumed that the rest of this statement was *if you ever catch me with one of those.* But maybe I'd been wrong. I was sitting on the couch, my hands still tied tightly behind my back. They'd gone numb a while ago, and it felt like that part of me was dipped into a black, airless void. I worried about nerve damage. I worried that I would never be able to bend my elbows properly again. But there was Cleo's cell phone, on the rug. I would have to try to pick it up. I'd have to scoot over on my butt and claw for it in the void behind my back.

IT WOULD BE easy to say that it was all Jean-Remy's idea, that he coerced me, because he was the one with the knife. He was bigger and more powerful. But what had happened next seemed more like a conversation. Jean-Remy and I were one part, and Cleo was the other.

He had spun me around so that I was facing her, and wrapped his arms around me. From there he unbuttoned my jeans. I saw Cleo wince as Jean-Remy pushed them down, then held me steady so I could lift my feet out. There was a tension between the three of us, and I believed that my body was the instrument; whatever Jean-Remy did to me was our message to Cleo. My tolerance of it was my own private postscript.

Jean-Remy got off the couch and I was spun around again. I felt something brush the back of my thigh. At first I thought it was accidental, but then I realized that it was Jean-Remy's finger. He was warning me. Letting me know where to expect it. I heard the clink of his belt buckle, followed by the swish of its release. He must have folded it in half, although that part was silent. And even though I had not asked for this, it felt inevitable. Jean-Remy's heavy hand on my back, guiding me to bend over the couch. Cleo's small sound of protest, because of course this was not supposed to happen.

The first stroke was cold, then instantly warm. Jean-Remy hit both legs together in a clean line, but I felt the point of contact spread out somewhat loosely, until it was immediately brought to order by a second blow. I gasped, and this made Cleo whimper again from behind her sock. Jean-Remy explained to her that he was not going to stop hitting me until she was quiet. "She's doing this for you," he said, his voice far away. I closed my eyes and waited.

There was nothing in the space between, only the grinding hiccup of the record that no one was ever going to turn over. I watched the pulp sizzle behind my eyelids. My lungs prickled, and I realized that I had been holding my breath. Then the belt hit me a third time, and the air rushed in.

PICKING UP THE cell phone was harder than I had expected. I had to lie on my side and fumble around, my hands as foreign and inept as the pincers on a claw machine. When I thought I'd got it, I pushed and squeezed, hoping to pry it open at the very least. I cursed Cleo for leaving me alone, even though I knew I deserved every second of agony. Maybe I would never get free. No one would come looking for me, and I would starve to death for lack of survival skills. But when I flipped over, I saw that I had succeeded in opening the phone and, in all my mashing of buttons, I had accidently called whoever was on the phone's speed dial. Oh shit, I thought. Fate! The fire in the stove had dimmed, and in all the fuss the record player had been mercifully bumped and was no longer skipping. Now it was just me and this little green square, calling a mystery person named "Hay Deli."

"Hi," said Hay Deli, breathlessly. Hay Deli was a man. Maybe I had woken him up. "Are you okay?" He sounded concerned already, like he knew that I needed someone to come untie me. "Hello?"

I lay my face against the open phone. How would I even begin to explain myself? Who was I to bother a stranger—even inadvertently—with my weird, complicated problems? But at this point, figuring out how to hang up with the tip of my nose seemed like more of a hassle than talking.

"Hello?" I said. "Can you hear me?"

"Yes," said Hay Deli. "Where are you? You sound strange." There was an eagerness in his voice that was deeply comforting to me, as if he did not even need an explanation to care about me. "Cleo?" he asked. "Cleo?"

And I knew instantly who it was, but could not yet piece together how I had magically gotten Tristan on the phone. Everything seemed to be connected as if by the stretchy ligaments of a dream.

"Tristan," I said.

"Yes!" Here, he laughed a little, as if in disbelief. "It's me. Please tell me you're alright." He had seen Cleo's number come up on his phone, and he was ready to do anything for her. Who knows how long it had been since she had last called him? Six months? A year? I felt the sadness of what I was about to do pass over me like a shadow.

"It's Drew," I said. "Cleo's not here."

BY THE TIME Jean-Remy had stopped hitting me, the air felt like it was on fire, and my skin felt like a mentholated salt rash. My pulse had migrated outside my body. It filled the room, throbbing. I was so dizzy and disconnected that I wondered briefly if Cleo could feel it too, like waves crashing over her skin. I heard her trying to say something through the gag, but the words came out like moans. The volume of these moans increased with a new sensation: Jean-Remy's fingers again, this time tucked beneath the elastic of my panties.

Did I think that he was going to fuck me in front of her? I really don't know. There had been so much talk and preparation. I had waited, anticipating his arrival for weeks, but during all that time, had I ever envisioned real sex? No. I felt the fingers edging my underwear down, little by little. He was taunting Cleo. He knew that she didn't want to see me fucked. I knew I didn't want either of them to see the disappointment that was my bare ass, but the fire was so low by then that maybe they wouldn't see much. I could deal with that. Still, I felt caught in a strange paralysis. True Drew had left long ago. Maybe she'd never gotten off the floor of the therapist's office. Maybe the body that I had been carrying around since I was thirteen was just a decoy. And in that case, what did it matter if I got fucked by a snooty, breve-drinking Canadian? Jean-Remy stopped when my panties were about halfway down, and I heard the faint clink of the belt being lifted. He wasn't getting ready to fuck me. He was going to hit me again. Before I could prepare myself, something cracked and I fell forward. I thought that there had been an explosion, the pain coming from behind me was so sharp and hot. But I realized as it struck again that Jean-Remy had been holding back the first time, and now he was wielding the belt with all his strength. I couldn't think of what to do or say. I felt stupid and shocked by the pain. With each blow I tried to push myself further into the couch cushions to escape it.

Stop, I thought. It was the only word that I could think of, and I knew it wasn't the right one. Jean-Remy didn't stop. The horizon across my ass where he was striking became a wall of fire in my mind, separating me from who I had been just minutes ago. Brave Drew. Willing Drew. Devoted Drew.

"Stop," I whispered.

TRISTAN FOUND ME in the living room. I watched him take in the surroundings for what must have been the first time. Here was Cleo's house. Her belongings and smells, mixed with her late husband's belongings, now further complicated by my unexplained presence, and the blood on the shag carpet. I hadn't even considered how I must have appeared, until Tristan switched on the light, and we both flinched for different reasons. I found that I was moved by the sight of him. There was a part of me—the part that, perhaps, wanted to justify all that had occurred—that believed Tristan was here to complete his role. He had always been the hero. It was so obvious.

"You were number one on her speed dial!" I said to him, turning and offering my wrists so he could saw through the rope with a pocketknife. I'd been dying to tell him, thinking it was a much bigger deal than perhaps it was. But still, it wasn't Jean-Remy, or Farid, or Lydia behind that button. It wasn't me. I hadn't even been told about the cell phone.

"Are you hurt?" he asked, sitting beside me on the couch. His hair had grown in, tufty and boyish. I wanted to touch it, but my arms wouldn't work. I could feel the adrenaline leaving my body, and I was scared to find out what heavy, painful thing would replace it. Was I hurt? Yes, but I suppose what he meant was *Are you injured?* And deeper than that, behind his innocence and integrity, what he really wanted to know was *Where is she? And is this her blood?* No.

"There was a man," I said. "He was hurting me, so Cleo broke his nose."

That was an oversimplification. And I could already see how I would twist the story so that Cleo could be the hero.

It was true that she had gotten Jean-Remy to stop thrashing me. She'd crawled her way over, and he had whirled around, leaving me folded over, crying into the cushion. When I turned, they were together on the floor. Maybe I saw what I wanted to see. Jean-Remy later claimed that he was helping Cleo undo her gag, but from where I was, it looked like he was on top of her, hands around her neck. My wrists were tied, and my entire lower half ached so bad that it felt like a different species altogether. Maybe I should have tried the safe word again before I acted. If things had not stopped right away, then I would have been justified. But I didn't. I limped over, panties hanging down, and did the only thing that my body felt capable of: I kicked him. I kicked Jean-Remy hard enough that he fell, catching himself on the raised brick hearth of the stove. He was unhurt, but he paused to look at his palm, the one that had landed on the bricks, as if checking for a cut. I don't know why I did it. Everything had become so conflated by then—our pretend selves in a pretend scenario trying to grapple with real feelings—that I had many factors to blame. All I know is that I saw an opening and I took it, telling myself that I was doing it for Cleo. All of this was for her. I kicked him again, as hard as I could, just as he was turning his head to look at me. My heel landed in the center of his face, and I didn't see the damage until later, when he peeled the mask away.

"HIS NOSE WAS *probably* broken," I said to Tristan. "Cleo drove him to the hospital." Tristan was helping me step into a pair of sweatpants. We had both decided that squeezing back into my jeans would be next to impossible. The way that he had sucked in his breath when he saw me told me all I needed to know about the state of my ass. Better to just cover it for now.

"I don't get it," he said. "Why help him?"

I wished I could explain to Tristan how morality felt like a stocking that had been stretched over my face and ripped away, again and again. How after enough of this, you had to fall back on the very basics of human decency.

"Because it was the right thing to do."

And I had felt guilty about what I'd done. I'd doubted my decision right away. After kicking Jean-Remy in the face, all the sickness flooded back into my throat. If I hadn't been crying—the ugly sobs of a girl unable to cover her face or wipe her snot—then I might have finally vomited. Things were only made worse by the fact that it was Jean-Remy who first tried to comfort me. Cleo, free from her ropes and gag, had gone into the kitchen to get a wet towel for Jean-Remy's face. He approached me, one hand holding his nose and the other outstretched, timidly, like I was a feral cat.

"Oh, Bug," he said. His voice was congested with blood. "We pushed you too far."

I spent the night at Tristan's apartment in town. It was a studio in an old brick building, above a pharmacy. I don't know why I had always assumed that Tristan lived in a log cabin, or an off-grid trailer. If he had lived atop a lighthouse, I probably would not have been surprised. His competence could have belonged anywhere. On the drive from Cleo's house, he touched my hand.

"You should know that I'm kind of seeing someone," he

said. I stared into the ashy halo of headlights in front of us. I had to sit sideways, resting my weight on my hip, holding my breath with every bump. My toes in Howie's boots felt miles away from the rest of my body. My wrists, where the rope had been, alternated between too hot and too cold.

"Please tell me it's not Diane," I said. After everything I'd been through, that might have been the thing that killed me. Tristan laughed nervously.

"No. Not Diane."

We were silent for the rest of the drive. I turned Cleo's secret cell phone over in my coat pocket, as if I were waiting for it to ring. I knew that it would not, and yet I still found myself clinging to the possibility that it *could*. We could still move past what had happened. Cleo and I could still open the café in the morning and tend to the small emergencies of The People—bagel shortages, botched drink orders, not enough protein, too much gluten. It was clear to me that these were the only crises I was qualified to handle.

"I'm trying to help you," she had said to me, and I'd realized that I had been backing away, as if afraid of her. She stood still. She was dressed. Her sneakers were on. She and Jean-Remy were ready to leave, and I was the only thing keeping them from doing so.

"Come with us," she said gently. "I can drop you somewhere for the night. Your mother's house?" I wondered if she was serious. If after everything we'd been through, she was just going to dump me back with poor Mary. And then it occurred to me that Cleo didn't know why this was such a terrible idea. I'd never talked to her about it. I'd made myself so small that I hadn't given her a chance to really know me.

"Let me at least untie you," she said when I didn't answer. Behind her, Jean-Remy held the towel to his face and looked at the ceiling. I imagined the blood in his nose oozing backward down his throat. I imagined sitting between them in the truck on the way to the emergency room, Jean-Remy buried in his towel, swallowing blood, Cleo silent and remorseful at the wheel. It wasn't just that the thought was unbearable—it seemed even more impossible than spending the night at my mother's house. There were suddenly so many places where I didn't fit. So many people who would probably be happier without me. I took another step back, away from her. It was irrational, but I felt that the rope holding my wrists together was the only threshold Cleo and I had left, and once it was crossed, we'd have nothing. We might return to work that week, but soon she would take me off Mondays, and then Tuesdays also. Before I knew it, there would be a sandwich board where the green-and-blue flag had once hung. There would be smart new employees wearing hats and up-to-code aprons, who didn't tease the clientele or threaten to throw muffins at them. Then, one by one, Cleo would find homes for Howie's horses. She'd explain that it had been a pipe dream to try to keep the herd together. It was all unsustainable. The idea that she and I could hold off the world. Do it all on our own.

"I'm sorry I brought you into this mess," she said.

I could tell by her tone that she was done with him. For real this time. Cleo was going to do this one last thing for Jean-Remy—drive him to the doctor to get his nose fixed—and then drop him. It occurred to me then that Jean-Remy's biggest error was that he had given Cleo exactly what she asked for. I suppose I had made the same mistake.

"I'm sorry I never brought you into mine," I said.

THE INSIDE OF Tristan's apartment was tidy. It was separated into a kitchen and bedroom by a floor-to-ceiling bookshelf, which held novels, biographies, and some film history books. Dylan Thomas? I had had no idea that Tristan was a reader, or that he was even an adult. On his counter was one of those cylindrical holders for wooden spoons. There were clean dishes on the rack. Houseplants that weren't dead. On the bedroom side, a TV had been left on with a paused PS2 game on the screen. Next to the controller on the floor, there was a half-eaten bowl of soup.

"I interrupted your soup," I said sadly, and sat on the edge of the bed, overcome by exhaustion. My body ached, and I knew that it was only going to get worse. The morning seemed impossibly distant, but also like wreckage atop a wave, ready to crash to shore. I felt sick again. If anyone ever asks me where remorse lives in the body, I will tell them that it's glandular.

Tristan pulled the blankets over me.

"Did I mention the speed dial?" I asked.

"Yes, you did." He crouched next to the bed. He would not get in.

"You're important to her—number one!"

"So important she disguised me as Hay Delivery?" He patted my shoulder lump.

"I know men who would kill to be Hay Delivery."

I asked Tristan if I could watch him play his game while I fell asleep. It was soothing, how nothing on the screen reminded me of anything from my own life. I liked Tristan's quiet concentration, his serious, forward-leaning posture. I knew that, whatever the point of the game, he was there to clean up, conquer. I was impressed by the breadth of his life, that it could reach into so many diverse corners, even after he had known someone like Cleo and lost her. I began to drift, but I did not want to sleep yet. Every time I closed my eyes, I saw Cleo trying to cut me free and the ridiculous fight I had put up, skirting all her efforts, shouting at her to leave me alone, until she did just that, laying the cell phone on the floor as one last offering. I was a delusional activist, chaining myself to her life when I knew already that it was too late.

"Tristan?" I asked.

"Hmm?" His little guy was swinging a sword at something that looked like a giant toad.

"What does it mean when a horse throws a shoe?"

He paused the game and looked at me.

"It just means they lost it. Are you sure you're okay?"

And then I could see it all unfolding: the stony field, the whisked, gray sky. The details ordinary yet poignant, like someone's home movie whirring on a projector. I had been looking the wrong way, searching for the wrong clues. My months of speculating—interrogating the farrier, smelling Thunder's breath, asking the horses to blink twice if they were guilty—hadn't brought me any closer to the answer, because the horses didn't matter. It wasn't about the horses at all.

I saw Howie out in his field, shirt buttoned tightly to his chin, belly puffed with self-knowing. He was leading one of the horses down the hill. Let's say it was Thunder, his mane lifted in the wind, showing its red undertones. I bet the farrier was due to arrive that afternoon, and Howie wanted to get the horses inside and brushed. It would line up with the schedule I'd seen in the manual, and it would explain the farrier's judgy attitude with me when I finally called him—maybe he had showed up that day to find Howie gone without explanation. Maybe no one had told him anything, and suddenly there I was, weeks late, wearing skinny jeans and boots that didn't fit, hovering annoyingly over his shoulder. Howie would have been leading Thunder with a lot of slack—Thunder didn't like to be restricted. He didn't like long, extravagantly trailing scarves either. Maybe the barn came into view, and there, standing at the gate, was a man, the ends of his white scarf reaching up like arms in the wind. Thunder would have seen him for what he was, would have lurched at the sight, possibly tossing his head, rearing, slipping on the loose shale of the incline. Later, they would discover the lead rope on the ground beside Howie, which means that he had unhooked it, probably as a safety measure when the horse had become unruly. *Hold on a minute. Stay right there!* Howie might have called down to the strange man, for the man's sake more than his own. And maybe the stranger had only been there to pick up a prop—it could have been that he already had it in his hand, waving it without knowing the effect that it would have. It's possible that he had been led to believe that the woman who lived in the house was unmarried, and he was just as surprised to see another person as Howie was. But once it happened, how could he stick around? How would he explain his presence there? Maybe he was not the only one hiding a spouse, a family.

Maybe—and this I would like to believe—he was the one who called for help, pretending to be someone else. He was good at that.

"Tristan?"

"Yes?" He paused the game again. I wasn't sure if I had been asleep or dozing in a waking dream. I wanted to tell him what I'd seen, but that would mean explaining everything, going all the way back to when Cleo and Tristan were together and happy, planting that seed of doubt. Tarnishing her perfect ghost. Perhaps even going as far as tarnishing the baby that never was. Tristan needed that baby to be his. I understood that much.

So, I said, "It's not Aurora, is it?"

He laughed.

"No. No more horse girls for me." He turned back to his little guy running on the screen, then added over his shoulder: "No offense." I huffed and rolled my body to face the wall.

"I'm not a horse girl," I said to the wall. "I'm a . . . I'm a Vespa girl."

"You are delirious."

He was right. But there was something to it. That thing I had been searching for on my scooter rides, that perfect bowl of green grass, the underside of a meadow flipping in the wind. The restlessness that had been the structure of my life. It was so familiar to me—if a place without a location can be familiar. I wanted to love her without having her because no one could have her. Cleo was the search. Cleo was the chase. Maybe Jean-Remy's belt had tricked me, momentarily, into thinking that I had found a loophole.

"Hey." Tristan was kneeling beside the bed now, looking at me with concern. "What do you need?" he asked. I looked at his kind face, his cautious, downward smile. Who was this man? I hoped that the new girl in his life, whoever she was, would try to figure him out better than I had. Tristan deserved someone who wanted to understand him, someone who knew how to receive his kindness. That was one of my many flaws: poor design. All devotion and no plan. No instincts to speak of. Thunder was the only one smart enough to turn on his heels and get the hell out of there. I felt a flash of love for him—for all of them, really. For the perfect knot that they made, one that I wasn't ready to escape from. Not yet.

"Take me back," I said, and I closed my eyes, waiting for Tristan's sweet and inescapable *no.*

ACKNOWLEDGMENTS

While writing *The Lonely Girl's Vegetable Patch*, I learned that the real-life Thunder had died. He was a big, sweet boy who never killed anyone, as far as I know. Certain human characters in this book and the real people they might resemble are also innocent, and loved. To one person in particular, I want to say: You are extraordinary and still a part of my life. I can't believe I let a mediocre man come between us.

There are so many people to thank. First is my agent, Reiko, also extraordinary. She should be reminded of this every day. Shout-out to her dad, Dennis! And my editor, Kameel Mir, who I believe this book was always headed for. I am beyond proud to have Feminist Press as my publisher. To the whole team: thank you!

Others who deserve recognition are: Alice Hansmann (who won't see this and therefore won't be shocked and embarrassed to learn that she is perfect), V. Hansmann, Camille Guthrie, Anna Hogeland, Janice Obuchowski, Rebekah Tracy, Tim Foley, Douglas Jowett, Laura Wolf Benziker, Kate Cooper, Renee Bouchard, Shellie Burdick, Linn Kirkpatrick, Elaine Henry Whalen, Kevin Whalen, Dare Chammings, Emma Peterson, Madalyn Olson, Fizza Hasan, Katharine King, Bob Guare, Felipe Stetson, and so many more. All these people kept me going in one way or another. Thank you, too, to *The* People, for being weird, relentless, and full of personality.

Thank you to my sister, Ava, for everything.

And Jamie, of course, who was there for all of it. I fucking love you.

GENEVIEVE PLUNKETT is the author of *In the Lobby of the Dream Hotel* and *Prepare Her*. A recipient of an O. Henry Award and the *Sewanee Review*'s Andrew Lytle Prize, her writing can be found in the *Sewanee Review, Electric Literature, Write or Die, Story,* and the *Southern Review,* among others. She lives in Vermont with her partner and their children.

The Feminist Press publishes books that ignite movements and social transformation. Celebrating our legacy, we lift up insurgent and marginalized voices from around the world to build a more just future.

See our complete list of books at **feministpress.org**

THE FEMINIST PRESS
AT THE CITY UNIVERSITY OF NEW YORK
FEMINISTPRESS.ORG